TORRID

NEW YORK TIMES BESTSELLING AUTHOR

ABBI
GLINES

JUDGEMENT SERIES
BOOK TWO

Copyright © 2024 by Abbi Glines
All rights reserved.
Visit my website at
www.abbiglinesbooks.com

Cover Designer: Sarah Sentz Enchanting Romance Designs
www.enchantingromancedesigns.com
Editor: Jovana Shirley, Unforeseen Editing
www.unforeseenediting.com
Formatting: Melissa Stevens, The Illustrated Author
www.theillustratedauthor.com

No part of this book may be reproduced or transmitted in any form or by any means, electronic or mechanical, including photocopying, recording, or by any information storage and retrieval system without the written permission of the author, except for the use of brief quotations in a book review.

This book is a work of fiction. Names, characters, places, and incidents either are products of the author's imagination or are used fictitiously. Any resemblance to actual persons, living or dead, events, or locales is entirely coincidental.

Torrid

Unbreakable
Jamie Scott

Guys My Age
Hey, Violet

Love the Way You Lie
Eminem

I Found
Amber Run

Back to Black
Amy Winehouse

Chasing After You
Ryan Hurd & Maren Morris

Playlist

Say You Won't Let Go
James Arthur

Easy On Me
Adele

You are the Reason
Calum Scott & Leona Lewis

If I Didn't Love You
Jason Aldean & Carrie Underwood

Nobody But You
Blake Shelton & Gwen Stefani

I Found You
Nate Smith

To the path we all chose for our story we call **Life**.
May we hang on through the pain so that we don't miss our happy ending when we reach that last chapter.

I

"There are only two mistakes one can make along
the road to truth; not going all the way,
and not starting."
—*Buddha*

Prologue

LIBERTY
Eleven Years Old

Think about Charleston, think about Mama D's fried pies, think about summer afternoons at the creek behind Dillard Holler.

Keeping my eyes closed tightly, I tried to focus on all the good things that had once been part of my life. Remembering what I'd had was better than facing what my life was now.

The pain never got easier. How many times had someone told me that time would heal the pain of loss or something dumb like that? I hadn't believed them five years ago after my grandmother, Mama D took her last breath; or seven months after that, when I'd clung to the side of my momma's casket; or six months ago, when my dad had been lowered into the ground. They had all been wrong or just lying because they didn't know what else to say. I didn't care if my dad was in a better place. He was supposed to be here with me. He was all I'd had left.

My eyes began to sting—an all-too-familiar reaction. I was so tired of crying. I'd done too much of it in the past five years. I tried once again to think about my life before we left our home in Charleston. The pretty yellow two-story house where I'd lived happily for the first seven years of my life. My Mama D's house sat right across the street. The day we had driven away with all our things in a moving truck, I'd felt like I was losing my mom and Mama D all over again.

That had been four years ago. Dad had promised me that day, as we drove south to Ocala, Florida, that I'd find happiness again. I'd have a new home with new memories. Our family would look different, but there would be love. He thought we couldn't move on if we stayed with the ghosts of what had once been. I disagreed, but then I hadn't wanted to move on. I had wanted to cling to what was left.

I'd lost Mama D and then Momma seven months later. It was the hardest year of my life. Dad held me, promising me he'd never leave. We would survive this. One day, we would have a fond memory and smile when we thought of them. He said it was us against the world. And I believed him. Until … he'd moved us.

Opening my eyes, I wiped at the tears that I hadn't been able to stop and stared at the bedroom that had become mine the week after Dad's heart attack. It had been my stepmother, Abilene's, crafting room and the only finished space in the basement of our home in Ocala. Dad had planned to finish the rest, adding a game room and a proper laundry room instead of the washer and dryer that currently sat in the open space across from my room.

The dirty laundry had been dumped on my bed—the single mattress that lay on the concrete floor. There were soiled towels, bloodstained panties from either my stepmother's period or her daughter's, along with other gross things that had spilled over onto the worn rug that only partially covered the concrete floor.

Taking a deep breath, I finally moved from the doorway and walked over to it so I could begin to sort them into the correct piles. My dad had always believed in having chores. He had said it taught you to respect your things and instilled a good work ethic. However, now that he was gone, I was the only one doing chores. I was the maid, the cook, their own personal Cinderella.

There had been other changes since my father's death. My bedroom had been upstairs, looking out over the front yard. Sissy, the sister my father had surprised me with after our arrival to Ocala, had always complained that I had a bigger room. It was a very small difference, but she had pouted about it since she'd moved in after the wedding that I wished had never happened.

Dad had hoped that my having an older sister would help heal the pain of all I'd lost. At least, that was what he'd told me when he explained that she was my actual sister.

Before my parents had met, he had gotten a girl pregnant in college. She told him after a bad breakup, and then she said she aborted the baby.

Six months after my mom's death, he received a message on Facebook from Abilene, the girlfriend from college, telling him he had a daughter. She had never gone through with the abortion, but he'd moved on by the time she was ready to admit to him she was keeping the baby. So, she had chosen not to tell him, but their daughter had been asking about him a lot lately. That was why he sold our home, packed us up, and moved us to this awful place.

Sissy came for visits at first. She'd stay the weekend. Dad then began inviting her mother.

It had gone from that to an engagement and now this. Me living in a home where I wasn't wanted.

I heard the footsteps overhead as the doorbell rang. There would be a lot of that this afternoon. It was Sissy's sixteenth birthday, and all her friends were coming over to get dressed with her. Abilene had rented out a popular restaurant in town for the party. I'd heard them talking about it for weeks. Not once had they mentioned my going. I didn't want to anyway.

I enjoyed the evenings when they left me here alone. It was the only time I felt any peace in this place.

The door to my bedroom swung open, and I turned to see Sissy walking in, her eyes locked on the laundry I hadn't washed yet.

"Please tell me you washed my pink Victoria's Secret bra with the little hearts on it," she whined.

"I just got home. I'm sorting things now," I replied.

"God, Lib, can you not be so slow? It's my birthday—not that you care. You've not told me happy birthday or given me anything."

I wanted to laugh. What was I supposed to give her? She'd taken my bedroom, along with the white furniture that my mother and I had picked out on my sixth birthday together. It was the last birthday that I'd had with my mom. She had taken the television that my dad had bought me when we moved into this house. I had nothing left to give her.

"Happy birthday," I told her, realizing I hadn't spoken to her today.

She was my sister. It wasn't her fault that her mother hated my existence. Sissy didn't hate me—at least I didn't think she did. She just wasn't nice.

She beamed a bright smile at me. Sissy was beautiful. Her blonde hair was the same color as Dad's, but the rest of her looked like Abilene. I was envious of her blue eyes and tall, willowy frame.

"Thank you, Lib. Now, if you could hurry with that laundry. Get mine done first, would ya?" she said.

The doorbell rang again.

"That's Hilly," she said, turning to hurry back out the door and up the stairs.

A loud scream startled me, and the clothes I had picked up fell to the floor. I took off running for the stairs.

What had happened? Was everything okay? My mind raced with terrible scenarios.

Then, I heard my sister's squeal. "OH MY GOD!!! MOM! You got me a car!"

I stopped and stared up the dark stairwell. She'd gotten a car for her birthday. If Abilene couldn't afford to buy me new uniforms for school, how could she afford a car for Sissy's birthday?

Sighing, I closed the door and turned to go back to get Sissy's underthings. There was no point in caring. I needed to be happy that Abilene had kept me after my father's death. Like she had told me many times, I could be in a foster home.

"When you think it's bad, baby girl, remember, there is someone out there who would give anything for what you have."

Mama D's words came back to me, and for the first time in my life, I questioned her wisdom.

One

LIAM
Present Day

When I slung open the door to the bar, I'd had to stop at for shelter on my way back to Ocala from Miami, the cool air inside chilled my rain-soaked body. The thunder rumbled louder, and I closed off the storm behind me, wiping what water I could from my cut—not that the leather hadn't seen its fair share of rain before. Reaching up, I ran my hand over my face and tried to get rid of the droplets clinging to my beard, not that it did much good.

Glancing around, I took in the place. There hadn't been a lot of options when it got hard to see the road through the downpour. Place wasn't bad. It wasn't an actual bar though. It looked more like a pub. A waitress walked by, carrying a tray of food. I wasn't hungry, but the cheese-covered fries, with what looked like bacon crumbles, were appealing.

The curly-haired waitress turned to me and smiled as her eyes drifted down my body. "You can have a seat wherever you'd like," she told me.

Too young, darling, I thought to myself as I nodded my head and made my way to the bar. I wasn't sitting at a table where Miss Barely Out of College could serve me.

The younger they were, the clingier they got. Daddy issues was not for me. I'd learned that lesson the hard way. Besides, I had a daughter who had just turned twenty-five and two grandsons now. For Madeline, my daughter, I chose not to mess around with anyone her age or younger.

I wasn't a fucking saint. I owned a strip club, and I didn't include the girls who worked for me in the no-touch zone. If one wanted to suck my dick and I needed it, I let them. Regardless of age. But that wasn't dating or relationships. It was just club business. A life Madeline wasn't a part of. She didn't have to know.

Sitting down on a stool far enough away from another person so I didn't chance one trying to talk to me, I looked at the whiskey options.

"What can I get you?"

The sexy Southern drawl caught my attention, and I snapped my gaze to the bartender who had just walked up as she slid a cocktail napkin in front of me.

Fucking hell. Long, dark hair was braided and draped over her left shoulder. Brown eyes, the color of warm honey, outlined by thick black lashes. Full red-painted lips. And those big, perfect tits …

Jesus, the cleavage in her tight black tank top made my dick twitch.

"What's your best whiskey, darlin'?" I asked, giving her a smile that always worked with women.

She glanced back at their selection. "You talking price or taste? Because the two are not the same," she said, lifting a bare shoulder. The smooth olive complexion didn't seem like a tan, but the kind of skin tone one had been blessed with at birth.

"Taste," I replied.

The corner of her lips tugged slightly. "Agreed. One more question: do you prefer rye or wheat?"

"Rye," I told her.

When the smile finally touched those lips of hers, a dimple appeared in her right cheek.

"Elijah Craig Single Barrel it is," she said, turning to walk over to the liquor shelf.

My eyes dropped to her ass, and I sucked in a breath. She lifted her arm to reach the bottle, and her tiny waist flashed me, but I couldn't focus on it because my gaze went back to her round ass. It was the right kind of juicy that would bounce perfectly when she was being fucked.

She turned around, and I jerked my gaze back up to see her eyes narrow as she came back over to me.

"Were you checking out my ass?" she asked.

I rubbed my bearded jaw. "Me and every man in this bar."

Amusement lit her pretty brown eyes, and she took a glass, then set it in front of her. "Which MC are you a part of?" she asked as she free-poured the whiskey.

"Judgment," I replied. "What gave me away?"

She nodded her head at my cut. "The leather vest. Patches." She pushed the glass over to me and studied the patch on front, and then her eyes widened as she straightened back up. "President, huh? Impressive."

I picked up the whiskey. "You didn't ask if I wanted ice."

She smirked. "I've been pouring drinks long enough to know a man who looks like you doesn't want it diluted."

Unable to help myself, I dropped my eyes back to her mouth, then her set of natural double D's. She was young. Too young.

A man down the bar called out, and she left me to get him a drink. I turned my eyes and watched her ass and the long, toned legs that were on display. Maybe if I didn't ask her how old she was, I could take her out of here to the nearest hotel tonight and fuck her. Clenching my jaw, I tore my eyes off her.

The sexy doctor I'd asked out last week before heading down to The Judgment's sanctuary in Miami to handle club business was thirty-six. Still young, but more than ten years older than my daughter. There was potential with her. She was someone I could bring around my daughter. Possibly settle down with. I was looking at fifty in a few years, and the idea of having someone to come home to was becoming more appealing.

Staring down at the glass in my hand, I tried to remember what Dr. Dillard looked like. Her platinum-blonde hair and big blue eyes had reminded me of Etta. Wincing, I took a drink. Etta was another lifetime ago. Young love that had never been meant to be and ended too soon. Etta would always be nineteen and perfect. She didn't get to grow old. Her life had been taken before she had that chance, and until I had found our daughter, I'd thought my heart had been taken with her.

"Ready for another?" that sultry voice asked me.

Lifting my gaze, I looked into the eyes of the brunette stunner I had no business lusting over. I was forty-seven. There was a good chance her dad was my age.

"Yeah, might as well. The storm hasn't let up."

My eyes followed her as she went for the bottle of Elijah Craig, not giving a shit about her age. That was definitely a prime piece of ass. The man who got to bend her over and fuck that tight cunt was one lucky son of a bitch.

I dropped my eyes back to the glass before she turned around and caught me ogling her ass again.

"Where were you headed when the storm brought you in here?" she asked, pouring another drink into a new glass.

"Home," I said, looking up at her. "Been in Miami, handling club business, but I moved my home here to Ocala a few years back."

She pushed the glass to me. "So, you're the president, but you don't live where the biker club is located?"

I smirked. That was a really long explanation that started with finding my daughter after searching for nineteen years. "Complicated."

She chuckled. "Complicated. That makes two of us. That's why I'm here too."

The flash of sadness in her eyes caused an uncomfortable feeling in my chest. She was too young for that look just yet. Sure, life was one shit show after another until you were dead, but a pretty thing like that shouldn't know it this soon. Didn't seem right. But then I kept imagining her naked and full of my cock, so my sympathy might be a little lust-driven.

"You not from around here?" I asked.

She started to shake her head and stopped. "Well, not really. I was born in Charleston. I like to think that's where I'm from. My dad brought me here when I was a kid, and bad decisions kept me here."

"We've all made those and suffered," I replied.

The sigh that she let out caused her tits to lift and fall enough to gently bounce. Fuck! I had to stop looking at her tits. She was clearly going through some shit. An old man perving on her wasn't what she needed.

"I guess," she replied, and then a smile touched her lips. "My Mama D used to say, 'Mistakes happen, and cryin' a bucket of tears over them is silly. Because wisdom is built from a pile of mistakes.'"

I grinned. "Mama D sounds like a smart woman."

She nodded. "She was. The older I get, the more her sayings mean to me."

I wanted to ask who Mama D was and where she was now, but the way she was talking in past tense, it sounded like the woman was no longer walking this earth.

"Liberty! You can leave early. Shawn is here, and we aren't busy enough for both of you," a woman with red hair, pulled tight in a bun on top of her head, called out from the other end of the bar.

The girl in front of me sighed. "Great," she muttered.

"She talking to you?"

She nodded. "Yeah, that's the owner. I was supposed to work a double today. I was gonna get a ride from one of the servers to the bus stop after work." She looked back at my glass. "Want me to get you another before I leave?"

The defeated look on her face didn't sit well with me. I liked it when she smiled.

"No, I'm good. Rain has mostly stopped. I'll close my tab and head on out," I told her, trying like hell not to say more, but I already knew I wasn't going to be able to do it. "You need a ride?" Yep, there it was. I couldn't leave her here to walk to a bus stop in the rain. I didn't know where the closest one was, but if she was hoping for a ride, I was assuming it was a good distance.

She pulled her bottom lip between her teeth and glanced toward the windows, then back at me. "Yes, I, um, I do, but I don't want you to go out of your way or anything."

I slid a hundred-dollar bill toward her and stood up. "I won't be. Go get your things and meet me outside."

"I need to get your change," she said, taking the money.

"No change."

She frowned. "That's a fifty-six-dollar tip."

I nodded. "Yeah. See you outside."

I didn't wait for her to argue before I headed for the door.

I shouldn't have done that. Putting a woman on the back of my bike was something I never did. But here I was, offering to give a ride to the sexy bartender because those eyes of hers did something to me.

Stepping into the humid, thick air that came after rain in the summer in Florida, I tried to take a deep breath.

Think about the doctor. She was who I was taking out tomorrow night. She was old enough. She was also a fucking doctor with an Ivy League degree. I could be proud of who I brought around my daughter and grandkids.

Picking up my helmet, I adjusted the strap so it would fit on Liberty's head. I was helping out a girl who needed a ride. I'd want someone to help my daughter if she was in this position. Probably wouldn't want someone like me doing it though. Not that it even mattered. Madeline would never be in this position.

The door to the bar swung open, and out sauntered Liberty, the hot-as-fuck, too-young bartender.

God, that body.

Why wasn't some man here, ready to pick her up? She should have a guy ready to drop whatever he was doing when she called him. Maybe there was one, and he was at work. I hadn't asked.

She reached me, and I handed her the helmet.

"Better put this on."

Her eyes dropped to it, and she glanced back up at me before taking it.

"Your man busy?" I asked.

She paused and looked at me as if she didn't understand me.

"A girl who looks like you has a man. Where is he?"

The pain was back in her eyes, and I wanted to let out a string of curses. I didn't like it when she had that sad expression.

"I did," she said softly. "I … he …" She took a breath. "I walked in on him and his sister-in-law two weeks ago."

What?

"His sister-in-law? Are you saying they were fucking?"

She nodded.

What kind of idiot had she been dating?

"They've always had a weird, flirty relationship, but, well, she's married to his brother. I didn't think anything of it until …"

Goddamn.

"Where am I taking you, darlin'?" I asked.

She slid the helmet on her head and struggled to buckle it. I stepped closer and took it from her hands, then fastened it, making sure it was secure before letting go.

"Bus stop. It's two miles that way," she said, pointing east.

I shook my head. "No bus. Where is home?" If I was gonna take Little Hot and Sexy on my bike, then I might as well get her home.

"The Ocala Inn on Second Street," she replied.

I tensed and studied her for a moment. "Why are you staying in a motel?"

"Because I was living in my boyfriend—ex-boyfriend's apartment," she replied.

And he'd been fucking his sister-in-law.

I threw my leg over the bike, then held out my hand to her. "Come on, darlin'," I said, trying to ignore the shit going on in my chest.

I didn't want to care about this girl. She wasn't my responsibility. She had a good job, and I was sure she'd find her way.

Her slender hand slid over my palm, and I closed mine around hers so that I could steady her while she climbed on behind me. This was the first woman to ride on the back of my bike, and I didn't even know her.

"Wrap your arms around me and hold on tight," I told her.

She leaned forward, and I closed my eyes to breathe through my nose as her hands moved over my abs. My teeth clenched tightly as her soft, full tits pressed against my back. My dick swelled inside the tight confines of my jeans.

Think of something else.

"Is this good?" she asked close to my ear.

I didn't trust my voice, so I just nodded.

This was probably a big fucking mistake.

Two

LIBERTY
Six Weeks Later

Please answer the phone. Please, please, please, I silently pleaded as I held it to my ear. My grip tightened on the phone as I waited.

This was the third time I had called Sissy in the past two days, and the other two times, I'd left messages that she hadn't returned. If I had anyone else to ask, I would, but I had no one.

My sister and I rarely spoke. I would call her on holidays and her birthday, but that was about it. I knew if I didn't call her, there would be no communication between us. She was the only family I had, and even if we had never had a close relationship, I didn't want to lose touch with her.

"What, Liberty?" she snapped into the phone.

I wanted to weep with relief. She had answered.

"Hey, Sissy. How are you?" I said cheerfully as my stomach churned from nerves.

"I'm busy, but you continue to call and don't seem to understand that not all of us have bartender hours."

I licked my lips and took a deep breath. "Yeah, I'm sorry about calling. I just … well, I needed to speak with you. I was wondering if I could stay at your house for a few weeks. Just until I can find an affordable place to live."

Silence. Not good.

I started pacing in the motel room that I couldn't keep paying for while saving enough money for an apartment. Even working doubles several days a week, I wasn't making enough to get my own place and save up for a car.

"What happened to the grocer's son?" she asked tightly.

My ex-boyfriend's father owned the Gabler Groceries chain. I had been with Wallace Gabler on and off since my senior year of high school. Then, four years ago, I moved in with him permanently. He talked marriage and forever. I was never sure that was what I wanted with him, but he was the only constant in my life. The one who loved me, and when I needed anyone, it was Wallace who was there.

Until two months ago, when I caught him cheating on me. I had no idea how long he'd been sleeping with his sister-in-law. But it had happened, and I had needed to see it. That had been the slap in the face to wake me up. Wallace was not my future. He had never been the one. He was just all I'd had.

"We broke up. I've, uh, been staying at a motel, but I need to save money so I can get my own place."

She sighed. "Can't you just make up with the Gabler boy?"

"He cheated on me," I explained.

She muttered a curse. "How long are we talking?"

"A month?" I asked hopefully.

"Jesus Christ, Liberty. You are thirty-one years old. When are you going to become an adult? I didn't go through all those years of college to take care of you because you chose not to get a degree."

I bit down hard on my tongue to keep from responding to that.

Her mother had paid for her education. I hadn't had that luxury, and I couldn't afford it. I tried to get student loans but with no credit and no cosigner I couldn't get approved. When Abilene kicked me out at eighteen, I couldn't go to school and work enough hours that would pay for my housing, get me a car, and feed me. I'd used the bus, eaten little, and lived with four other roommates for almost two years and even then, I was barely making the payment plan the junior college had set up for me. I finally gave up.

"I'll clean your house and stay out of your way. You won't even know I'm there," I assured her.

"Fine. I'll be home about six. But one month, Liberty. That is it. I have a life, you know."

I almost let out a sob as relief washed over me. "Thank you."

She ended the call without another word, and I sank down on the end of the bed. Living with Sissy wouldn't be easy, but I had survived worse, growing up with her mother. I could handle this until I had enough money put away to get my own place.

My suitcases were already packed, and the money I had tucked in my purse was my entire savings. One thousand six hundred and ten dollars. A month of not having to pay for this room, and I could get an apartment close to the bar. That way, I could save my bus money by walking and then be able to afford a car. I should have never let Wallace convince me to sell my car and use a company car. He'd gone on and on about how unsafe mine was and that it was bad for the environment.

Like always, I did what he wanted. Somewhere along the way, it had become a pattern I hadn't noticed I'd fallen into.

I dropped my gaze to my flat stomach and knew I didn't have any other choice. I had to save money. This had to work. Things weren't just about me anymore.

Standing back up, I took both my suitcases and rolled them to the door. Reaching for the knob, I glanced back at the bed. The night I had invited the biker named Liam inside after he gave me a ride after work six weeks ago changed my life.

I had been attracted to him the moment he sat down at the bar. He was everything Wallace wasn't. He was tough, dangerous, sexy, and older. I liked all of that.

Then, after the ride back here, being pressed to his muscular back with his bike vibrating between my legs for twenty minutes, I was more turned on than I could ever remember being in my life. I had asked if wanted to come inside not expecting him to. When we walked into the room, he backed me up against the wall and claimed my mouth like he owned it.

The dirty words that came from his lips was a turn-on I hadn't known I was missing. He seemed to be as hungry for it as I was. We had sex three times that night. It was incredible. I even lost count of my orgasms.

Wallace had never brought me to an orgasm during sex. He had always pumped a few times and groaned his release, then pulled out, taken off the condom, and gone to sleep.

Liam was nothing like that. He'd gone for hours.

I had used that memory to get myself off for weeks after hoping he'd walk back into the bar again. As the days passed and he didn't return, I started realizing he wasn't going to. I'd had a life full of disappointments. Liam was just one more to toss onto the mountain of others.

When my period was late, I didn't think anything of it. I'd gotten off the pill when I left Wallace because it wasn't something I could afford and I didn't need it at the time. I figured it was messing with my cycle. Up until this week, when I woke up and ran to the bathroom to vomit. The nausea was gone by the time I had to go to work, and I chalked it up to something I had eaten the night before.

But the next day, it happened again.

The two blue lines on the pregnancy test appeared almost immediately, and I knew nothing would ever be the same.

I had googled The Judgment MC and Liam's name. I didn't know his last name, and that made it difficult. I couldn't find a contact for any of them. They weren't on the internet. Apparently, bikers didn't do social media.

I opened the door and pulled my luggage outside into the sweltering August heat.

Liam didn't want to be found. He'd left that morning before I woke up. No letter. Nothing. I lay there, hoping he'd gone to get breakfast. But five hours later, when I had to go to work, he still hadn't shown up.

Here I was, six weeks later, knocked up, and I didn't even know the father's last name.

Three

LIAM

With my hand fisted in Pandora's hair, I held her in place as I shot my load down her throat. I let out a deep groan of satisfaction as she gagged, unable to breathe. Fuck, I had needed that. She was by far the best cocksucker we had at the club.

Slowly I released her hair, then let my hand drop to the armrest of the leather office chair I was sitting in behind my desk. Pandora looked up at me, clearly pleased with herself as tears ran down the sides of her face, and she wiped the mess off her mouth.

I patted her cheek. "Thanks," I told her.

She gave me a sultry smile and stood up. "Anytime."

Closing my eyes, I laid my head back and waited for the door to close behind her. That was one of the best things about Pandora. She wasn't clingy or needy. She sucked my cock like a whore and then went back to work. Not all the girls who worked at Devil's were like that. Some wanted on my cock because they wanted the power they thought would come with it.

I opened my eyes and reached to tuck my dick back in my jeans and zip them up, then glanced at the time. If I didn't leave now, I was gonna be late, and I still needed to change into something else. The doctor I'd been casually dating for a little over a month had asked me to attend a fundraising event with her tonight for the children's wing of the hospital. It wasn't formal, and the children were attending, so I'd agreed.

She was nice enough, and she was too damn busy to be clingy. There were no demands for something exclusive, and that made dating her easy. Sure, there were things about her that I wasn't crazy about, but she was gorgeous, successful, and independent. She didn't need me to take care of her.

The vanilla sex, however, wasn't the best, and I had been sending for Pandora and the use of her mouth more often lately. Hell, I'd even bent Bellatrix over the bar last week and fucked her after she arrived for work, flirting with me and offering her cunt to release any of my stress. I'd sworn I wasn't going to fuck any of the girls again after that. How was I ever going to settle down if I couldn't keep my dick out of the strippers? I had to stop it.

I'd told Madeline about the doctor, and she'd been fucking giddy. Happy that I was seeing someone that I could have a future with. If I could get past the boring sex, then, yeah, maybe.

Standing up, I shrugged off my cut and went to hang it on the hook beside the door, then tugged my shirt over my head and went to get the long-sleeved dark blue oxford shirt I'd brought to wear. The jeans were staying, and so were the boots.

Once I had the shirt buttoned up and tucked in, I went to the desk to grab the brush I kept in the drawer and pulled my hair back neatly, then used the black hair tie to secure it at the nape of my neck. My eyes went to the pack of cigarettes I had hidden in there. I was trying to cut back, but just in case, I tapped one out and stuck it in the pocket of my shirt before heading to the door.

Tex was starting up the stairs as I came down them. His mouth quirked in amusement as he looked at me. "Damn, Prez. You look almost respectable. Date with the sexy doc?"

He was having too much fun with the idea of me dating a doctor.

I grunted in response.

"I was wondering why you drove the Charger in today," he said.

Until I'd started dating the doctor, I rarely drove my Charger. I was always on my Harley unless I had to go get my oldest grandson. But seeing as how I didn't put women on the back of my bike, I always took the Charger on our dates.

"Make sure the club is closed up tonight before you leave and try not to need me," I told him.

He nodded. "Planning on it. Country is coming in tomorrow, and I'm headed to Miami."

I knew he'd be going back to The Judgment sanctuary soon. He'd been here two weeks, and he never stayed this long at a time.

"Okay," I replied, walking past him. "I got my phone on me if shit comes up."

"Keep the ringer on this time," he called out, and I paused.

"That was one fucking time," I ground out through clenched teeth.

"Well, that one time, all hell broke loose, and you were needed."

He was never going to let me forget it either, and he would never know that my phone hadn't been on silent at first. I'd put it on silent after the first time he called, and then I'd placed it upside down so I wouldn't be disturbed.

"You handled it," I replied.

"If that's what you want to call it. You ever gonna tell me where you were?"

I started for the door. "No," I snarled, then shoved open the back entrance to get away from Tex and his nosy questioning.

He had called me just as I ripped the top off the gorgeous brunette bartender I'd given a ride to. I hadn't been going to let anything or anyone keep me from stripping her naked and sinking my cock into her cunt.

All the shivering and squirming she'd done on the back of my bike had been impossible to ignore. I'd been so goddamn hard when I got to the motel where she was staying that when she invited me in, I no longer gave a fuck that she was too young for me.

I'd taken her like a crazed man who couldn't get enough. Several times.

Shaking my head, I tried to push away the memories of her plump ass bouncing while I slammed into her and she begged me to do it harder.

I jerked the car door open with more force than necessary and climbed inside. Staying away from that bar and that girl had been damn near torture, but I'd done it, and I would continue to do it. She was trouble.

I was supposed to be at my date's house in ten minutes, and I didn't need to show up with a hard-on from thoughts of another woman.

"God, that was tedious and exhausting."

I glanced over at the doctor as she closed her eyes with her head lying back on the seat.

She'd been impressive tonight. Everyone had seemed to adore her. The woman knew how to charm a room.

"The whiskey was good," I said because other than that, I didn't have much else to say about it.

The event had been a lot of wealthy, uppity, educated folks trying to outdo each other. No one seemed to remember it was about the kids. I'd had nothing in common with any of them.

She laughed. "That's good. I wish I'd drunk some. I've had a shitty day, and this month is going to be trying on me."

Her job seemed stressful, not that we talked about it much. Maybe she did, but she talked a lot, and I tended to zone out.

"What's happening this month?"

She rolled her head over to the side to face me as I drove toward her house. "Did I ever tell you about my sister?"

We had talked very little about her family. Unless it was one of those times I had zoned out.

I shook my head, seeing as she didn't seem to remember.

"Well, she's a disaster. Our father spoiled her. She was always his favorite. She got everything she wanted. Like the bigger room even though I was five years older than her. He called her baby, but no endearments for me. Even on his death bed, it was her name he whispered on his last breath." She sighed heavily. "Her spoiled life led to her dropping out of college. Dating this rich guy since high school who won't ever marry her. She was just his easy fuck. She can't keep a job, and the one she has now is a shitty one. Anyway, her rich boyfriend dumped her again, and she basically demanded that I give her a place to stay. I'm giving her a month."

She sounded like a bitch.

"You're more generous than I'd have been."

"Mom died two years ago, and she didn't even come to the funeral. She called me, and that was it. Nothing else. Then, she shows up on my doorstep with her suitcases like I should kiss her feet that she came to see me."

Who doesn't come to their mother's funeral? Jesus.

"I worked so hard in school to get scholarships, and then I got student loans. I busted my ass through medical school while she was off, traipsing around, never visiting Mom or me. Sleeping with that boyfriend for his money. It would have broken our dad's heart to see what she'd turned out to be."

Their father had clearly ruined her by having a favorite.

"Seems like he chose the wrong daughter," I said.

"Yeah, that's what Mom use to say," she replied with a sad smile on her face.

I pulled into the driveway of her three-story home. It was massive for just one person, but she'd explained she bought it with her future family in mind. The thought of my living here and having a family with her, however, wasn't appealing. I liked my farmhouse and land. But if I listed out the pros and cons of settling down with her, the pros side would win.

"I'd invite you inside, but, well, she's in there. Probably eating all my food and lying in the living room, watching television like she owns the place."

I should feel disappointment that there would be no sex with her tonight, but I was more relieved than anything. I leaned over and pressed a kiss to her lips. She smelled expensive, and I liked that. Her lips were a little hard from the filler she'd just had injected into them, but her minty breath was nice.

"Good night," I said as I ended the kiss.

"Good night, Liam. Thanks for tonight."

I nodded my head. "My pleasure."

I waited until she made it to the door. I should have probably walked her to it, but I wasn't thinking. I'd been ready for her to get out so I could go home and enjoy a quiet evening on my front porch with Ozzy—my Great Dane—and a beer.

Four

LIBERTY

Shawn glanced down at my chest, then cleared his throat. I tugged at the Abernathy's tank top that was part of our work uniform, feeling self-conscious. I knew what he was thinking. I'd noticed it, too, in the mirror when I got dressed earlier today. My boobs were bigger. I hadn't known that happened with pregnancy. There was a lot I didn't know. I needed to see a doctor, and as soon as my Medicaid was approved, I would.

"You, uh," he said, running his hand through his wavy brown hair, "look good tonight, Lib."

I had to see if I could get a bigger-sized tank top.

"Thanks," I replied tightly.

He was a complete man-whore. When he had first started working here, he asked me out regularly. Even though he knew I had a boyfriend. Eventually he stopped and we'd found a comfortable working relationship. Then, when he found out we broke up, it resumed. I had finally gotten to a place where I didn't dread seeing him, and now, I had to deal with his propositions all over again.

"Looks like sorority girls just sat down there. Your favorite," I told him. "You take that end. I'll stay on this end."

He glanced down there, then back at me. "Was that a jab?" he asked.

I shook my head. "Not at all. Just pointing out the obvious."

He took a step toward me and glanced back at my chest again. "If you gave me a chance, Lib, I could change your mind about me."

Yeah, well, buddy, I am three years older than you and pregnant. Not happening.

I raised my eyebrows and shook my head. "Go see what the sorority girls want to drink."

He sighed and gave me one last look before he left me to deal with the customers we already had. I finished refilling two of their drinks and was about to go get a case of beer when Virginia walked in from the back office. I wanted to groan in frustration. She always sent me home when there were two of us on a night like this. Which sucked because I needed the money.

Her husband, Tom Abernathy—whose father had opened the bar fifty years ago—would not send me home. If he were here and anyone was leaving, it would be Shawn. I was the harder worker. But Virginia liked Shawn's looks even though she was thirty years older than he was.

"Liberty, you can go. Tonight is going to be slow."

I started to beg her to let me stay, but her eyes dropped to my chest, and I changed my mind. I didn't want her asking questions about my overflowing cleavage. The last thing I needed was for her to know I was pregnant. I knew they couldn't legally fire me for being pregnant, but I had worked here long enough to know Virginia could find loopholes when she wanted something. She could cut my hours drastically or put me in the back, doing something that I didn't get tips from. They liked their servers and bartenders to be young and attractive. She would have my pay cut until I had to quit.

"Okay," I replied, quickly turning away from her and handling the customers I had left before going to get my purse.

Two of our regulars closed their tabs and tipped me. I wiped down the area and went to let Shawn know I was being sent home. He groaned and bitched about him not getting to leave. I thought about asking him to tell Virginia he wanted to switch, but then I thought about my boobs and changed my mind.

She was busy talking to one of the servers when I went and grabbed my purse and headed for the door.

It was already dark on my walk to the bus stop. The two-mile trek wasn't convenient, but for now, it was all I had. Spending money on an Uber every time I went to and from work would eat into my savings. After one week at Sissy's, I knew I had to save quickly and get out fast. If she let me stay a month it would be a miracle. It was clear she was already changing her mind.

The bus ride took thirty minutes when a car ride would have been more like ten. My eyes felt heavy by the time it stopped and I got out. Thankfully, the walk to her house was just under a mile. I made my way down the sidewalk and fought against the sudden fatigue. I'd been dealing with that lately too. Exhaustion coming out of nowhere.

Tonight, I would google *pregnancy* on my phone and read about other things I should be expecting. What else was going to change on me soon?

There was a classic Dodge Charger in the driveway when I finally made it to Sissy's house. I knew she was dating some guy because she'd mentioned it the first night I got here. But there had been no signs of him.

This must be the guy. Nice wheels. That one had to be early to mid-seventies but looked like it had just been driven off the lot it was in such good condition. Dad had loved classic cars. He would have been our here drooling over that one. I doubted my sister even knew that about him.

Sissy was as gorgeous now as she had been when we were younger. She was also a successful pediatrician and had wealth to go with her looks. I was surprised she wasn't already married.

The door was unlocked, so I didn't have to dig out the key she'd given me. I stepped inside, quietly listening for any sounds. If she was going at it somewhere, I did not want to walk in on that. I moved toward the stairs but there were no moans or headboard banging coming from her bedroom.

I wanted a bottle of water, but I wasn't sure if she had some romantic dinner planned.

I made my way down the hallway toward the kitchen, and I heard Sissy's laughter. It was further down, near the great room. Sighing in relief, I went into the kitchen and grabbed a water. There was something in the oven that smelled fantastic, but I knew I wasn't going to be offered any of it. My stomach growled, so I went to the pantry to get a protein bar from the box I'd bought on Monday before heading back to the staircase.

I heard the deep timbre of a man's voice but couldn't make out what he was saying as I went back to the foyer.

Climbing the stairs, I grew tired again and looked forward to a shower and bed.

I closed the door to the bedroom, then walked over and sat down on the bed to take off my shoes. My feet ached since I'd been on them since ten this morning, and all the walking I had done to and from the bus didn't help. At least it was keeping me fit. Who needed a gym membership when they walked almost six miles a day?

I took a drink of water and lay back on the double bed. I would close my eyes for a moment, then go get a shower.

When my eyes snapped back open, I stared at the ceiling, realizing I'd fallen asleep. I sat up and looked at my phone to check the time. It was just after eleven. I'd been asleep for over three hours. Curling up and going back to sleep sounded appealing, but I sniffed my tank top and could smell the bar. Scrunching my nose, I stood up. I would sleep better if I was clean.

Opening the door slowly, I looked down the hall to see Sissy's bedroom door closed. It hadn't been when I walked by it earlier. She was either asleep or was in there with her date. I went back to get my bag of toiletries because she had informed me that I wasn't to use any of hers. There weren't any in the guest bathroom anyway, and I assumed she had taken them before I arrived.

Just as I stepped out into the hallway, I heard a loud moan coming from her room, and I paused before continuing. When I reached the door to the bathroom, she let out a scream that made me wince. The man must have a big cock.

"Oh, YES!" Her high-pitched voice made me cringe.

I hurried inside to close the door and muffle her sounds. I didn't need to know what she sounded like while having sex. Although I was curious about the man she was dating. I wondered what he looked like. Was he a doctor too? Probably wore expensive Armani suits. Hopefully, he was hearing impaired.

The warm water sprayed from the showerhead, and I quickly stripped my clothing and climbed into the bath-shower combo. I had gotten good at rationing my supplies when I was younger. Abilene had only supplied me with toothpaste, soap, and deodorant every two months. I'd had to wash my hair with the bar of soap. As an adult, I spent very little on things like that. I could make them last much longer than the average person. Although I did purchase shampoo and conditioner for my hair. Having to brush my hair after just using soap on it had been horrible. The one time I'd asked for some conditioner, she'd slapped me across the face and called me a spoiled brat, then sent me to my room in the basement without dinner.

I was not going to think about that time in my life. It was behind me. I had survived without her help. When she had died, I hadn't even shed a tear. She meant nothing to me. I had called Sissy to tell her I was sorry for her loss, and she'd hung up on me.

Feeling refreshed after rinsing off, I dried my hair with the towel the best I could, then wrapped it around my body. Sissy had given me one towel and told me that I wasn't to touch her other towels. This one had a hole and several stains. It looked like something she cleaned with. I wondered what her towels looked like. I was sure they weren't like this one.

I brushed my hair, then my teeth before putting my things back into my bag and peeking out the door to make sure the coast was clear. When I saw no one, I tiptoed out and headed to my room. Just before I reached it, I heard the click of a door behind me and turned to see a man stepping out of Sissy's room.

Knowing I needed to hurry and get inside my room before he saw me, I started to turn away when he looked over at me and our eyes locked. Recognition slammed into me like a semitruck, and the bag in my hand fell to the floor.

The shocked look on his face quickly morphed into a disinterested glance before he turned and walked away.

I couldn't breathe or move.

Liam.

My sister was dating Liam.

I slid my hand over my stomach as I finally sucked in some much-needed oxygen. *Oh my God.*

Five

LIAM

My fist slammed into the punching bag as I cursed. Sweat rolled down the side of my face, and my breathing was ragged. I'd been at this for almost an hour. I ignored the burn in my arms and stomach as I continued.

Ozzy sat across the room, watching me. He was starting to appear concerned. I didn't normally hit the bag this long. I usually moved on to weights. But I needed to hit something. Leaving the bed of the woman you were dating after some less than enjoyable sex and finding the hottest fuck you'd had in God knew how long standing in the hallway, wrapped in a bath towel that barely covered her pussy, was the worst kind of luck a man could have.

To make matters worse, you found out that the sexy, sweet, sad beauty you'd fucked like an animal wasn't sweet or sad. She was a complete spoiled bitch. Which made a lot more sense because, seriously, a girl who looked and fucked like that one shouldn't be in need of a ride ever. She should have a list of names a mile long to call.

Even with all the shit I now knew about her, my dick had still gotten hard minutes after getting off in her sister's cunt.

I might be here all day, hitting the damn bag. The war of emotions inside my head wasn't easing up. I was dating a woman who checked all the boxes for a perfect catch. The settling-down type. She had it all. The sex wasn't great, sure, but did I expect married sex to be great? No. Even good sex would get boring after some time anyway. You couldn't build a relationship on sex.

Yet every time I'd closed my eyes last night, it was the younger sister that I had seen. Naked, on her hands and knees, while I slammed my cock into her tight cunt. Her ass.

I shouted angrily as I hit the bag. Why couldn't I let that memory go?! She wasn't the only hot ass I'd fucked.

Dropping my arms, I stood there, breathing hard as Ozzy tilted his head, still watching me. "Be glad you're neutered and not ruled by a tight pussy," I told him, taking off the gloves and tossing them onto the weight bench.

Just three more weeks, and she'd be out of her sister's house. I could stay busy and cut down on the time I saw Selena while she was there. Once Liberty left her house, we could go back to the regular pattern.

Unless Liberty told her. Which could happen. Although I'd fucked Liberty before I ever went on that first date with Selena. It might not matter to Selena though, and I couldn't trust Liberty not to lie just to hurt her sister. From what Selena had told me, it sounded like something she might do.

I stalked over to my phone and picked it up. Selena hadn't called, which was a good thing. She was one to face issues, not bury them. If she'd spoken to Liberty and found out I'd fucked her, then she'd have called me.

The worst that could happen was, she'd stop seeing me. I wouldn't be heartbroken. I wasn't in love. She was just something that might become something more. I liked the way we sounded even if the way I felt wasn't deep.

Maybe I should just break it off. End this now.

Ozzy stood up and walked past me toward the stairs, ready to go back up. Sighing, I grabbed my towel and wiped the sweat from my face, then nodded at him to go on.

I would figure it out later. Right now, I had to call Micah, my vice president, and deal with shit that had gone down at one of our clubs in Miami last night. Toxic Throttle was our most popular location down there, and it got rowdy more often than not. Once club business was handled, I had to get to Devil's and sign off on some bills.

If I kept myself distracted, then I wouldn't have time to think about Liberty or Selena.

I stood on the driveway outside my house, waiting for Madeline's Mercedes G-Wagon to come to a stop, then went to open the back seat door. My oldest grandson, Cree, beamed up at me, making all the bad shit melt away.

"Papa!" he shouted. "I came to see you!"

I started unbuckling him from his car seat. "And I've been waiting out here since your momma called and said you were headed this way. Come tell me all about this new horse I heard you got with your dad last week."

His eyes went wide. "It's big and black! I got me a cowboy hat, too, just like Dad's."

I lifted him from his seat and held him in my arms as he wrapped his little arms around me. Looking over his shoulder, I smiled at my daughter. She was older now than her mother had ever been, and there wasn't a day I didn't wish Etta could have seen her grow up. See her now. Know the boys.

"Thanks for this, Dad," she said. "Fawn is keeping Eli for me. She'd happily keep them both, but Cree said he needed some Papa time."

When he spotted Ozzy walking this way, he wiggled to get free, and I kissed his head and let him down. Those two were tight.

"No need to thank me. I need some Cree time myself, and you know Ozzy enjoys his attention. Where is Blaise taking you?"

She blushed, and it amazed me that after six years and two kids, those two still acted as if they'd just fallen in love. It wasn't something you saw often, and knowing my daughter was worshipped by her husband made it easier to accept he was also the boss of the Southern Mafia. That had been a hard pill to swallow at first. But the man would kill an entire town before he allowed anything to hurt her or their boys. A father couldn't ask for more than that.

"He won't tell me. Just that he wants me to himself. He loves our boys, but he can be selfish with me at times. I don't mind though," she said, smiling. "Fawn is going to come pick him up tomorrow afternoon," she said.

Fawn was Blaise's stepmother. Once his father had married Fawn, he had stepped down as boss and handed the title and responsibility that came with it to Blaise.

"No rush. I cleared my schedule the moment you called," I told her.

She narrowed her eyes. "How are things with the doctor?" she asked, then grinned.

I shrugged. Didn't want to talk about that. I sure as hell couldn't tell Madeline what I'd done. I wanted her to be proud of me.

"It's good."

"I want to meet her. Maybe I can have the both of you over for dinner one-night next week," she said with a hopeful look in her eyes.

I nodded.

If we were still dating then, I'd do that. I wasn't ready for that step, but I guessed I could go ahead and take it if Madeline wanted to meet her. I might start seeing things differently once I saw how well Selena fit into my life.

"I looked her up online. She's gorgeous," Madeline told me.

"Yeah, she is. She's a good person too."

Madeline closed the space between us and hugged me. "I want that for you."

I wrapped my arms around her and felt my chest tighten. When she stepped back, she glanced over at Cree running around the yard with Ozzy, who was as tall as he was.

"Come give me a big kiss!" she called out to him.

He paused, then spun around and came barreling back this way.

When he flung himself into her arms, I watched them, wishing I'd been there when she was that little. That I'd raised her. She'd had a rough life, growing up, and I hated to think about it. I felt like I'd failed her by not finding her. Even though I had exhausted every lead I got.

I had so much to make up for, and I feared I never would.

Six

LIBERTY

Darkness was dancing at the corners of my peripheral vision. I blinked several times and took a deep breath. I had worked a double today, and the walk from the bus stop to the house was proving to be more difficult than normal. My head felt light, and I walked over to a lamppost and held on to it while I tried to wait out the spinning. I had to find a way to make this stop. This was the second night in a row I'd felt faint on my walk back to Sissy's. Tonight was much worse.

The rumble of a bike barely registered in my head as I gripped the post tighter. The darkness was creeping in. I could not black out on the sidewalk at eleven at night. Maybe if I sat down. The loud engine got closer, and I decided to wait until it passed before I sat. It would look odd to whoever was passing by.

The bright light from the bike slowed, and I felt a sudden flutter of panic. Were they stopping for me? I had to go. I had to walk. It was late, and this was dangerous. The engine cut off behind me, and I forced my feet to move and focused hard on the ground in front of me. I could do this. I was going to be fine.

"Liberty." A deep voice barked my name, and I froze.

I recognized it. In fact, since he had walked out of Sissy's bedroom a week ago, I'd had a difficult time not thinking about him. Seeing him while I was fighting to stay conscious was not ideal.

"What the fuck are you doing?" he asked, sounding angry or annoyed.

He wasn't going to leave me alone. I turned around to look at him, and I wished I hadn't.

"Walking back to Sissy's," I replied as my head swam. I reached for the streetlamp again to make sure I stayed upright.

"This is how you're gonna thank Selena for letting you crash at her place? Stumbling home drunk late at night? Are you that fucking selfish?"

What? I blinked, trying to understand what he was saying. *Drunk?*

I shook my head. "I'm not drunk. Just got off work," I replied.

He glared at me as his eyes did a quick inventory of my outfit. The world spun a little, and I closed my eyes for a moment. I was going to pass out. Right here on the sidewalk in front of this man.

"Where are you coming from?" he asked. "And you can't stand up! If you're not drunk, then what the hell is wrong with you? Did you take drugs?"

I swallowed and shook my head, opening my eyes. "No. I'm coming from work."

"Did you already lose the job at Abernathy's? Because that's miles from here. You didn't walk from there."

"The bus stop isn't," I said, opening my eyes up.

"The bus stop?"

I nodded. "Yeah. Remember, I use the bus."

"Why can't you stand up without help? Don't fucking lie to me! Selena doesn't need this bullshit. She's had a stressful day."

Selena. Sissy had hated that name as a kid. All anyone called her was Sissy. No one had even known her name was Selena back then.

I opened my mouth to say something, but the blackness overwhelmed everything, and I heard Liam curse before I faded.

Blinking, I opened my eyes and stared up at the ceiling of the bedroom I was using in Sissy's house. Confused, I tried to remember how I had gotten here. Slowly, the memory came back to me—fighting to keep from passing out and … Liam. I sat up too quickly, and my stomach rolled. I took a deep breath and stayed very still.

The nausea began to ease off, and I looked down at my clothes. I was still wearing my work outfit and my tennis shoes. It looked like someone had dropped me on the bed sideways with my feet hanging off the side and walked out. It had to have been Liam.

I started to stand up when the door swung open, and Sissy stood there, clearly furious.

"Oh, good. Your drunk ass is awake. Get your things packed up and get out."

I shook my head. "I'm not drunk. I wasn't drunk. My blood sugar was low. I didn't eat enough, and I worked two—"

"Shut up! I should never have agreed to let you stay here. I knew better than to help you. I don't want to hear your bullshit excuses. Get your things and go."

Where was I going to go? I looked out the window. It was dark outside. How late was it?

"I don't have anywhere to go," I told her.

She shook her head. "I do not care. You can't stay here. I want nothing to do with this disaster of a life you live. The fact that my boyfriend had to pick up your drunk ass because you'd passed out on the sidewalk and bring you here is humiliating."

Her boyfriend. She'd not called him that before. When had the title changed from guy she was dating to boyfriend? He wasn't anything close to a boy. He was a man.

I was still weak and feeling woozy, but asking her for something to eat or to let me get some sleep first was pointless. I went to my suitcase and began to pack it.

"You have twenty minutes to get out of this house," she snapped, then turned and walked out of the room.

I would have to get an Uber and a motel room. I couldn't bring a baby home from the hospital to a motel. I needed a new plan. Perhaps I had enough money saved to get a studio apartment in a less desirable part of town. One that wasn't too dangerous, but not in the best of shape. I could make it look better. Spend some money on sprucing things up.

Trying to think positively, I packed, stopping to steady myself every few minutes. Once I had all my things ready to go, I pulled both suitcases down the hallway. I was going to have to get these down the stairs. Glancing back at Sissy's closed bedroom door, I sighed as I decided on how

I could do this. I didn't have the strength to pick either of them up.

Finally sitting down on my bottom, I slid down a step and laid a suitcase flat, then eased down one step at a time, taking it with me. With the thudding sounds of my body and suitcase sliding on the stairs, I expected Sissy to come out of her room to shout at me, but I didn't hear her door open. I eventually made it to the bottom with the first one and stood it up, then headed up to get the second one.

When I reached the top, I heard a loud moan coming from her room, then the thump of the headboard. Standing there, I listened, unable to end the torture as Liam and Sissy screwed. My eyes stung with unshed tears, and I knew I had to get out of here. Away from both of them.

The pain in my chest was one I was familiar with. It was from the rejection and not being wanted. Well, I'd be damned if my child ever knew that feeling.

Determined, I got the second suitcase down the stairs faster and headed for the front door.

I didn't need anyone's help. They could all go to hell. I would figure this out.

Seven

LIAM

Selena: Sorry again about last night. Thanks for your help.

I read the text twice, trying to think of how to respond. Whatever Liberty had been on was strong, and I didn't think Selena knew what she might be up against.

Me: Have you spoken to her this morning?

I sent it and waited.

Selena had told me last night she'd been worried that Liberty was on drugs. I'd been uneasy, leaving her there last night after dropping Liberty in her room. Liberty could bring some dangerous shit to her door if she was messing with heavy drugs. I'd seen death in my club because of this kind of thing.

Selena: She got up this morning, packed her bags, yelled at me, and stormed out of the house. She's gone. I couldn't help her. She refused to even talk to me about it.

Sounded like drugs all right. I could normally pick out a female like that a mile away. Liberty had fooled me though. I'd been too distracted by that face and her world-class tits and ass that I hadn't noticed the signs.

> **Me:** It's for the best.

I slid my phone in my pocket and headed out of the house after rubbing Ozzy's head and telling him I'd be back later. I needed to make up my mind about Madeline's invitation to bring Selena to dinner.

I found myself not looking forward to being around her simply because I wasn't feeling anything more for her than friendship while I was starting to see the signs of her wanting more. She didn't deserve to be strung along, believing we would become a couple when I wasn't into her. Not the kind of way a man needed to be if he was going to be exclusive with one woman.

I got on my bike and debated on my next move. Going to Miami for a few days was probably needed. It would give me space, and I could be around to deal with club stuff. I cranked up the Harley and headed south. A week away, and I would be more clearheaded and ready to make a decision about Selena.

I made a quick stop at the service station to fill up and call Devil's to let Tex know I was headed to Miami. With him back for the next week, things would be under control here. My gaze veered to the next exit up ahead and the Abernathy's sign that could be seen from the interstate. Deciding to do a little investigating for Selena since I was leaving town and not sticking around to help with anything that came up with Liberty, I turned on my blinker and headed toward the bar I hadn't set foot in since the night I'd taken Liberty to the motel.

Pulling into the front, I parked my bike and got off. It was early still, and the sign said they opened at eleven. That was thirty minutes ago. Not much of a crowd at this time of day. I took off my helmet and headed inside.

Behind the bar was a guy unloading a cart of clean glasses onto the shelf. He glanced back at me as I made my way over there. Only two tables had people at them, but there was no one sitting at the bar. He put the glass in his hand down and turned to me.

"Can I get you something?"

I pulled out a stool and sat down. "Bud Light," I told him.

"Tap?" he asked.

"Yeah."

He picked up a tall glass from the cart.

"Liberty still work here?" I asked.

He paused and looked back at me. "Yeah. How do you know Lib?"

Lib. Him shortening her name like that annoyed me, but I didn't want to think about why.

"She working today?" I asked, ignoring his question.

He glanced toward the back, looking unsure of how to answer. "Uh, yeah," he finally said.

I followed his gaze. "She here already?"

He slid my drink in front of me. "Listen, I don't know you, and I don't feel comfortable telling you Lib's personal stuff."

I cocked an eyebrow. "When she's on shift next isn't personal. Just a question."

The guy didn't say anything.

"Did she work last night?" I asked.

He nodded. "She worked a double yesterday."

"What time did she leave here?"

He tensed up and shook his head. "Why do you want to know?"

The little dickhead was getting on my nerves.

I picked up my beer and took a long drink before setting it back down. "What time do you close on Sundays?"

"Ten," he replied.

The back door opened, and my gaze swung to see who was walking through. It was an older man with a bald head and a large belly. He was headed in this direction.

"Shawn, there are two more carts with glasses to get out before the lunch hour hits. Speed it up."

The guy in front of me nodded then went back to unloading glasses.

I turned my attention to the older man. "You the manager?" I asked.

He nodded and smiled. "Tom Abernathy. I own the place. How can I help you?"

"Does Liberty still work here?" I asked.

The way his brows drew together instantly seemed as if he didn't like me asking questions either. "She's been working here for five years," he said in a less than friendly tone.

Five years? Selena had said she kept losing her jobs. Did the man have her confused with another employee? I doubted she'd been here long enough for him to remember who she was.

"You sure about that?"

The man's shoulders snapped back as he tried to make himself appear taller. "Liberty Dillard has been working for me for five years. Of course I am sure. I'm the one who signs her paychecks. What business do you have with her?"

I took another drink, studying the man. Would he lie for her? Did that hot body of hers in the tiny shorts and tight tank she wore here have him drooling over her? Men could easily be led by their dicks.

"I'm friends with her sister. Checking to see if she's where she says she is—that's all. Her sister has reason to be worried about her."

The man's face turned red, and his eyes widened. "The same sister who kicked out a sick girl in the middle of the night? That sister? The same one who can't be bothered to give her a ride home so she has to walk to the damn bus station two miles away? Why don't you tell that sister she can go to hell for me, yeah?" he said angrily, then swung his gaze to the bartender. "Let him finish his beer and then make sure he leaves."

The other guy glanced at me nervously and then nodded. I got one more glare from Tom Abernathy before he stalked away. I waited until he was gone before asking the bartender anything else. I wasn't leaving until I had some answers. Liberty was good at playing the helpless-female-in-need act. I'd fallen for it myself.

Sounded like Liberty had called in sick and blamed Selena for it, lying about getting kicked out. Ole horny Tom had believed her completely.

"How long you been working here, Shawn?" I asked.

He tensed and looked over at me. "Three years, and Liberty has been here since before me," he replied, seeming to already know what I was going to ask next.

Two witnesses to back up Liberty. Why would Selena lie about something like that? But then maybe she didn't know. If Liberty never called her and hadn't gone to their mother's funeral, Selena might have assumed she was still not keeping a job. That wasn't a big reach. I couldn't blame her for that.

Fine. So, Liberty wasn't a flake when it came to a job. That didn't wipe out all her other transgressions. The reason I was here had nothing to do with her work ethic anyway. I wanted to be sure she wasn't about to bring any danger to Selena's door if she was messed up with some lowlife druggie.

"Do you know if she's seeing anyone? Maybe hitting the party scene after work?"

Shawn was putting another glass up when a smirk touched his lips. He didn't look at me. "Liberty broke up with her boyfriend a couple of months ago. She doesn't party at all. Works too damn much." He cut his eyes to me. "I don't know what her sister has told you, but these questions don't fit her. The only thing Liberty is guilty of is being too damn stubborn to let someone take her home after work."

She'd had no problem letting a stranger almost twenty years older than her give her a ride after work on his Harley, but I didn't say that. Whatever life she did live, she kept it out of the workplace. I had to give her props for that. I wished the girls who worked for me could do the same thing. They loved bringing drama to work with them.

I finished my beer and laid a twenty on the bar, then stood up.

"Thanks," I told him and headed for the door.

Last night was still going to bother me, but Selena had a security system, and she was at the hospital more than she was at home. I didn't need to stick my nose any further into this. Liberty checked out with her employer and coworker. Granted, both were men, and they probably fantasized about fucking her every chance they could, but they hadn't looked like they were covering anything up.

Getting back on my Harley, I tried to shove all thoughts of Liberty out of my head. Cranking it up, I turned to drive out of the parking lot when the sight of her bent over a bush, holding her long brown hair back, caught my attention. I parked my bike in a parking spot closer to her, watching her.

I was a few feet behind her when she straightened and her shoulders slumped forward. She let her hair go, and it cascaded down her back. I waited for her to turn around. I might not have seen her face yet, but I knew that ass. It was Liberty, and I was positive she had been vomiting just now in the bush.

When she turned around, her eyes locked on me, and then they widened. She was already pale, but the shock, then fear that flashed in those honey-brown irises unsettled me. I was missing something. Overlooking it because I didn't want to see Liberty for anything more than the spoiled bitch she had been to her sister. Trying to remove Selena from the equation, I took in Liberty's appearance. She was dressed for work. It looked like her top was a size too small. Probably helped with the tips.

"What are you doing here?" she asked, her voice hoarse.

I raised an eyebrow. "Checking to see if you're gonna bring any trouble to Selena's door while I'm away."

The flash of hurt in her eyes before she dropped her gaze to the ground didn't fit. What did she have to be hurt over? I'd caught her before she even hit the concrete last night and carried her the rest of the way to the house since I couldn't ride with an unconscious woman on my bike.

"I'm not at Sissy's anymore," she replied. "And I don't think she'll have a change of heart." Liberty didn't look my way again but started to walk toward the back of the building.

"She opened her home to you, tried to help you, and you threw all that in her face this morning and left. She's going to worry about you. Are you really that selfish?"

Liberty stopped walking. Her back went rigid, and she stood there for a moment, saying nothing. I started to think she was going to ignore me and leave when she finally turned back around to face me. Her brows were drawn together, as if she was trying to figure out what I'd said.

"Selfish? Me? That's what you think?"

A hard laugh fell from her full lips. Without the red lipstick, they were a pale pink. I liked them better that way. Not that I should like anything about this woman. But I was a red-blooded male, and she was a sexpot.

She tilted her head back, letting her waves of thick brown hair fall back over her shoulders as she stared up at the sky. I said nothing but waited to see if she was going to explain or elaborate.

When she looked at me again, she no longer looked angry. There was a quiet determination in her expression. "I need to get to work. If you are done accusing me of things that you know nothing about, I'd appreciate it if you left. Sissy is in no danger of me coming near her again—I can swear that to you," she said, then spun around before taking long strides toward the back entrance of Abernathy's.

I watched her go, wishing I didn't give a fuck about her being mixed up with bad shit. She had so much potential, yet her father had really ruined her. Men bent over backward to do her bidding. Her life had been too easy, whereas Selena had had to bust her ass to get to where she was now. I was sure there was jealousy there, causing Liberty to lash out at her sister.

Fucking women.

She stopped and took the handle of a suitcase I hadn't noticed before and rolled it toward the door. There was another one behind it. Why did she have her suitcases here?

When she'd left this morning, she must have gone somewhere. Had a plan at least.

I watched her pull both suitcases inside and waited until the door closed behind her.

Turning back around toward the bushes, I walked over to see if I'd been right about her throwing up. I had been. Looked like she'd lost her breakfast.

Glancing back at the building, I thought back to last night. She'd been pale. I'd caught her before she hit the ground when she fainted. More than twelve hours later, she had thrown up what she had eaten for breakfast. She was still pretty damn pale. Selena had said she woke up and grabbed her things and left. She hadn't mentioned her appearing sick. Why would she run off from the roof over her head when she wasn't feeling good?

Unless there was another reason she was sick and didn't want her sister to find out …

Fuck.

Eight

LIBERTY

The lunch crowd had cleared early, and that meant Shawn and I could take turns having a lunch hour. Monday nights weren't normally busy, but you never knew what could happen. If I was released to go home early, then I'd have to suck it up and get another motel room for the night. I needed to find somewhere a little cheaper though. Seventy-nine dollars a night wasn't awful, but it was more than I needed to spend. If I could find something for around sixty dollars, then spending a few dollars on some food wouldn't cut into my savings too bad.

"Liberty," Virginia called, and I turned to see her standing at the other end of the bar.

"Yes, ma'am?" I asked, hoping she wasn't already sending me home. I needed today's tips to cover tonight's motel cost.

"I need to speak with you in the office," she replied in a clipped tone, then turned to head back in that direction.

I glanced nervously at Shawn, who was watching me.

"Don't look like that," he said. "You're the best employee they have. She's probably going to give you a raise or some shit."

Virginia had never liked me. She sent me home every chance she got, and if she did the schedule, I was barely on it. That didn't really matter though because the others she scheduled more all ended up asking me if I wanted their shifts because they didn't want to work so much.

I had done my best to win her over for the longest time, but eventually, I just let it go. I did my job and ignored her disdain for me.

"You know she's not my biggest fan," I said under my breath.

He grinned. "No, but Tom is."

I shook my head and sighed before leaving the bar to go follow her back to the office she and her husband shared. If she had some reason to fire me, I was truly screwed. With no job, nowhere to live, no vehicle, and pregnant, I was going to be in trouble. Possibly homeless by next month.

The door was open, and Virginia was sitting on the edge of her desk, facing me, when I walked inside the room.

"Close the door," she told me.

Dread pooled in my stomach as I closed it behind me. Taking a deep breath, I turned to look at her. Her arms were crossed over her chest, and her expression was tight, making the wrinkles in her cheeks more severe.

"Have a seat," she said.

Every step I took felt heavy as I made my way to the faded blue sofa that sat across from her. Slowly, I lowered myself to sit, then stared up at her, waiting for whatever it was she had brought me in here for.

She stood up and let her hands fall to her sides. Lifting her chin a little higher, she cut her eyes toward me. "You're a dependable employee," she began. "I'll admit, in the beginning, I was sure you would take advantage of my husband's easygoing nature, but you never have, like many in the past did. I appreciate that. You work more hours than any other employee we have. Again, that is an asset most places of business do not have."

She sighed heavily then, and the tiny bit of hope I'd suddenly gotten was dashed.

"I was even willing to overlook the fact that you are clearly pregnant." She paused and looked at me pointedly, as if daring me to deny it. When I said nothing, she nodded once. "I'm right then. The bigger boobs, weight loss, looking pale after long shifts, getting sick out by the bushes before you come in to work. I know the signs."

A cold sweat broke out on my skin. I didn't know where she was going with this. She'd said she'd been willing to overlook it, but I was in her office for a reason.

"Today, a man walked into our pub, asking about you. Now that wouldn't be an issue because, well, look at you. Many customers want to know when you'll be working, where you are if you're not here, but this man was different. You don't run a place like this one in town and not know who to steer clear of. You recognize the kind you want as regulars and the kind that can cause problems. Liam Walsh is the president of The Judgment MC. Normally, that would be okay. The Judgment don't cause issues here in Ocala, and although they own strip clubs and other ill repute businesses, they keep their hands clean for the most part." She studied me. "How well do you know him?"

I shook my head. "Not very well." My voice cracked. "He is dating my sister, but she and I aren't close."

Telling her he was the one who had gotten me pregnant wouldn't help me save my job.

She leaned back against the desk again, sitting on the edge. "His daughter is married to the head of the Mafia. You don't live in Ocala all your life and own a business without knowing that the Southern Mafia is based here under the guise of their wealth and racehorses. We want no connection to them. Not even a minuscule one. I've let someone go before for a much smaller connection to the Mafia than yours. You have family dating a man linked with the Devil himself. I can't bring that to our doors. I'm sorry, Liberty, but I need you to get your things, and I'll give you your last paycheck tonight. When you leave, do not walk back in those doors again. Not even as a customer."

My throat felt as if I'd swallowed a ball of yarn and it was lodged inside. I was losing my job. This was real. All because of Liam. I wanted to argue my case and beg her to not do this, but I knew it would do no good.

I'd not known who Liam's daughter was. We had never discussed it. Would this cause me problems? My baby?

Standing up, I struggled for words. I was in shock. Liam wasn't just connected to the Mafia; he was linked by marriage.

Oh God. I swallowed.

"I … I didn't know. I'm—I'll go," I stammered.

She nodded, and for once, in all the years I had worked here, I saw a touch of sympathy in her expression even if it was fleeting.

"If you can, stay clear of him. For your own good."

I should never have thought my situation couldn't get any worse. It had just spiraled to a new level of low.

"Okay," I replied in a whisper.

She picked up something off her desk and held it out to me. "Tom wanted to add some extra to it."

I glanced at the check to see that it was one hundred dollars more than it should be. Every little bit helped at this point.

"Thank you," I said, the words feeling thick on my tongue.

Turning, I left the office and headed for the room where we kept our personal items while working. Both my suitcases and my purse were in there. I felt like I was functioning on autopilot. Distress, shock, fear all battled for first place, and I didn't have the energy to fight them.

I rolled my luggage to the employee entrance, then glanced back once. It wasn't that I loved my job, but this had been my one small shred of security I clung to, and now, I didn't have it either. I shoved the door open with my shoulder and pulled my luggage out one at a time before letting it fall closed with a heavy thud behind me.

Not wanting to stop and linger, I kept walking, unsure if I was going to go all the way to the bus or to the nearest motel. I had a little over a hundred in cash from tips tucked in my pocket. I could use it to get a place for today and perhaps look for a job the rest of the afternoon.

"Are you pregnant?" a deep voice demanded.

Startled, I swung my gaze over to the parking lot to see Liam standing beside his Charger instead of his Harley, wearing a pair of dark sunglasses, his leather biker vest, and a pair of jeans. His jaw was clenched tight, and although I couldn't see his eyes behind the glasses, I felt the threatening scowl directed at me.

"Leave me alone, Liam. You've done enough," I said as my own anger began to burn inside my chest.

He was the reason this was happening.

He took a step toward me, and I refused to back away like a scared little girl. It wasn't like he was going to hit me. I squared my shoulders and glared at him.

"Are you pregnant, Liberty?" he asked again.

"Why do you want to know? I seriously doubt Sissy is interested in my life," I snapped.

"Answer me," he said, his tone going a touch more intense.

"Yes!" I all but shouted.

He might as well know. It wasn't like he was going to help me, and even if he wanted to, I wasn't sure how safe that was. His connection to the Mafia didn't make me feel comfortable.

"Is it mine?"

Of course he would ask me that. His opinion of me was pretty low, and I would blame that all on Sissy, but I was the one who had opened my legs for him hours after meeting him.

"Does it matter?" I asked him.

He stalked toward me, and I backed up until my back hit a tree behind me. Liam stopped inches from his chest touching mine. I tilted my head to stare up at him. I could feel the anger pulsing from his body.

"Maybe not to you, but it does to me," he snarled. "Is it mine?"

I could lie, but then I feared the repercussions if he ever found out the truth.

"Yes," I bit out.

My heart was hammering against my chest as panic began to build inside me. What did this mean now? What was he going to do?

"You could be lying," he said in an accusing tone.

God, this asshole. He had asked me, and now, he wanted to claim I was a liar.

"If you weren't going to believe me, then why did you ask?!" I shot back at him, then shoved against his chest, wanting some space. He didn't budge.

"I want a paternity test," he said, then stepped back and grabbed the handle on my luggage I'd left when I backed away from him. "Get in the car."

I shook my head. "I'm not going anywhere with you."

He picked up both suitcases. "Yeah, you are," he replied, then began walking toward his car with my things.

I hurried after him. "Put them down! You can't force me to do anything!"

He didn't even slow down. His long strides only quickened.

My mind was racing as I tried to think of a way to stop this. I didn't need a paternity test. I hadn't had sex with anyone but Liam in the past four months.

Wallace's lack of interest in having sex with me should have been a clue that our relationship was going downhill. But we had both been busy, and there hadn't been much time—or so I had thought then. I hadn't been off my birth control when I was with Wallace, and I'd had two periods since the last time I'd had sex with him.

Liam wasn't going to believe me even if I told him all that. To him, I was a woman who fucked strangers that picked me up at work.

"Why do you want a paternity test? I'm not asking for your help. I didn't plan on demanding anything from you."

He opened the trunk of his car and slid a suitcase inside, then put the other in before closing it, barely looking at me. I stood there, watching him, waiting on an answer. I did not want to get in that car.

Jerking his door open, he looked at me finally. "I take care of what is mine. What we did was reckless, and I'm old enough to know better than to fuck some bartender who has no self-respect. But I did, and if you're carrying my kid, then I will take care of both of you. I'll take full responsibility. Now, get in the goddamn car before I put you in it myself."

I glanced at the pub, knowing there was no help for me inside there. In fact, if Virginia saw Liam, she'd be even more determined to get me out of here. She'd probably shove me inside his car herself.

He had my things, and right now, I had nowhere to go. I was out of options.

Giving in, I walked over to the passenger door, opened it, then climbed inside.

Nine

LIAM

We drove in silence as I made the decision to take her to the club and keep her in my bedroom upstairs beside my office instead of taking her to my house. Tex used the other room up there, and I was going to need him to let me stay there instead. I'd send him to my house. Ozzy would need someone there with him at night anyway.

I had to make sure she wasn't lying. That baby could be her ex's or some other random dude she'd fucked. Until I knew if it was mine or not, I wasn't letting her stay in a motel or walking to bus stops and passing out. But I sure as hell wasn't taking her to my house. I didn't take women there. It was my one place that was an escape. My solace. Having her invade it would tarnish that.

My hands gripped the steering wheel tightly. I didn't want that woman to be the mother of my child. The idea of having another kid, raising it the way I'd missed out with Madeline, appealed to me from time to time. However, giving a kid a mother like Liberty felt like I'd failed it before it was even born. There was a good chance it wasn't mine though. I had to stop thinking the worst.

I had fucked her three times that night. The last time, the condom broke, and when I felt it, I immediately pulled out. I was almost positive I'd gotten out in time. It was very unlikely this kid was mine. She had probably fucked the ex raw regularly. I flinched at the thought and hated myself for it.

I didn't want her to be pregnant with my kid, but my dick sure as hell wanted to sink inside her cunt again. She'd been one of those fucks that was hard to forget. Damn her and her bouncy, round ass.

I flicked my eyes over to her tits and swallowed. They were bigger. That was why the top seemed too small.

"What year is this Charger—'70?" she asked, interrupting my inner turmoil.

"Seventy-four," I replied.

"Must have cost a fortune," she said, running her hand over the seat beside her thigh.

"It was my dad's. He bought it new in '74," I told her.

She didn't need to start seeing dollar signs with me. If the kid was mine, I wasn't putting her up in some luxury life.

"Wow," she whispered. "It looks new."

I wasn't going to talk about my father or anything else personal with her.

The man who had given me life had beaten me my entire childhood. He put a bullet in my mother's head and then my nanny's head years later for doctoring wounds he'd left behind with his whip. I grew up as the son of a drug lord. I was raised to one day take over the gang he had started. Luckily for me, the majority of them were killed, along with my father, when anarchy inside the ring went down.

I was free to build a different life from the one that still managed to infiltrate my nightmares at times. I'd lost Etta because of him, and not one day since his death had I mourned him. He had tried to create a monster, but I had never truly bent to his will. I'd only allowed him to think I had.

The club didn't open its doors to the public for two more hours. Only VIP members were allowed in right now. The parking lot held only a few Harleys and a handful of expensive cars. I pulled around back and parked beside my Harley, which I had driven here after seeing Liberty this morning and traded it out, knowing I'd more than likely be getting her and her luggage after her shift.

"You brought me to a strip club?" she asked.

"I brought you to my strip club," I corrected her, opening the door and getting out.

The scent of coconut and honey that she put off was starting to make me edgy. She'd smelled like that between her legs too. Whatever lotion the woman wore was an aphrodisiac. I didn't need a reminder.

Not waiting to see if she was getting out, I went to the trunk and pulled out her two suitcases. This couldn't be all she owned, but I wasn't in the mood to ask. Until I knew whose baby she was carrying, I didn't care about anything that had to do with her.

Slamming the trunk, I saw her standing beside the car, staring up at the building. I wasn't taking her in the front entrance. She was going directly upstairs, where I intended to keep her. I didn't need the rest of them knowing what was going on just yet. The thought of Madeline finding out that I might have gotten a thirty-one-year-old homeless bartender pregnant made my stomach clench. I didn't even want to think about how embarrassed she would be. She had been so damn happy about me dating a doctor who was at least closer to forty than thirty.

"This way," I said, carrying her suitcases toward the back entrance.

I set one down to punch in the code. When the light turned green and it buzzed, I pushed the door open. I grabbed the suitcase and went inside with both of them. I heard her step inside before the door closed and headed for the stairs. She'd have a private bathroom, bedroom, and a television. I could leave her there, and besides when I took food up to her, I could pretend like she wasn't here.

Opening the door of the room I barely used, I held it for her with one of the suitcases, then went the rest of the way in to set her other one down.

"Bathroom is in there. Remote for the television is there," I said, pointing to both. "Don't leave this room. I'll have food sent up to you."

She was just inside the door frame, looking around at it. "How long are you going to keep me in here?" she asked, swinging her eyes to me.

"I'll take you to have a paternity test done first thing in the morning," I told her, wishing I could use the private doctor that Blaise Hughes kept for the family's needs.

He'd done a swab here once for one of Blaise's men, and the results had been quick. But then the baby had been here too. I wasn't sure how that worked when the woman was still pregnant. Regardless, I knew Blaise's doctor would get things done faster, but keeping this from my daughter was more important. If this wasn't mine, then she never had to know about it.

"Then what? I doubt results are same day. Are you locking me up in here until you get them?"

I hadn't thought that far. I knew I couldn't keep her here. I wouldn't want to. I was here almost every day. Having her that close all day long would be an annoyance in many ways.

"We will cross that bridge when we get to it. For now, you're here." I walked past her and out the door. "Close the door. Don't leave the room."

She said nothing as I turned and walked back toward the stairs. I needed a drink and a blow job. Possibly several of both.

Ten

LIBERTY

The banging on the door woke me, and I groaned as I opened my eyes. It had been almost four when I finally fell asleep last night. The music from the club had been so loud; it'd vibrated the walls in the room. Squinting, I looked toward the only window. It was tiny and too high to look directly out of it. But the sun was bright as it poured inside.

"Liberty!" Liam's voice called out.

I yawned as I sat up and ran a hand over my messy hair before standing to go to the door. He had come up twice yesterday with a tray of food and bottles of water. He hadn't said anything but sat it outside the door, then knocked and left. It could have been someone else who had brought it for all I knew.

I unlocked the door and opened it to find Liam dressed in his usual attire with his hair pulled back in a ponytail and a scowl on his face. I should be the one scowling.

"Get dressed. We are leaving in ten minutes," he said, then turned to walk away.

"What time is it?" I asked, stifling another yawn.

"Seven thirty."

Three and a half hours of sleep. Awesome.

I closed the door, then headed for the bathroom. I was thankful I'd taken a shower last night. Ten minutes didn't leave me time for much. I hurried to dress and do my morning routine, then pulled my hair up in a ponytail. Slipping on a pair of sandals, I looked around, trying to remember where I had left my purse. When I spotted it on the small chair in the corner, I went to get it, then made my way to the door. I wasn't sure how long I had taken, but I felt fairly certain it was under ten minutes.

Liam was leaning against the wall with his arms crossed over his chest when I opened the door. He barely glanced at me. "Let's go," he snapped before going to the stairs.

I wasn't in the mood for more of his attitude, so I decided to remain silent.

I'd googled the test on my phone last night, and I knew what they were going to do and that it would take up to seven business days for the results. I was not living in that room for seven days. I needed to get a job, but right now, I was too tired to argue with him. Mornings were not my thing.

"I'm pretty sure you need an appointment for genetic testing. I doubt you can just walk in when they open," I stated the obvious when we reached his car.

There were no other cars in the parking lot this morning. Just his car and his Harley sat out back. I wondered what time all the strippers had left. Did they go at it all night?

"I have an appointment," he said, unlocking the doors.

Once we were inside, neither of us spoke while he started the engine and pulled out onto the street.

"It'll take about three days to get the results. Until then, you'll stay at the club," he informed me.

"Try seven business days, and I'm not spending all that time up in that room. I have to find a new job, look for a place to live. You can't just keep me locked away. It's illegal, not to mention inhumane."

"I have connections. We will know in three days. You can handle three days. Why do you need a new job? Did you do something to get fired?"

The accusation in his voice had me wishing I had something I could throw at his head.

"Yeah. You. I did you."

His eyes swung over to look at me. "You got fired because of me?"

I crossed my arms over my chest. "Yep. Your reputation got me fired. They don't want anyone connected to you or your family coming in there."

He didn't say anything, and I figured he was trying to find out just how much I knew about his life. I wasn't going to offer the information. Not while he was treating me like trash that had been dumped in his lap.

"When we have the results, we will take it from there," he replied after a few moments.

"I don't have time to sit on my ass for three days. I need a job and somewhere to live. Because regardless of the results, I do not want to live with you, and you don't want me to either. That much we can agree on."

His knuckles turned white; he was gripping the steering wheel so tightly. I jerked my gaze off him to look out the window.

"If the baby is mine, I will provide for you. I take—"

"Responsibility. Yeah, I heard that already. But here's the thing: when you find out this baby is yours—because I can assure you without a doubt that it is—you aren't going to control my life."

"You walked out of Selena's and burned that bridge. You have nowhere to live and can't afford a place, or you wouldn't have asked your sister for help. Getting a lease approved after just starting a new job will be damn near impossible. If it's my kid, then I will make sure you're not living in a box on the side of the road. That you eat properly and aren't walking home from work at midnight, passing out on the street. Do I want it to be mine? Fuck no! But if I messed up and it is, then I'll do my best by it. That includes taking care of its mother."

Angry tears burned my eyes. I didn't look at him. I kept my eyes on the passing cars and tried to get control of my emotions.

I had known he didn't want this baby to be his but hearing him actually say it was hard.

I'd had a dad who loved me. He wanted me. Even after he was gone and I lived a life of hell with Abilene, I'd always had my parents' love with me. I knew the ones that mattered most had loved me.

Would I have chosen to get pregnant? No. But that was neither here nor there. I was pregnant now, and I realized I wanted this baby. It would be the only real family I had. Sissy might be my blood, but we weren't family. We never had been. She wouldn't allow it. My baby would be born with a mother who wanted it and loved it. But hearing its father say he didn't want it cut deep. I didn't want my child to know that kind of rejection or lack of a father's love.

We rode in silence until he pulled into a parking lot at a medical building. I had managed to not cry, and I was thankful for that. I reached for the door handle to get out of the car and get some distance from him.

"I have some office work I need done, like filing and paperwork that needs to be scanned and entered into our system. If you want a job, then until we get the results in three days, you can do that for me. I'll pay you two fifty a day."

I didn't want to work for him or be near him. But it was unlikely I'd find a job today where I could make seven hundred fifty dollars in three days. That would be enough to get an apartment, but Liam was right; without a job, a lease would be hard to get.

"Fine," I muttered, opening the door and getting out.

In three days, he'd find out he was going to be a dad again. To a kid he didn't want. Until I knew what he was going to do about it, I could stay at the club and work. Sleep would be difficult, but I'd manage. I'd slept in worse places.

Once we were in the waiting room, Liam walked up to the window and spoke to the lady while I stood back and waited. He was only up there briefly when he turned and motioned for me to follow him as he headed to the door that was being opened by a nurse. That was fast service. There were at least six other people in the waiting room.

The nurse smiled at me. He was a tall ginger with blue eyes. "Miss Dillard," he said, and I nodded. "I'm Holden, and I'm going to be taking your blood. Do you need to use the restroom before we get started?"

I shook my head. "I'm good."

"Very well then, come with me."

He led us into a room with two tall chairs and some equipment. "You can both take a seat," he said. "I'm going to swab

Mr. Walsh's cheek first, and then we will move on to drawing your blood."

I'd known this involved my blood sample, but I hated needles. I'd hated them all my life. I felt the familiar panic that came when I knew I was getting a shot or having my blood taken. Not wanting to appear childish, I clasped my hands tightly in my lap and took deep breaths. It was just some blood work. I was an adult. This was fine. I wouldn't look at the needle. Just a little poke—that was all.

"Are you okay?" Holden asked, and I realized he was speaking to me.

My eyes darted up from the spot on the floor I'd been focused on, and I gave him a forced smile, then nodded.

Lie. I was not okay.

His brows drew together. "Are you sure? You've gone pale. Do you need some juice or something?"

I shook my head, holding on to a smile I did not feel.

He didn't seem to believe me, and he studied me for a moment, concern etched on his face. He swabbed Liam's mouth, then placed it in a vile before turning back to me.

"You're still pale. I'm going to get you some juice. Not sure what we have, but we should have something. I don't want to take your blood if your blood sugar is low."

"My blood sugar is fine," I told him.

He opened his mouth to argue again, and I sighed in defeat. I was going to have to admit the issue.

"I don't like needles."

He visibly relaxed as understanding crossed his face. "I see," he said. "That's common. Why don't you take a few deep breaths for me?"

I could feel Liam's eyes burning a hole in the side of my head. I knew he was probably annoyed, and I refused to look at him. So I had a fear of needles and I was a grown woman. He could get over it.

I took deep breaths, as instructed.

"I'll make this quick," Holden said. "Tell me something about yourself. What do you love to do?"

I stared at him, and he grinned.

"It'll distract you."

I doubted it, but I was willing to try anything. Although I didn't have much time for things I enjoyed to do. Lately, every day felt like another day I had to wake up and fight to survive. When was the last time I had done something fun?

"Gardening," I said finally, and a smile touched my lips.

His eyebrows shot up. "Gardening, huh? I can't keep a cactus alive."

"My Mama D had the most amazing flower gardens. She would plant everything and anything. She could save a plant on the brink of death and bring it back to life."

Memories of her always seemed to make bad days better.

"Your grandmother?" Holden asked.

I nodded. "Yes. My dad's mother. We spent hours in the sun, planting things. I don't have a yard or a chance to do that now, but I have a scrapbook. I pick up brochures with flower gardens, cut out pictures I like, and save them so that when I do have a yard one day, I'll have all those ideas to work with."

Wallace used to make fun of my book full of flowers and plants. I never cared. It made me happy to sit and look over all of them. Daydream about the day I could plant gardens that would make Mama D proud.

"I like that," Holden said as he untied the rubber strap around my arm.

I looked down to see the bandage taped at the bend of my arm, then jerked my gaze back up to meet his. "You got it already?" I asked in amazement.

He nodded. "Yep, and I think I might just take up gardening."

A laugh bubbled out of me as I turned, remembering Liam was beside me. I'd forgotten about him. He was studying me as if I were some curiosity he'd never seen before and wasn't sure what to think of it.

He stood up, turning his attention to Holden. "I was told three days until I get the results."

Holden nodded. "Yes. We got the instructions to expedite this. You'll get a call in three days' time."

"Let's go," he said to me as he walked around me.

"She might need a moment," Holden said, turning to me. "Are you weak or dizzy?"

I shook my head and scooted off the chair to let my feet fall back down to the floor. "I'm fine."

"All right then. Good luck."

I had needed someone to be nice to me today. I liked Nurse Holden. "Thanks."

He glanced over at Liam, and his smile fell before he nodded, then turned to walk away. Shifting my attention to Liam, I saw the scowl in place that I assumed was only reserved for me. He didn't say anything more, but headed for the exit. I hurried to keep up and tried hard not to think about what the future held.

This man was determined to hate me, and we were going to have a child together. I needed all the luck I could get.

Eleven

LIAM

One thing I knew for certain: if this kid wasn't mine, she'd have some poor fool doing her bidding and paying her bills in no time. She'd had the fucking nurse ready to propose to her over a damn story about flower gardens. Hell, I had even caught myself mesmerized, but it was brief. I'd snapped out of that real damn fast. Liberty was a prime example of the woman Hall & Oates had written the song "Maneater" about in 1982. She was a goddamn pro.

We didn't speak on the ride home even though I wanted to call her out on that bullshit tale about her grandmother. If she'd had a grandmother who spent that much time with her, then she'd not have ended up as a selfish, manipulative brat.

"I'll send up something for you to eat, then show you what I need done with the files," I told her, wishing she didn't have to be in my office to get it done. I would find somewhere else to be today.

"Okay," she replied.

No questions or comments. That wasn't like her.

I glanced at her before stepping inside the back entrance to the club and wished I hadn't. She didn't even have to lay that charming shit on so thick, and she'd still have a man's attention. Selena was a beautiful woman, but when it came to physical looks, she couldn't compete with Liberty.

Cursing myself mentally for comparing the two of them, I went inside. Selena was a good person, and it was unfair to her to do that even if it was something I never said aloud.

Tex was coming down the stairs and stopped, his eyes swinging over toward us. My internal cursing intensified when his gaze landed on Liberty and his eyes lit up with interest.

Not now, you horny-ass fucker. Not this one.

"If she's new, I approve," he said with a thick drawl, tilting his head and moving so he could get a better look at her.

"She's not," I snapped, annoyed.

He seemed to struggle to take his eyes off her. "Why not?"

"Because she's not. Let it go."

Finally, he managed to tear his lust-filled gaze off her to look at me. "Is this up for debate?"

Clenching my teeth together, I shook my head. "Don't," I warned him.

"Hi. Since he's not going to introduce me because his rude setting is always on where I am concerned, I'm Liberty," she said, stepping up beside me and holding out her hand to his.

Tex's eyes dropped to her hand, then slowly moved back up, pausing on her tits with a smile stretching across his face.

Fucking hell. Could she not just keep her mouth shut and go upstairs quietly?

"He's not normally rude to beautiful women, sweetheart," Tex said, taking a step closer to her and holding on to her hand for longer than necessary. "Makes me wonder what you did to ignite his grumpy side. Because looking at you, I can't imagine anything that would make a man annoyed with you."

"Well, you see, he's dating my sis—"

"That's enough!" I barked, then pointed to the stairs. "Up now!" I told her before she blurted out shit Tex didn't need to hear.

Her hand fell away from his grasp, and those honey-brown eyes of hers flashed with anger. "See what I mean?" she said, stepping between us and toward the stairs.

"Prez, what the fuck is wrong with you?" Tex asked, watching her ass as she headed up. I could see his eyes eating up the view as he licked his lips.

"She's off-limits," I snarled.

Once she was finally out of sight, he looked back at me. "Why? Because I need a real good reason, Prez. That's one hot piece of prime ass."

"Because I said she was. She's mine." As much as I didn't want to give her that label, I knew it was the only way to keep the others back.

He gave me a shocked look. "That is not the doctor," he said. "That cannot be a doctor."

I rubbed my temples with my thumb and forefinger. "No, it's not."

He let out a low chuckle. "Guess I'd change course, too, if that sweet thing walked across my path. But you might want to be nicer to her. Unless being a dick to her is what gets her wound up for a good fuck."

"It's not what you think," I said, wishing he would let it go.

Both his eyebrows shot up. "I think you're banging that perfect, plump ass and unloading in her every chance you get because you're a smart man. So, are you saying that ain't what's happening?"

"She's Selena's sister. I'm keeping her here for a couple of days to do some work for me while she relocates. That's all anyone needs to know."

Tex ran his hand over his mouth, trying to cover his amusement. "That's the doctor's sister, and you are giving her a job to do in your office upstairs for a few days."

I sighed and headed up the stairs.

"Is that why you sent me to your house last night? And if so, why the fuck did you stay down here until two before you went to bed?"

"I'm not fucking her, Tex," I ground out.

"You keep her all cozy up there with you much longer, and you will be."

I shook my head and kept going up. I was over this conversation. He didn't need to know anything more. No one did. I had three days to decide what I was going to do if the baby was mine.

Liberty stood at the top of the stairs with her hands on her hips, looking pissed. That stance put those tits of hers on display in a way I didn't need.

Did she not own a baggy shirt? Was everything tight and too short?

"This door is my office," I said, opening it and walking inside.

It wasn't until she followed me in that it dawned on me that my office was going to smell like her now. Just fucking great. Maybe I should let her go on a job hunt. I mean, there was a big chance that in three days, she would no longer be my concern and she'd need a job.

Jerking my chair out from under my desk with more force than necessary, I sat down in it. "How would you get around to find a job if I let you go look?"

She was thirty-one, and she didn't own a fucking car. How pathetic was that? Could she not have pulled her life together by this point? If she worked all the time, why hadn't she bought one already?

"The bus," she replied, crossing her arms over her chest. That only pushed her tits up more, but at least it was better than when they were on complete display.

"That's a lot of walking," I pointed out.

"I've had to do it many times in my life."

I leaned back in my chair and looked at her. "Why is that? You're thirty-one. Why don't you have a car?"

She visibly tensed, and I realized I'd struck a nerve.

"I had a car in the past; I just don't have one at the moment."

I reached for a cigarette. "And why is that?"

"That's not an easy question to answer. There is a lot to that story."

I just bet there was. She had to make up all the excuses as to why she had chosen this path in life when she could have had the same life as her sister. They'd been offered an education. She hadn't wanted it.

I stuck the cigarette between my lips and lit it. "Always something with you, isn't there?" I said, standing back up. "The stack of files right there, they need to be put back in those cabinets, where they belong. It's in alphabetical order. Once you're done with that, go back to the bedroom. When I have time, I will show you what needs to be scanned and how to use the scanner. I'll have that food sent up," I told her as I walked past her and out the door.

I expected her to say something, but she didn't say a word. I wasn't going to be able to stay up here with her. The harder my dick got when I thought about how tight her cunt was, the more I lashed out at her.

If the baby was mine, I was going to have to find a way not to do that.

Twelve

LIBERTY

A knock on the door interrupted my reading about the first trimester of pregnancy from a website I'd found on my phone. I looked at the time to see it was a few minutes after seven. I had finished the filing hours ago, but after Liam had brought me a chicken sandwich and fries for lunch, I'd not seen him again.

Swinging my legs off the bed, I walked over to the door to open it. I wasn't going to sit in this room all day tomorrow. If he wasn't going to show me the work he needed me to do, then I was going to find a job.

Jerking the door open, I was ready to tell him just that, but it wasn't Liam.

A blonde with a lot of makeup, lashes that could not be real, and pasties on her nipples stood there instead, holding a tray of food. Her eyes did a quick once-over of me before they snapped back up to my face. There was a flash of displeasure before she gave me a smile that didn't meet her eyes.

"Liam sent me up with your dinner," she said, holding the tray out for me.

"Thank you," I replied as I took it.

She didn't make a move to leave. I glanced at her stiletto heels with rhinestones and the barely there string of red satin that was supposed to be panties before walking over to the bed to set the food down.

"Who are you?" she asked me.

I turned back to her and wondered what excuse Liam had given her for me being up here.

"Liberty Dillard," I replied, not giving her any more information than that.

"Are you the doctor?" she asked, her gaze doing another scan of my body.

"Nope."

She tilted her head to the side, and her gaze turned haughty. "Whatever you're doing with Liam, he isn't going to keep you."

I let out a laugh. "God, I hope not."

It looked like she was going to say more when I heard footsteps on the stairs. She tensed and glanced back toward them.

"You weren't sent up here to chat, Pandora. Get back to the floor," Liam's voice commanded.

She spun around, giving me a view of her naked ass before hurrying to do as she had been told. I went over to close the door behind her when Liam's eyes met mine. Pausing, I waited to see if he was going to say something. When it appeared he wasn't, I decided I would.

"If you don't want to show me what to do tomorrow, then I'm going on a job search," I told him.

"Got busy with some things today. I'll show you in the morning." His voice was deep with a raspy edge to it, like he was tired.

For a brief moment, I felt concern. Why was he tired? Had something happened? But I shook it off. I was exhausted from little sleep last night, but he didn't seem to care about me.

Tightening my grip on the knob in my hand, I closed the door and locked it.

Turning back to the meal he'd sent up to me, I wasn't that hungry, but I knew I should eat something. For a strip club, the food wasn't so bad. Today's sandwich had been tasty. The fries were even better. I hadn't expected good food where women pranced around, dressed like the blonde Liam had sent up here.

Pandora. I rolled my eyes at that name. I wondered what her real name was.

Did they all have ridiculous names like that? I was curious about what the floor looked like and how many of them there were. Did they get onstage and dance? I doubted Liam was ever going to let me go inside the club, but that didn't mean I couldn't sneak down there.

Sitting on the bed, I looked at the chicken fingers. No fries this time. I lifted the cover off the other dish to find a salad. Did they actually serve salads at a strip club? The idea made me want to laugh. I could just picture some man sitting there with his salad covered in ranch dressing, eating while Pandora swung her leg around a pole in front of him.

My phone dinged, alerting me of a text, and I reached over the bed to get it from the side table. Sitting back up, I stared down at the screen, and although the number was one I didn't know, the small portion of the text I could see on my lock screen told me who it was. The name there wiped the smile from my face. I had blocked Wallace's phone number when he started calling and texting me nonstop.

Sliding my finger to open the text, I debated on even reading it. If he had really wanted to talk to me, he knew where I worked—or had worked. Not once had he tried to find me. Not that it would have changed anything. He'd been cheating on me. Even if I wanted to forgive him, which I didn't, I was pregnant with another man's baby. Wallace and I were over.

> **Unknown Number:** It's Wallace. I've been calling and texting you for weeks. It took me until yesterday to figure out you'd blocked me. I miss you, Liberty. I fucked up, babe. I'm so sorry. It meant nothing. Janie means nothing to me. You were working all the time, and I felt like you were drifting away from me. Please talk to me. Let me take you to dinner. That little Thai place you love. I'll get reservations. We can talk. I know you're hurt, and it kills me that I caused it. I love you. I will always love you. Don't let this end us.

Sighing, I dropped the phone onto the bed and reached for my salad. That was another version of the other texts he had sent, except this time, he seemed less angry with me for leaving and was taking more responsibility for his actions. At least he was admitting he'd messed up and not telling me I'd pushed him away. Taking a bite, I chewed as I stared back down at my phone.

I had believed I loved him once, but the day I walked in on him and Janie, it hurt, but not the way it should have. My heart didn't shatter. I'd felt betrayed and stupid for not seeing what was going on. All their flirty banter. The times they'd both worked late, going over orders. Janie had been given a job at Gabler Groceries main office, where Wallace worked. His older brother, Janie's husband, was the face of Gabler Groceries and went to the stores across the southeast to oversee how they were running. He traveled a lot, but he made three times more than Wallace did. It was a sore point for him.

Another text came.

Setting down my salad, I picked up my phone to read more of his pointless words. He was wasting his time with this.

> Unknown Number: Please, baby. God, I miss you. I went by Abernathy's yesterday, and that guy bartender who always flirted with you said you didn't work there anymore. Where are you now? He didn't know where you were living. I'm worried about you. How are you getting around? You don't have a car. You left the company one here. I want you to have it. I'll give it to you if you come see me. If you need a job, I'll give you one. You can work at the main office with me. I know you need me. Don't suffer because of my screwup. Call me.

He was offering me a job now? I rolled my eyes. He had never wanted me to work at the main office when we were together. I'd even mentioned applying for a position that came open, and he shot me down. Some excuse about his father being against hiring girlfriends. He said it got messy. Janie had been hired once she was married into the family. As for that car, he had given it to me after he convinced me mine was a piece of junk and I needed to get rid of it. That I was a danger to others and myself, driving it on the road.

I finished my salad and one of the chicken fingers without another text from him.

When I was in the shower, I heard the phone ringing and stayed under the warmth of the spray longer, just to avoid seeing it was him that called me. I needed to block this new number, too, it seemed. He was relentless. How long before he contacted me from yet another number? And if he was so worried about me, why had it taken him until yesterday to go looking for me at Abernathy's? I didn't want to play his games anymore. I had finally stopped relying on him, and it was going to stay that way.

I should just respond and tell him I was pregnant and that it wasn't his. That would shut him up.

Thirteen

LIAM

My son-in-law, Blaise Hughes; his enforcer, Huck Kingston; and the psycho who was his best friend, Gage Presley, filled my office, along with Tex and Drifter—a member of The Judgment since the beginning, who had relocated with me to Ocala to help with Devil's. We had emptied the club and closed down early last night, and then I'd contacted Blaise to tell him who had walked in my doors.

"You sure it wasn't just some snake tat someone copied?" Huck asked me.

I leaned back in my chair and shook my head. "I fucking wish it were. He had on the vest too."

Blaise's expression didn't show any emotion. He glanced over at Gage, who showed enough rage for both of them. I knew he was making sure Gage stayed in check and didn't stalk from the room to go hunt the man down and slice his neck. At least not until we knew more.

"The LA Vipers believe they killed every member of the Florida Vipers three years ago," Huck said.

I nodded. "Either they missed one or there is a new start-up. I can't imagine one single man is walking around with the tattoo and vest on. It's a statement. Could be he has no idea about the connection here and walked in blind with Diamond last night or he did it on purpose."

Blaise showed the first sign of annoyance with a small flicker in his eyes. "If he's wearing the vest and the tat is the same, he knows. It was meant as a statement. How long has Diamond been working here?"

I glanced at Drifter. He'd know the exact date we'd hired her.

"Seven months ago next week, but the background check done on her was clean—"

The door opened behind him, stopping whatever else he was going to say. Liberty stepped in, her gaze sweeping the room before settling on me.

Fucking hell! What was she doing? I'd had breakfast sent to her, along with a message for her to stay in her room until I came to get her.

"Go back to your room," I demanded.

She flared her eyes at being ordered around. I didn't give a shit.

"It's not *my* room," she snapped, and then her mouth softened into a smile. "I was unaware you had company. I just came to tell you that I was leaving to go search for a job."

I did not have time for this bullshit!

"No," I replied, not wanting to do this in front of any audience but especially this one. The last thing I needed was for Blaise to tell my daughter about some girl staying in my room at the club.

She placed a hand on her hip, causing her tits to sway slightly under the sundress she was wearing. Did she not have on a goddamn bra?! I swore to God I was going to lock her in that fucking room.

"I didn't come to ask for permission, Liam," she said tightly but managed to continue smiling at me like we were having a friendly discussion.

It was at least a three-mile walk to the closest bus stop, and at eight this morning, it was over ninety degrees. It was probably close to, if not at, the one hundred mark right now. She couldn't walk three miles in this heat.

Shoving the chair back, I stood and stalked toward her. At least she had the good sense to look worried as she took a step back out of the room.

"This will just take me a minute," I told the others before slamming the door behind me and crowding her until her back was against the wall.

"Do you know who is in that office right now?" I asked her through clenched teeth.

She inhaled sharply, lifting her chin up in defiance. "I don't care. I told you last night, I'm not sitting in that room all day. I need a job."

Leaning down, I placed my palm flat on the wall beside her head. "The fucking Mafia, Liberty. They didn't stop by for a chat. Did you notice how quiet it was last night? That was because some shit went down, and now, we are dealing with it. So, I need you to take your ass back into that room and stay there until I come and get you."

Her eyes glanced behind me at the closed door. There was the briefest glimpse of fear in them. At least she was smart enough to understand the situation. Maybe she'd listen to me then and stop being a fucking brat.

When her eyes swung back up to meet mine, that moment of fear was gone. Determination shone bright in them instead. "I'm sorry I interrupted. But I'm leaving. I'll be back this evening."

I heard the door open, and I tensed. Looking back over my shoulder, I saw Gage leaning against the doorframe with an amused grin.

"Am I interrupting?" he asked.

I sighed. "I'm coming. Just give me a minute."

He looked from me to Liberty, then smirked. "All right, but we don't have all day."

Cocky fucker.

I turned back to Liberty, anger radiating through every cell in my body. I was going to have to explain her. Blaise would have questions, and I had to make sure whatever he told my daughter didn't make this look like something it wasn't. It also couldn't be the truth. I hoped Madeline never had to know about this. I just needed that paternity test to come back negative.

The door clicked closed.

"It's a hundred fucking degrees outside, and the closest bus station is three miles. You might not care about your health or safety, but until I know if that baby you're carrying is mine or not, I fucking do. So, take your ass back into that room and stay there. I don't have time to argue with you. That man who just came out here is a damn psycho. I have to get back in there."

She blinked, then bit her bottom lip nervously. I tried real hard not to look at her plump lips because even now, when I hated her, I wanted a taste.

Shoving off the wall and stepping back to get distance from her, I pointed to the bedroom door. "Go."

Thankfully, she didn't say anything more and walked toward it instead of the stairs. I waited until she was inside before going back into my office.

Glancing at Drifter, I nodded my head toward the hallway.

"Make sure she doesn't leave the room," I told him.

He didn't question me and left to go do as he had been told.

I walked back over to the desk, feeling every pair of eyes in there locked on me. I could almost feel the amusement coming from Gage.

When I sat back down, I looked at Blaise. "Sorry about that."

He raised an eyebrow. "That's not the doctor."

I didn't ask him how he knew what Selena looked like. I already knew how he worked. The moment I'd started dating the woman, I was sure he'd had a complete background check done on her. He probably had a file with every tiny detail about her in it, along with several photos. Blaise allowed no one into Madeline's life until he checked them out thoroughly. That meant anyone who was connected with me too.

"No," I sighed. "It's her sister."

I couldn't lie to him. There was a good chance he had a photo of Liberty in that file of his. He'd know all of Selena's relatives.

"Half-sister," Huck replied.

My eyes shot up to the tall brick wall of a man who stood with his back against the wall and his arms crossed over his chest. He lifted his shoulder in a small shrug. "I was there when Levi got all of Dr. Selena Dillard's information in. I saw the photos and the family tree. Six wanted to know if the sister was single."

Six. Another one of Blaise's men and one of the few who wasn't already claimed by a woman. He was a regular here. Bellatrix was his current favorite.

Well, Six, she's pregnant. Stick with the strippers. Less drama.

"She's dating Marlow Gabler's youngest son," Blaise said.

Not anymore. Looked like they didn't have the updated information on Liberty.

I shrugged as if I didn't know her current relationship situation, like it didn't matter to me. I had to be careful. I might be Blaise's father-in-law, but lying to him wasn't something he'd forgive. Even if this wasn't his business.

"As much as I love a good soap opera, can we get back to the fact that there was a motherfucking Viper in here last night? If one of them survived and they are rebuilding, then we need to know," Gage said.

Blaise stared at me for a moment more, as if trying to decide if he should be concerned about Liberty being at my club, before glancing over at Gage. "You take Huck and go question the girl. Find out what she knows. Levi is already looking into things on his end. If they have a paper trail, he'll find it."

"Diamond is being held downstairs. Drifter can take you to her," I told them.

Gage stood up and followed Huck from the room. Blaise didn't move. His focus remained locked on me.

When the door closed behind the others, he leaned forward, narrowing his eyes slightly. "You need to tell me something, Liam?"

I wanted to tell him my personal shit was just that. Mine. But I also didn't want to have a bullet removed from one of my body parts today either. He wouldn't kill me, but that didn't mean he wouldn't shoot me.

I leaned back and smoothed my beard with my hand. Leaving out anything would bite me in the ass. Levi could find anything on the internet, and if he couldn't, Wilder Jones, their very own cyber genius, sure as fuck could.

"The week before I went on my first date with Selena, I was on my way back from Miami. It was storming, so I stopped at Abernathy's to get a drink until the rain lightened up. Liberty was the bartender. We talked. I enjoyed her company. The crowd was thinning out, so her boss let her off early, but she didn't have a ride." I paused, wishing like fuck I could stop this story now. "She was staying at a motel—she'd broken up with her boyfriend, who she had lived with recently. I went inside. We ..." I stopped again.

He raised his eyebrows. "Fucked?"

I nodded. We had definitely fucked. Several times.

"Anyway, I left, didn't think I'd see her again. But she called her sister, needing somewhere to stay until she could get a place of her own. Selena took her in."

I was hoping that would be enough.

Blaise tilted his head. "Why's she here?"

Dammit.

I leaned forward, putting my elbows on the desk. "She and Selena had a falling-out. She had nowhere to go. And ... she's pregnant. Until I know if it's mine, she's here. I would appreciate it if you didn't tell this to Madeline. I don't want her to know I fucked some thirty-one-year-old bartender I didn't know and knocked her up if I didn't, in fact, knock her up. If it's mine, I know I'm gonna have to tell her. But I ..." I rubbed my temples, why hadn't Liberty just stayed in her room.

"You don't want her disappointed in you. Why? Because you got a woman pregnant from a one-night stand or because she's only six years older than Madeline?"

I frowned. "Both."

He nodded and stood up. "I don't keep things from Madeline that affect her. What you do affects her. But I'll wait until you know if it's yours. No reason she has to know about her father's sex life otherwise."

There was that at least. If it wasn't mine, she'd never know. I had a small amount of relief. If the baby was mine, I'd have to tell her eventually.

Blaise shook his head as a low chuckle came from his chest. "Siblings with a twenty-five- year-old age gap. Jesus," he said in an amused tone.

I didn't want to look at it like that. It made me feel like an even bigger disappointment to Madeline.

"Could be worse," he said as he headed for the door. "It could have been one of your strippers."

Fourteen

LIBERTY

When Liam walked into my room, I was writing down another phone number for a job I'd found while searching online. I hadn't wanted to do what he'd ordered me to do earlier, but he had a point. Walking three miles in that kind of heat was dangerous. I had to think about the baby. It wasn't just me I was abusing anymore.

"My office," he said before turning and walking out.

I set my phone down and glared at his back before getting up and following him. Was this how it was always going to be with him? Once he knew this was his baby, what would happen then? I sure as heck wasn't going to stay in that room, and he wasn't going to tell me what I could and couldn't do.

"How good are you with computers?" he asked me as he walked behind his desk.

I glanced at the large flat screen desktop computer that sat on the left side of his desk. "Meaning what exactly?"

He lifted his gaze to meet mine. "Meaning how good are you with computers?" he repeated, sounding put out by my question.

"Well, I'm the end of the millennials. I grew up with computers. I can work one just fine, but if you need me to fix one, I can't do that."

He gave me a scowl. "Why would I ask you to fix one?"

I shrugged. "I don't know! Why would you ask a thirty-one-year-old how good they were with computers when that's all my generation has known?"

He rolled his eyes and pulled out the chair. "There are receipts that need to be scanned and put in the digital file."

I walked over to look at the pile of paper receipts and picked one up. "Why are you doing it this way? Just go paperless and have the receipt emailed to you. Then, you can save it from the email to your file. Less paper, less time."

He stared at me for a moment, and I waited to see what tongue-lashing I was about to get next.

His eyes dropped back to the stack of papers on his desk. "How do I set up going paperless?"

Was he serious? The man was mid to late forties, not eighty. Why was he still keeping his records like it was the '90s?

I scanned the receipt and found the website for the business listed on it. "Do you have the logins for these companies?"

His brows drew together. "Uh, yeah. I go online to make most of the orders. I have to call in a few, but I have a login for all the accounts to check order statuses."

"Perfect. I'll log in to each one, change your billing to paperless, and go ahead and start pulling the receipts on your account that match these, then just download them to the file on your computer."

He rubbed his jaw and almost grinned. "You're making my head hurt. But, yeah, if you know how to do that and I can get rid of all these piles of paper, then do it."

I smiled at him, and he just looked at me. It wasn't the normal seething glare I had grown accustomed to; it was almost … as if he didn't hate me.

His eyes darted away, and he moved back from the desk, then waved a hand in that direction. "Go ahead and sit down. Do your thing. Whatever. I need to get back to things downstairs." He grabbed a piece of paper. "I guess you need logins and passwords."

I shook my head. "Not if you have used this computer to get into the accounts before."

He looked at the computer, then back at me. "Yeah, it's where I do most of my ordering."

"Then, your passwords should be saved in your system settings. I just need the password for this computer, seeing as how my fingerprint and yours are not the same."

He let out a small laugh. "You mean to tell me that this thing saves my passwords?"

I nodded, trying not to gawk at how little he knew about his very expensive Mac. "Yep."

"Damn. All the times I had to change passwords because I couldn't remember them …" He shook his head and actually grinned. "It's Ozzy1998," he said, motioning to the computer. "The password," he added.

I sat down. "Ozzy with two z's?" I asked.

"Yeah."

I typed it in, and the screen unlocked. "Got it," I replied, then looked up as he headed for the door. "Who's Ozzy?" I asked.

He glanced back at me briefly. "My dog."

Frowning, I thought about the year. It couldn't have anything to do with his dog. No dog was twenty-six years old.

"And the year?" I asked. "He can't be that old."

This time, Liam didn't look back. He paused and when he didn't reply, I realized I'd hit a sore spot. I hadn't meant to, but normally, passwords were important things so you didn't forget it.

"The year I met Madeline's mother," he replied, then closed the door behind him.

I stared at it, letting that sink in, and then my eyes dropped to my stomach. He had loved his daughter's mother. Enough that he was using the year he'd met her as a password. I placed a hand over where my baby was growing inside me. He didn't love this baby's mommy. He barely tolerated me.

It was getting harder and harder to remember the man I'd met that night at the bar. The handsome biker who flirted with me. Asked me questions about myself. Gave me a ride after I got off work. Then ... showed me what sex could be like. I'd been clueless until that night.

Before Wallace, I'd only had sex one other time when I was fifteen years old, and it wasn't because I wanted to. The guy who took my virginity raped me. He was one of the boys Sissy had brought home from college. She blamed me when she walked in on it. Abilene had kicked me out of the house that night.

I had trusted Wallace with that information when I was seventeen. Wallace took his time winning my trust and easing me into a sexual relationship. He said the reason I didn't reach an orgasm during sex was because of being raped.

I had believed him until I had sex with Liam. I'd lost count of my orgasms that night.

Shaking my head to clear it, I turned back to the screen. I had a job to do, and thinking about Liam wasn't helping me any. That would just lead to me being sad and probably crying. I'd felt like doing that a lot lately. But I'd read on a prenatal website that it was to be expected.

Fifteen

LIAM

Pulling a cigarette from my pocket, I stared down at it, then tossed it on the bar with a curse and reached for a bottle of Jack instead. Opening it and not bothering with a glass, I turned it up and took a long pull.

"Guess that one's yours now," Tex drawled.

I slammed the bottle down onto the counter and glared at the empty stage. I'd been so fucking sure. I had convinced myself that this would be fine. It was just a precaution.

FUCK!

I took another drink.

"What did I miss?" Tex asked, sounding concerned.

I couldn't talk about this with him. Not yet. I was still trying to wrap my head around it.

The past two days had gone smoothly. Hell, this morning, I'd not even been annoyed when Liberty walked into my office. She had organized and updated so much shit in two days' time that I felt like a weight had been taken off my shoulders.

It had all been fine. Good even. Until five minutes ago, when I had gotten the call that the baby she was carrying was mine.

I'd pulled out, goddammit! Yeah, sure, I'd shot my load all over her ass immediately, but still, what were the fucking odds?! Did she not take birth control? She was thirty-one and had been living with a guy.

I took another drink, wishing something would make this go away. I couldn't have a kid. I was a grandfather, for God's sake. One day, Cree and Eli were gonna go to school with their aunt or uncle.

I winced, closing my eyes and sucking in air.

How did I tell this to Madeline? *Sorry, honey, but I got a one-night stand pregnant.*

This was a disaster.

Speaking of disaster, the woman having my kid was a disaster. She was too young and unfit to have a kid. She didn't even own a car or have a home.

"All right, Prez. You're worrying me," Tex said, reminding me he was there.

"Everything okay in here?" Drifter asked as his heavy footsteps drew closer.

"I'm not sure. He's drinking straight from the bottle and hasn't said a word," Tex told him.

They'd know eventually. Blaise would be expecting me to tell him today. Or for me to tell Madeline. He wasn't going to keep it from her.

Lifting my gaze, I looked at Tex, then at Drifter. They were both watching me as if they didn't know what to do with me. I took another drink.

"You trying to tie one on before ten in the morning?" Drifter asked. "That's not like you. Something bad happened."

I let out a hard, humorless laugh, then set the bottle down with a hard thud. "You could say that," I agreed.

"Do we need to call in backup?" Tex asked as he studied me closely for some sign of why I was trying to get drunk before I even had breakfast.

I shook my head.

"Okay then, you're gonna have to tell us something. You can get as shit-faced as you want, but we need to know what's up," Drifter urged me.

I took in a deep breath, then let it out. I didn't even know what I was gonna do with her now. I hadn't made plans. I'd stopped even thinking about it. The thought of this being the outcome had been nonexistent because I was sure it was the ex-boyfriend's.

Selena had texted me last night, saying she had been given tickets to a concert this weekend. It was some new band that claimed to play country music. I'd suffered through several of their songs when she'd played them at her house. What they sang wasn't country music. Not by a fucking long shot. I'd agreed to go even though I shouldn't have.

"Liberty is pregnant," I said, my voice sounding raspy. I took another drink before looking at them. "It's mine."

"Fuck," Tex muttered.

Drifter ran a hand over his hair; his eyes had gone wide, but he didn't say anything.

"I fucked her one night. Several times, but one night. That was it, so I didn't think it was mine," I ranted, then took another drink. It no longer burned, going down. "But the paternity test results came back, and it's mine all right. She had said it was, and I thought, *Hell, she fucked me hours after* we met. *She probably did that shit all the time.* Guess she wasn't lying about that."

Tex pulled a barstool out and sat down. "I mean, this is a shock, but if you gotta have a baby momma, that is one hot—"

"DON'T!" I warned him before he started that shit again.

He held up both hands. "Sorry. I was just pointing it out. Now, you can fuck her *raw* all you want." He said *raw* like he was envious.

"I'm not fucking her," I growled.

He frowned. "Can I ask why?"

"Leave it," Drifter said to him.

Tex shrugged. "I'm just trying to figure it out. You know he's gonna take care of her. It's his kid. He isn't about to just let her go. So, why not enjoy what he has?"

I wasn't going to be able to let her go. The baby was my responsibility too. She couldn't take care of herself, much less a baby. Did she even have a doctor?

"I don't know what I'm going to do," I admitted. "Trying to get over the shock at the moment."

"That's understandable," Drifter said. "But, I mean, it's like getting another chance. You didn't get to raise Maddy. You'll get to be in this kid's life."

I shook my head. "This isn't the same thing. Madeline was Etta's. Mine and Etta's. I don't even like the woman who is having my baby. I'm not moving her in my fucking house and playing family with her."

"Well, I wouldn't be against moving her into mine—"

I slammed the bottle down, shutting Tex up.

"Too soon?" he asked.

"Jesus, Tex, shut the fuck up," Drifter told him.

I had to go talk to her. Telling her I was the father was pointless. She'd already known, or she'd been hoping I was and bluffing. It wasn't like I could trust her.

"Why do you hate her so much?" Tex asked.

I wouldn't be telling him or any of the others all she'd done in her past. Maybe it was stupid, but I couldn't tell that shit to anyone. She was the mother of my unborn child. I might not like it, but I'd be damned if I let others think bad about her. She needed someone to take care of her, and it looked like my inability not to sink my dick into her had just given me that role.

Sixteen

LIBERTY

Without him saying a word, the moment he walked into the office, I knew the results were in. I stopped what I'd been working on for him and dropped my hands into my lap with a sigh.

"I see you got the call with the lab results," I said, going ahead and laying it out there.

He smirked, and that surprised me. I hadn't expected him to do anything remotely close to smiling.

"I sure did," he replied with a slight slur to his speech.

I narrowed my eyes and studied him as he walked in, closing the door behind him.

"Guess we should talk about it. What we're gonna do now," he said, not sounding at all upset.

I glanced at the time on the computer screen. It wasn't even twelve yet. Was he drunk?

"You don't seem as bothered as I thought you'd be," I pointed out.

Another curl of his lips. "You didn't see me before I drank a fifth of Jack," he said, then sank down into a chair across from the desk.

My eyebrows shot up. "You're drunk?"

He shrugged. "More or less. I don't know. Does it matter? I've got a thirty-one-year-old baby momma, and I'm so close to fifty that I can reach out and touch it."

I sat there as he chuckled briefly before his eyes drifted down to my chest and stopped.

"You keep prancing around with those big tits bouncing, I'm gonna jerk your shirt up and suck on your fat nipples. Should be wearing a bra."

I tensed as the nipples he was referring to hardened and a shiver ran through me.

He tilted his head and leaned forward, still looking at my boobs. "You liked that," he said huskily. "They got pointy real damn quick."

I swallowed as his heated gaze moved back up to my face.

"You trying to push me until I'm burying my cock in that tight cunt again? Is that why you aren't wearing a bra? Making me look at them. Remembering how pretty they bounce, just like your ass."

The tingle between my legs startled me. He was definitely drunk. What was wrong with me? Why was I reacting to this? He didn't like me.

"I need bigger bras," I said, hating that I sounded affected. "My others don't fit."

His tongue darted out as he licked his bottom lip, looking at my breasts again. "They were great before, but Tex is right;

they're fucking spectacular now. I bet they'd look even better with my cum dripping from them."

I shifted in the seat as the tingle morphed into an ache. What was he doing to me? I had to snap out of this. The man didn't really mean what he was saying.

He stood up then, and I sat, frozen, while he walked around the desk. My breathing turned into more of a pant as he got closer. I should say something. Get up and run to the other side of the room.

"Take that tank top off for me. Let me see those pretty titties," he urged.

I wanted to. I knew I'd regret it, but my vagina did not seem to care. She wanted his hands and mouth on her.

He stopped in front of me and ran the back of his fingertips down my right arm. "Show me, baby."

He moved his left leg in between mine, then reached down and grabbed the shoulder straps of my top and began to slowly tug them up. The soft cotton rubbing over my sensitive nipples caused a whimper to work its way out of me. He shouldn't be doing this. Sober Liam was going to regret it. I didn't want to be the source of more of his regrets. I was almost positive I was ranking in at number one already.

"Liam," I croaked out as the bottom part of my boobs felt the air. He continued until I had to raise my arms or have a tank top covering my face. I didn't think he cared either way. As long as he could get to my boobs.

"Good girl," he rasped, tossing my tank top to the desk, then lowering himself to his knees in front of me.

His eyes were locked on my chest, and I watched, unable to speak as his large, tanned, weathered, and tattooed hands covered them and squeezed.

"Fuck, that's more than a handful," he said, then leaned in and licked at my right nipple, rolling the tip of his tongue around it before pulling it into his mouth.

When the edge of his teeth scraped it, I slightly came off my seat from the pleasure.

While he enjoyed one with his mouth, he squeezed and used his thumb to flick and play with the other. I began rubbing my thighs together, no longer able to sit still.

His hand grabbed my thigh, then shoved it to the side, opening my legs for him. I was close to begging him to do something. I'd never had such a strong sensation stirring down there before. Not like this anyway.

When his moved under the leg of my shorts, I wanted to weep with joy. I should probably care about the small gushes I felt inside my panties since he'd started this, but right now, I didn't care about anything other than getting my release.

Thick fingers slid inside the crotch of my panties, and I let out a strangled cry.

"Fuck, that's a wet pussy," he growled as he let my nipple he'd been sucking on go. His hazel eyes were almost black now as he stared at me.

"Oh, please," I begged, grabbing his shoulders and moving my hips so that I rubbed against his hand.

More of the wetness gushed from me, causing his eyes to flare as it coated his fingers.

"That's a horny little cunt," he said, then slid his middle finger between my folds. "You've soaked your panties and your shorts."

That should embarrass me. It might later but right now, I just needed more. My mouth fell open as my breathing came in fast, hard gasps.

Liam's hand left my shorts, and I cried out, panicked that he was going to stop. His fingers began unbuttoning my shorts.

"Stand up," he said. "You're all wet. I need to get these off you."

Yes, okay. Whatever. Just touch me some more.

I stood, and he pulled both my panties and shorts down. When they were at my ankles, I lifted my foot, slipping it out of my sandal first, then did the same with the other. Liam took my panties and brought the crotch to his nose and inhaled while staring up at me.

"You smell even better than last time, and you were fucking delicious then," he snarled, tossing the bottoms aside. "Put your hands on the table, baby, and open your legs."

He no longer sounded drunk, but honestly, I didn't care. I just wanted him to make me come. I had never needed to come this bad in my life.

His tongue ran between my opening and then flicked my clit, causing my knees to buckle. Another gush came from me, and Liam let out a growl that vibrated against me, bringing me very close to my peak.

My hands gripped the table tightly. I was going to explode.

Both his hands grabbed my bottom, kneading it and pulling my cheeks apart as he licked from the front all the way to the back. My eyes flew open as he ran the tip of his tongue around the untouched puckered hole.

"Liam," I panted as his fingertip did the same then he spit on the hole and pushed the end of his finger in gently. "Oh God," I choked out.

His mouth was back between my legs as his finger continued to ease in just a tiny bit more before pulling out. The build was there. I felt the first wave of delirium as it crested, and I cried out his name. His tongue left me then, and I fell forward onto my elbows, gasping.

The sound of a zipper registered in my orgasm-hazed thoughts, and then I felt the heat of Liam's body as he moved in behind me. I fisted my hands, lifting my head to look back at him. The swollen head of his erection nudged against my entrance, and I let out a low moan.

"Fuck, that dripping pussy," he said with his eyes on my butt as he plunged into me. His fingers dug into my skin, and he let out a deep rumble. "How the fuck is it tighter?" he swore, and then he pulled back and pushed in harder. "It is. Christ! It's motherfucking tighter."

I pressed back, meeting his thrusts, and his eyes lifted to meet mine before dropping back to my butt. He let go of me, then watched my bottom as he rocked into me. His hand came down hard on one side with a loud slap, and I let out a startled sound.

"Fuck, I love seeing this juicy ass bounce." His voice sounded deeper than normal.

"GOD, Liam! Please, harder," I begged, needing to feel him deeper.

The way his girth stretched me was like nothing else.

His hand grabbed my ponytail, and he pulled it back, then smacked the other cheek with his free hand. "You want to be ridden hard? Hmm? Is that it? You've been a bad girl, and you want to be fucked like one?"

I was going to come again.

"Yes!" I gasped out. "Please! Spank me!"

"Goddamn!" he swore as he started slamming into me with so much force that the desk began to scoot and the things on it were rattling. "Take that dick! Naughty little slut with a tight cunt that keeps squirting. Hungry for my cock."

His dirty words kept coming, and the pulse between my legs grew so intense that I begged and bucked beneath him until it broke free and I screamed his name.

"Jesus! Fuck! GAH!" Liam roared behind me, and I felt the heat of his release as it shot into me with every thrust of his hips.

For a moment, we were silent as we stilled. This was even more spectacular than it had been in the motel room, and that had been life-changing. How had it gotten better?

Liam stepped back from me, and his cock slid out. The trickle of warmth I felt oozing between my thighs was him. He'd not worn a condom. But I guessed it wasn't like he could get me pregnant since he'd already accomplished that. There were other things to worry about. Like the fact that he had sex with God knew who.

I stood up and turned to face him. His eyes met mine as he zipped up his jeans.

"I'm clean," he said. "I get checked regularly and was just tested last week, but I will go get another one just to be sure." His nostrils flared as he looked behind me, then reached for my tank top and handed it to me. "Get dressed."

Here was where the regret came in. I'd known he was going to feel this way, and honestly, I should too. But I didn't. Because that had been insane, and I wanted more of it.

I slipped my top on and went to pick up my panties, separating them from my shorts. I needed new ones, but I didn't have any in here, so I put them on quickly, then my shorts. When I turned back to Liam, he was sitting in the chair with his head in his hands and his fingers threaded in his hair. My stomach sank.

Why did this thing between us have to be bad? When he was nice, I liked him. And we were very good at the sex part.

He let out a deep sigh and dropped his hands from his head and looked up at me. "That shouldn't have happened. I drank too much, and, well …" He shook his head and leaned back in the chair. "Fuck," he muttered.

That annoyed me. Why was he so upset? Was it because he had feelings for Sissy? That thought made me feel sick. Did he not like me because I was going to be a problem with their relationship? He had no idea how bad it was going to be. When she found out, she would lose it. But she wasn't pregnant with his baby. I was.

"The amount of your cum pooling in my panties right now says you enjoyed it just as much as I did," I said, angry that he was acting like this.

He looked at me and tensed, then shook his head. "Don't say shit like that," he warned me.

I lifted my shoulders in a shrug. "I'm just pointing it out. If you thought they were wet before, then you should—"

"SHUT UP!" he shouted.

I crossed my arms over my chest as the feeling of rejection began to sink in. As if I hadn't dealt with that enough in my life. Having it come from the man whose baby I was carrying was a hard blow, no matter how used to it I should be. This hurt.

A knock at the door stopped whatever else I was about to spew from my mouth, and I was thankful for the interruption.

"What?" Liam barked.

It opened, and the tattooed, green-eyed man with a pierced tongue stepped inside. Liam had called him Tex. His gaze darted to me quickly, then went back to Liam.

"Sorry, but it's important," he said.

Liam swung his eyes back to me. "Go to the bedroom. Pack up your things. I'll be there shortly," he said.

Pack up my things? I should be relieved. He wasn't planning on holding me hostage. Instead, dread started to creep in. What was he going to do? Take me to a motel and leave me? Or would he possibly take me to his house? Did he have one? Yes, he had to have a house.

The thought of living with him, in a home, not this club, sent a thrill of excitement through me. He didn't want me, but maybe if I was given a chance, I could change his mind about me. It wasn't like I could get this man to love me, but maybe he could like me. We could be friends even. Possibly friends who had sex because I really wanted more of that.

Seventeen

LIAM

"I know this is bad timing, but I waited until I was sure you were done and had time to dress," Tex said.

I ran a hand over my face. What the fuck had I just done? I could still smell her on my beard, and, dammit, my cock was getting stiff again. I had to wash her scent off me.

"Sounded like you decided against the not-fucking-her plan," he was amused.

"It was a mistake," I snarled.

"The floor shaking and the cursing, shouting, and screaming didn't sound like a mistake. I was close to needing to rub one off, listening to her."

The instant fury that unleashed inside me was the slap in the face I needed. I didn't like that he'd heard her. He didn't need to know what she sounded like when she was fucking. It made me want to rip his head off, and that was a problem. Because having any kind of reaction to her, other than just making sure her needs were met because she was carrying my child, was bad.

That woman was not my future. She wasn't what I needed or wanted. I was ready for someone stable, with a level head, a little older, successful. Someone like her sister, which wouldn't be happening. I'd already decided it probably wasn't going to before I found out I had knocked up Liberty, but it was a definite no now.

"I was drunk and weak. Yes, she's got a hot body, and you put that shit in my head about not needing a condom with her. I snapped. Won't happen again," I told him. "Now, what is it that you came in here for?"

He nodded his head toward the door. "Police are here. Diamond was found dead in her apartment about an hour ago. To make matters worse, Whisper was the one who found her. She hadn't been answering her phone, and she was supposed to cover her shift here tonight. Anyway"—he shook his head and winced—"it's bad. They did some fucked-up shit to her. Even fucked her with a knife."

Jesus Christ. A sick knot settled in my stomach as I stood up, no longer having to worry about a hard-on. That had taken care of it.

"Do they any leads?" I asked, walking around my desk that had moved forward at least five inches since I'd come in here.

"They have a witness, a neighbor, saying a man came out of her place around five this morning. They described the Viper she had been with, and we can't find him. She'd claimed he was a guy she'd met at a bar the night before. All the information she had on him—name, number, car—none of it is legit. So, she either lied to cover for him or he lied to her."

Fucking hell, these women and dating gang thugs. What was their problem? Had none of them learned from the mistakes of the past? I'd already had one of them shot dead in my club due to a damn gang.

I started for the door.

"You should probably know that it's Harrison and Millow. Due to our relationship with them, they were following me up the stairs when we heard things. They might have heard more than you'd have liked before Drifter took them back inside the main room."

A burning in my chest that I didn't recognize or like started up, and my hands fisted. I had to get her somewhere that wasn't near me. I didn't trust myself with her. Not if this was how I was going to react to shit like this. Harrison and Millow

had walked in on me getting head before, and I'd taken my time finishing, blowing my load in front of them—that was how much I hadn't cared.

Knowing they had heard Liberty, I cared. I cared so much that I wanted to put my fist through a wall. Which meant she had to go.

Three hours later, I'd given the detectives all the information I had, made some calls, and let Tex and Drifter know I'd be back late tonight.

Liberty's suitcases were by the door when I opened it. I looked across the room to find her curled up on the bed, asleep, wearing some new shorts and a top and a pair of Converse. I'd expected her to start yelling at me the moment I walked in since I'd sent her in here and said I'd be with her shortly.

When she was sleeping, she looked so damn sweet that it was hard to think any of the shit I knew about her was true.

The night I'd spent with her in her motel room, I had stood over her, watching her sleep for a hell of a lot longer than I should have. I hadn't wanted to leave. Maybe years ago, when I had been younger and didn't have grandsons and a daughter who was in her mid-twenties, I could have taken this ride with her. Jumped in, knowing full well that she was a bucketload of red flags, and fucked her until I had my fill. Soaked in those killer eyes of hers and plump lips. Listened to her laugh and smiled at the sound of it. But not now.

I was well past that stage in my life where messed-up girls like her were fun. She was having my baby. I'd share a kid with her. A kid who was going to need me because its momma couldn't be trusted to do right by it. We hadn't talked about if she even wanted to raise a kid. As far as I knew, she'd hand it over to me and walk away.

That right there was why I was doing this. Getting her somewhere safe and far away from me. The Judgment Sanctuary was our club compound in Miami, and it was surrounded by security gates. She could go out to the pool there, freely roam around outside, and I would be hours away. I'd show up for doctor's appointments, then come back to Ocala. She wouldn't be alone. She'd have Nina and Goldie, who were both a little too fucking giddy about this. Leave it to the ole ladies of two of my original members to think me knocking up a woman was a good thing. They'd baby the fuck out of her.

I walked over to her and shoved all doubts about my decision away before touching her shoulder. "Liberty."

She blinked a few times, then looked up at me.

Damn that woman and her eyes.

Space. Lots of fucking space. This was the right thing.

"Time to go," I told her and turned to walk over to the luggage.

I heard her yawn, and then her feet hit the ground.

"Where are we going?" she asked in a raspy voice.

"Miami," I told her and started walking, carrying one of her suitcases in each hand.

"Miami?" she repeated.

"Yeah. The Judgment Sanctuary is there. Big compound, nice pool, some women you'll like."

She followed me down the stairs, not saying anything else. When we got outside, I unlocked the doors to my Charger so she could get inside, then went and put her suitcases in the back. If the traffic wasn't terrible, I should return before closing time.

I climbed into the driver's seat and started it up.

"How long will we be there?" she asked.

"You will be there your entire pregnancy. I'll get you set up with an OB-GYN tomorrow and come back for the appointments."

"You are leaving me there? With people I don't know? Why can't I stay here? I'll get a job and an apartment."

The panic in her tone was not going to get to me. This was the right thing to do. She just didn't realize it yet.

"You're pregnant with my baby, Liberty. Because of me, you lost your job. I am going to take care of you and the baby. We will address where you want to live and what you want to do once the baby is born. But while you're pregnant, you need somewhere safe to live. You can't live upstairs at a strip club. This is the best option."

She didn't say anything, and after a few minutes, I thought we were done talking, so I reached for the radio to turn it on. I sure as hell didn't want to discuss what had happened in my office.

"So, that's it. We fucked, and now, you are shipping me off. To get me away from you so, what, that you won't fuck me again or because you think I'll be clingy? Because rest assured, as much as I obviously enjoy what you do with your mouth and cock, I do not stay where I am not wanted."

Guessed I wasn't so lucky. She was going to talk about it, and the more she said *fuck* and *cock*, the harder said cock was going to get.

"I was drunk, and you weren't wearing a bra. I got carried away. That's a mistake. We aren't going to be a couple. We are in two different eras in our life. But we are having a kid together. We need to get along. Accept it. Work together. Fucking will add shit we don't need. When the baby gets here, we need to have a common ground. Not a lot of messed-up shit that will hinder us working together."

"I didn't ask you to take care of me. I'm not a charity case."

"I know you didn't ask. But I got you pregnant, and now, your needs are my responsibility. The way you were overworking yourself wasn't safe for the baby. You'll have a much healthier pregnancy with me taking care of things. No stress."

It sounded better, the more I talked about it. I glanced at her to see her hands fisted tightly in her lap and her bottom lip between her teeth.

Fuck, was she about to cry? God, I hoped not. I didn't know what to do with an emotional woman. Another thing Nina and Goldie would be better at. I wasn't cut out for any of this shit. She was fucking lucky.

Eighteen

LIBERTY

He was gone. He'd left me like an unwanted pet, dumping me here for strangers to deal with.

I'd managed to fight back the tears until I could get back to the room he'd taken my luggage to and told me to use. It was his room here, and no one had ever used it but him. I was the only one with the key, and I was welcome to treat it like my own home.

Goldie and Nina had been really sweet and seemed to understand that I needed to be alone. Both of them looking at me with sympathy and pity had just about sent me over the edge into a fit of tears.

I reached up and wiped away another tear that had rolled down my face as I looked around the room. It was huge. There were no windows, which was different, but it wasn't confining due to the size of it.

A king-size bed with a black down comforter; a flat screen TV that was the size of one of the walls in the room I'd slept in at the club; a black leather sectional sofa with a coffee table that was made up of two motorcycle tires, stacked on top of each other; a square metal Harley Davidson sign that had smooth, rounded edges; a weight bench, a stand with rows of handheld weights, along with weights for the bench press, placed neatly in the corner, all filled the open space.

There was a bearskin rug, which I really hoped wasn't real, that covered the floor over by the sofa and coffee table while a soft gray rectangular rug lay in the center of the room. There were some framed albums that were signed, it seemed, and a few biker week posters on the walls.

The private bathroom attached to the room was equally impressive with a big walk-in shower with two showerheads. One was the kind that hung from the top, releasing water like rain, and the other could be detached and held in your hand. The tub looked like it was a Jacuzzi that could fit four people. The walls were black with white marble countertops and brushed nickel finish.

Wallace had a nice apartment. It was considered luxury. However, it was nothing remotely close to this nice.

I'd never seen anything like this in person. In magazines and television maybe.

All of that, however, didn't make up for the fact that Liam had just brought me here to get rid of me. It was humiliating and insulting. Yet he was right. If I had to do this on my own, I would work a lot of hours on my feet, and that would be harder later in the pregnancy. It wasn't safe for me to be walking to the bus stop at night. If something happened to me, it happened to the baby. I had to think about that.

So, I'd kept my mouth shut while he listened to classic rock on the radio the entire drive down here. The only time we spoke was when he stopped for gas and asked me if I wanted anything or needed to use the restroom. That had been it.

I stared at the big bed and tried to decide if I wanted to lie down or go get something to eat in the kitchen. I hadn't gotten anything at the service station, and I was starting to get a little hungry. Perhaps there was chocolate or ice cream. I could eat my feelings.

I checked my appearance in the mirror and then splashed some cold water on my face and patted it dry. I didn't want to look like I'd been crying. They already felt sorry for me. No need to make it worse. When I was sure my sobbing fit didn't show on my face, I headed back down the long hallway with the black walls to the stairs.

There were a lot of rooms up here, but the only one he'd shown me was this one. All the others belonged to members. I wondered who lived here with me.

Footsteps caused me to pause, and I waited to see who turned the corner on the first flight of stairs. It was a man with blond hair, pulled back loosely in a bun, and brown eyes the color of chocolate. He was tall with wide shoulders, and since he was just wearing The Judgment vest with nothing underneath his well-cut arms and chest were on display. I realized I was staring and felt my face warm.

"Um, hi," I blurted out. "I'm Liberty."

The only member I'd met when I arrived was Brick, Goldie's husband—or her ole man, as she had called him.

A smile stretched across his face. "You're Liberty," he replied, then held out his hand. "I'm Country. It's nice to meet you."

I shook his hand, uncertain of what to say. "Uh, you too."

He let my hand go. "I hope you're going to the kitchen because Nina and Goldie are stressing the fuck out over you not eating before you came up here."

I hadn't meant to make them worry.

"I am," I replied. "I just needed to freshen up a bit."

His gaze swept over me quickly, not stalling anywhere or making me feel like he was checking me out. "Seems like you accomplished it."

I laughed, not sure what he meant. "Okay, well, I guess I'll see you around."

He stepped out of my way so I could continue down the next set of stairs.

"Yeah, my room is three doors down from Prez's, on the left, if you need anything. I mean, at night—" He shook his head, and it looked like he was blushing. "That is not coming out right. What I am trying to say is, I am here at night if something happens. Goldie and Nina normally go back to their houses. Sometimes, they stay here, but not a lot. Dolly and Micah are here a couple of nights a week. They're down on that end. Anyway, just, uh, make yourself at home."

He wasn't sexy in the way that Liam was, but he had a certain appeal. Not that it mattered. I was pregnant. I wasn't shopping around for a man. It would likely be years before I got to have sex again. At least today's experience had been medal-worthy. It would have to last me for a long time.

"Thanks," I replied, then continued on down.

Taking a deep breath, I tried to still my nerves before walking into the kitchen with what sounded like a lot of people that I didn't know, but who all knew their Prez had dumped me off here. His unwanted, pregnant one-night stand.

Pushing the heavy red door, I walked inside, ready to get this over with.

Goldie—an attractive woman with dark red hair, styled in a pixie cut—looked up from the food she was dishing onto a plate and smiled brightly at the sight of me. That eased my nerves considerably.

"Liberty," she called out, and I made my way over to the counter.

The talking seemed to quiet, and I felt as if everyone was staring at me. Curious about the woman their boss had left here.

Nina turned around from the stove and gave me a smile before turning to look out at the room of people. "All right, this is Liberty. She belongs to Prez. She's staying here in his room. Everyone understands she has free rein and is not to be touched," Nina called out.

There were grunts, agreements, mutters, and other things going on behind me, and I knew I needed to do something. Not keep my back to them like a weirdo.

I turned and gave a small wave and smiled.

There were more men than women. Men of all ages, in leather vests, with tattoos. The women were, well, interesting. Barely dressed for the most part, and they appeared a little hard, as every single one shot less than friendly looks at me. At least the men seemed welcoming enough. Maybe.

"Nice to meet you, Liberty," an older guy, who was a little on the heavy side, called out.

A few others said similar things. I did my best to acknowledge them, then looked back to Goldie.

"I'd say they're harmless, but that would be a lie. The girls are nasty. Most of them are in the porns that the club produces. There are a few club whores. Don't worry about any of them though. You are under Prez's protection. No one is going to bother you.

"Now, what would you like to eat? We've got dinner all laid out. Most have already eaten, but I set a plate back for you with everything on it. I wasn't sure what you'd want. I will tell you though that the shrimp is fresh caught and the cheese grits I made to go with them are Prez's favorite," she said, taking a plate from the oven and uncovering it.

There were so many different items on it that I just stared.

Nina laughed as she came up to the counter with a flat iron skillet she'd pulled from the oven with homemade biscuits on it. "You need one of these. I make the best biscuits. Just ask anyone here."

"Just 'cause she's Prez's baby momma don't mean she gets all the hot biscuits," a man with bright red hair and a goatee said, coming up beside me. He shot me a wink and grabbed a biscuit from the skillet.

Nina slapped at his hand, and he just laughed, then stuck the biscuit in his mouth before he walked off.

"That was Fox. He always says stupid shit. We ignore him," Goldie said.

I knew she was trying to cover for him calling me Liam's baby momma, but that was all I actually was to the man. If it quacks like a duck …

I shrugged. "Doesn't bother me."

Goldie leaned in closer to me. "You're more than that, or he wouldn't have brought you to us and put you up in his suite."

Nina slid a biscuit onto my plate. "She's right. Now, eat up. You are too tiny as it is. Not that I wouldn't shave off my hair to have your boobs and ass, but other than those areas, you are too thin. You need some food."

Goldie chuckled. "She'll try to fatten you up. It's her calling in life. Until I met her, I didn't have these thighs," she said.

Brick walked up behind her and grabbed her leg, making her squeal. "These are my thighs. Don't be bad-mouthing them."

Goldie's eyes warmed as she tilted her head back so her husband could kiss her. It was more like her mouth was his source of oxygen. I had to look away. It felt voyeuristic.

That must be wonderful—having someone like that.

My mom and dad had had it. When I was little, I always thought that I'd have it, too, someday.

But then Mom died. Dad married Abilene, and looking back now, I knew he never loved her like he had my mom. That wasn't my fault, and her taking it out on me was unfair. I was a kid who'd lost her parents.

The older I got, not having someone who loved me so completely, I'd wondered if it was me who was inadequate.

"We sure this was an accident?" a man asked, and I glanced over to see a guy with black hair, blue eyes, and dark skin standing beside me, smirking. "Prez is a smart man. I can see why he left it unwrapped with this one."

"Easy," Brick said in a deep, scratchy voice, his eyes glaring at the other guy.

"Just stating what we're all thinking," the man said.

"Don't go stirring up a fight tonight. She just got here. You behave," Nina said, pointing her finger at the man. She looked over at me. "This is Lick, and ... well, he's just—"

"An asshole," another feminine voice said.

His gaze looked past me, and he winked at whoever it was. I shifted to see a woman with heavy makeup, fake lashes, and overly plump lips a lot like the stripper who had brought me food at the club. She was wearing a halter top instead of pasties and a pair of shorts that were closer to panties. The stilettos were stripper material too.

"Amethyst," she told me. "I'm on my way to Toxic Throttle, but I had to swing by and see our new face. It ain't every day Prez brings home a woman."

Someone else laughed. "He only did it once, and that was his daughter. Not a baby momma."

Amethyst sent whoever it was a sour look, then turned back to me. "Pinch is a douche," she said with a roll of her eyes.

"You're supposed to be at Toxic in ten minutes," a man barked out.

She saluted him. "I'm going." She looked back at me. "Good luck around here."

"Now, try my cheese grits," Goldie said, drawing my attention back to her.

There was one thing for certain: I wasn't going to get bored around here.

Nineteen

LIBERTY

I couldn't remember the last time I'd slept so late. Without windows to let in the sunlight and no alarm to wake me up for work, it was after ten when I walked downstairs. Nina greeted me with more of her biscuits. The smell of bacon, eggs, and sausage turned me off, however. I took a biscuit, thanked her, and made my way out the back of the clubhouse.

The pool was lovely with plenty of shade and seating. I continued to walk around, breathing in the fresh air and taking small nibbles from the buttered biscuit. Without the fried meat tainting my senses, the biscuit settled my stomach. There was so much property here. The front entrance was all parking lot and Harleys, but back here, there were palm trees and green grass.

"You're out early," a familiar drawl said from behind me.

I turned to see Country standing against the side of the building with a cup of coffee in his hand.

I smiled. "This is not early."

He lifted a shoulder, and a crooked grin curled his lips. "It is for here. Most of the guys stay up all night and sleep until noon. I'm normally the only one out here in the morning."

He took a drink from the mug in his hand as he studied me.

"I was in bed before ten last night. I almost slept twelve hours," I told him.

"Eh, Prez's suite doesn't have windows, so I expect that's easy."

I glanced up at the second floor and noticed there were windows up there. "So, not all the suites are windowless?"

Country chuckled. "No, and the only suite belongs to Prez. The rest of us have bedrooms with a bathroom much smaller than his. When he had this place built, he chose not to have windows for security purposes. His former VP was his best friend; he thought the idea was funny and teased him about it."

I frowned. I knew so little about Liam, and I was carrying his child. Our child.

"Former VP?" I asked, curious why his best friend was no longer his VP.

"Tulsa Abe. I never met him—before my time. He was killed about fourteen or fifteen years ago, I believe it is now. His son, Micah, is the VP now. He was a kid when his dad died, and Liam raised him after," he explained.

Liam had lost his best friend and raised his son. Wow. I hadn't expected that.

"Where was Micah's mom?" The question came out before I could think about how nosy I sounded.

The hunger to know more about Liam and his life was new to me. But he was never going to open up to me. I would take what I could get.

"I've heard someone mentioned she died before Tulsa. I know Micah's younger sister is his half-sister. She has a different mom. Pepper owns a bar in town. Nice place. Nina and Goldie go with their ole men from time to time. You should go. You'd like Pepper."

One conversation with Country, and I knew more about Liam than I'd learned since I'd met him. At least it felt that way.

My gaze swept over the property, and I sighed, thinking of all the lovely plants and flowers that could spruce up the place. It was like a blank canvas needing some art. The grass was freshly mowed and a pretty green that made me think it must have a sprinkler system. Florida summers were rainy, but the sun could still turn things brown around here with its brutal rays.

"Who cuts the grass?" I asked, wondering if the men did it or if there was a landscaper.

Country chuckled. "Whoever draws the short straw on Friday night."

I laughed. "Really?"

He nodded. "Yep. Grass gets cut on Saturday morning. Now, granted, we have a John Deere riding lawn mower with a cover and AC, but no one wants to get up early on Saturday to cut grass after a late night of drinking."

Chewing on my bottom lip, I tossed the idea around in my head before looking back at him. "How do you think everyone would take it if I took over the mowing on Saturdays, and in return, I'd be allowed to plant some flowers? Just give the place a little color? I wouldn't overdo it."

Country took another drink from his mug while he looked out over the backyard. "I think you can plant whatever the fuck you want, and not a soul will complain. But I'm gonna just veto you cutting the grass now. Don't offer that. Some of those lazy-ass fuckers will let you do it, and then I'll be up every Saturday morning, cutting the damn grass because there is no way in hell I am letting you do it."

I frowned, placing a hand on my hip. "I am very capable of running a lawn mower. I have mowed lawns with a regular ole mower many times in my life. When I was growing up, my stepmom had me do it every week, and there was no seat or fancy AC on the thing she had me using." I finished my little rant, not appreciating the fact that he thought riding a mower was beneath me.

"Where was your dad?" he asked, his brows drawn together.

I swallowed. It had been over twenty years now, and time did heal, but not completely. "He died when I was ten years old. A few months before my eleventh birthday."

The sympathy in his brown eyes was immediate, and I could tell he regretted asking me. "I'm sorry to hear that."

"Thanks," I replied, hating that it felt awkward now. It always did when this topic came up.

"I'm still not letting you cut the grass. The mower is huge, and there are areas you have to get off and use a weed eater to reach things. I just can't allow a pregnant woman to do that kind of work. Especially out in this heat. You'd have to climb up in the mower and …" He paused, shaking his head. "Can't do it. Even if my momma hadn't raised me to take care of women properly, I wouldn't be able to stomach that. But you want to plant flowers? Go for it. I'll handle the others. They won't give a shit though. I promise you that."

My head was instantly turning with ideas. Over by the back entrance and around the pool area. I had my scrapbook full of all the inspiration I'd saved. I could go through it today and piece together the things I wanted to do. I would need to make sure it worked in this heat and in the shading the backyard provided. I didn't need to overspend. Even though I didn't have bills right now, I wasn't going to just stay here and give Liam nothing.

Once the baby came, I needed money saved to get a place of our own. I wished he'd allow me to get a job here. Maybe I could work at that bar his VP's sister owned. I'd ask about that next time I saw him. Although I didn't know when that would be. Perhaps I would ask the VP himself or ask Nina how to get in touch with Pepper.

"I'd need to find a nursery with affordable prices," I said more to myself than to Country.

"You tell me when you want to go flower shopping, and I'll give you a ride."

Twenty

LIAM

It had been a little over a week since I'd left Liberty at The Judgment Sanctuary. I'd considered calling her a few times to see how she was settling in, but decided against it. I called Nina instead to make sure she was doing okay. Since there was no cause for concern, I was able to relax somewhat.

Selena was becoming a bit of an issue. I had been dodging her calls and responding to her texts at a minimum. I felt guilty every time her name appeared on my screen. I knew I needed to make a clean cut with her. We hadn't been exclusive, but it was clear she had read more into whatever we'd been doing than was there. When Liberty wanted to tell her about the pregnancy, she could, but I was leaving that up to her. As for me and Selena, I intended to just stop seeing her.

She was probably the classiest woman I'd ever date. The fact that a doctor, with all she had going for her, was interested in the president of an MC club, who had long hair and tats, was surprising. Sure, I'd fucked high-class bitches before, but not dated them. I had just been their walk on the wild side. Didn't matter. Selena and I were done.

A couple of prospects were on the far right side of the parking lot when I parked. Looked like Pinch was working on his bike. The fucker always had something wrong with it. The others with him were taking a smoke. They all called out a greeting, and I just nodded my head and continued inside.

Liberty's first doctor's appointment was in an hour, and I'd come to take her and have church with the club officers. After, I thought I'd head over to Paradise Brew—Pepper's bar—and socialize with the men a bit before going back to Ocala. Normally, I'd stay the night, maybe two, but with Liberty in my bed, that wasn't going to happen.

Taking long strides toward the kitchen, in hopes that Nina and Goldie had something left from breakfast, I glanced at the stairs, wondering if Liberty was ready yet. I'd told her I'd be here at twelve and to be ready to leave. It was ten till that, so I had a few minutes to grab something to eat.

Shoving through the red door, I stepped into the kitchen and paused at the sight of Liberty standing there with an apron on, laughing with Nina, who looked to be rolling out some dough. Dolly, my VP's fiancée, was on the other side of Nina, watching with a huge grin on her face. They were clearly enjoying themselves.

Seeing Liberty happy like that gave me a funny feeling in my chest. She didn't laugh like that around me.

Nina spotted me first. "Prez," she said, stopping whatever she had been doing.

Liberty's gaze swung to mine, and her amusement vanished. "I didn't realize the time. I'm sorry," she immediately said and began to untie the apron she was wearing.

"I'm ten minutes early," I explained, then looked back at Nina. "Was hoping you had something to eat."

She nodded, laying the rolling pin down.

"I can fix it. You keep doing that, and then the filling is ready to go on the stove. Just cut it in round circles, like I showed you. Scoop it in the middle, fold it over, and seal it with the fork tongs. Tablespoon of butter per pie. Two to three minutes on each side. Be sure to use the iron skillet though. Mama D said that made all the difference," Liberty told her, then walked over to the fridge.

I watched her, not sure what to make of the fact that I'd walked in on Liberty teaching Nina how to make something.

"She's showing me how to make fried apple pies the way her grandmother used to. I've made them in the past, but they were from some recipe online," Nina told me, smiling, then glancing over at Liberty.

I looked at Dolly. "Micah here?" I asked, knowing he had to be if Dolly was.

He didn't trust any male around her. She was a sweet thing. Quiet and tiny. Her amber eyes softened slightly at the mention of his name.

She nodded, her cheeks a touch pink. "He went upstairs to take my things. He's here for church, but we're staying a couple of nights."

Micah had once lived here until he got pussy-whipped by Dolly. He put a ring on it so damn fast after she got out of the hospital due to an accident caused by his ex-girlfriend. At first, I'd worried it was because he felt guilty over what had happened to her, but I hadn't been here much to see the entire thing play out. The man-whore had been reformed by his sister's best friend.

"This is the plate you put back for Liam, correct?" Liberty asked Nina, pulling a plate out that was covered in aluminum foil.

"That's it," Nina replied as she went back to cutting out a circle of dough.

"You knew I'd come hungry," I said as I pulled out a stool and sat down across from Nina.

She glanced up at me. "I've been cooking for you long enough to know you," she said, and then she nodded toward Liberty, who was heating up my plate. "That one though makes me feel a tad bit inferior. I've yet to find something she can't do."

Liberty looked over her shoulder at Nina. "Don't start that. I can't make your biscuits or your fried chicken the way you do."

Nina chuckled. "Thanks for that, but if you tried, I have no doubt you'd excel at it."

"I want you to come help me in my flower beds at home," Dolly told Liberty. "Now that the house is finished, I feel as if the outside looks bare."

I had known Nina and Goldie would befriend Liberty and make her feel comfortable. Dolly would be a good influence on her. I hadn't expected to walk into my club and see Liberty fitting in so well. She hadn't been easy for Selena to live with, growing up, and the way she'd stormed out of her house, I'd been prepared to find out she had shown that side of herself here by now. She was sleeping in my suite. I knew everyone was letting her have her way because of me. I'd thought she'd be a little more demanding, not so … helpful.

Liberty placed the plate in front of me. "I reckon you can get your own drink," she said, then walked over to the stove and began to stir something in a pot.

Nina's eyebrows shot up as she looked at Liberty's back, then at me. There was amusement dancing in her expression, but she didn't dare smile. Standing up, I walked over to the fridge and got a bottle of water, then went back to my plate of food.

"Look what the cat dragged in," Micah drawled as he entered the kitchen. His hand patted my back hard. "How's big daddy?"

The laughter in his eyes when I looked at him wasn't surprising. He was a smart-ass, and the fact that I'd knocked up a one-night stand must have been an endless source of entertainment for him.

"Micah!" Dolly scolded him.

He turned his attention to her, and his smirk switched to that ridiculous lady killer smile of his. "What, Tink? I was just having some fun, baby."

She shook her head, trying to act as if she wasn't melting under his gaze. The two of them were a touch nauseating.

"I'm sure it's not fun for everyone," she hissed under her breath.

He cupped the side of her face and brushed his thumb over her cheek. I was trying to eat. I didn't need their public display of affection while doing it.

"Don't be mad, Tink," he told her, lowering his mouth to hers.

I decided it was best to just keep my eyes on my food.

"Liberty, got that soil you asked me to pick up," Country called out from the back entrance to the kitchen.

My eyes shot back up, and I paused with my fork halfway to my mouth. Looking at Liberty, I watched her beam brightly before putting her spoon down and hurrying around the corner.

"Thank you! You are the best!" she called back.

"No problem. Need anything else, just let me know," Country replied.

I could feel Micah's gaze on me, and I looked at him for an answer.

He wagged his eyebrows at me. "Good ole Country. You can count on him to make sure everything is handled," he said, then gave me a pointed look. "No, wait. Come to think of it, that don't sound like him at all."

He was determined to make me uncomfortable. Well, I was verging on pissed. I swung my gaze to Nina, who was also watching me for a reaction. She gave me a little shrug and went back to rolling the leftover dough after she cut out a circle.

When Liberty turned around, her eyes met mine, and again, the smile vanished. She said nothing, but went back to the pot to check on what was inside.

"You planting something?" I asked her when it seemed no one wanted to explain why Country had bought her soil.

Liberty's shoulders tensed, and she turned back to me. "Yes. I hope that's okay with you. I made sure the others didn't mind."

"It looks real nice out there," Nina said. "Never thought much about adding flowers and such, but she's sure made it pretty."

"Oh, yes! You should see it! She's brilliant. I need her to come to our house and help me," Dolly exclaimed with excitement.

Liberty's mouth lifted slightly at the corners. "I'm not done just yet," she said.

I took another bite and then washed it down with some water. "Been using that scrapbook you got for inspiration?"

I asked, remembering what she'd told the nurse and how I'd thought she was full of bullshit.

She nodded. "Yeah. First time I got to do that. I, uh, appreciate everyone being so nice about it."

Country was doing her bidding. Nina was making stuff that Liberty was teaching her. My VP's fiancée was trying to get her to come to their house and do their landscaping. Had she charmed the whole damn place?

"Hope it's not making the mowing any more complicated," I replied, and her face fell.

A worried frown wrinkled her forehead. I hadn't meant to sound like an ass, but the men weren't crazy about keeping the grass cut, and they had to get off and use the edger and weed eater enough as it was. The property wasn't small.

"Country has been handling the extra edging and weed eating," Nina said, giving me a sharp look.

"You don't say," Micah piped up, grinning like a damn fool.

I wasn't taking his bait. He could kiss my ass. By looking at Liberty, he thought there was more to this. He was wrong.

I shrugged. Guessed they had it all worked out. I finished my plate without saying anything more, then stood up.

"Ready?" I asked Liberty.

She closed the dishwasher she'd been loading and turned to me. "Yep."

"Thanks for the meal, Nina," I said before turning toward the door. "Delicious, as always. Tell Goldie I said thank you."

"Liberty helped me make breakfast. Might want to thank her instead," she replied.

I glanced back at Liberty, who gave me a forced smile, then took her purse from a hook and placed it over her shoulder. She was making breakfast? I studied her, finding this hard to believe. Cooking for this bunch wasn't easy. Why would she offer to do that?

"Can't wait to hear about your appointment," Nina told her.

"Me too! If you get an ultrasound, bring pictures," Dolly added.

Liberty gave them a little wave. "I will be sure to give you the highlights."

Shoving the door open, I headed out into the hallway just as Grinder was coming in from the back door.

"Prez," he said. "Didn't expect you until later. Church is at four, right?"

"Yeah," I replied.

His gaze shifted to Liberty as she followed me into the hallway, and he grinned. When did Grinder ever fucking grin?

"Liberty," he greeted her. "Didn't see you when I came into the kitchen this morning; you'd gone up to get ready. But them fried potatoes were something else. I had two helpings before Nina cut me off."

Was I in the motherfucking twilight zone?

I looked at Liberty, who was blushing.

"I'm glad you liked them. I know Goldie does them different, but Nina wanted me to do them the way I knew how."

"The general consensus is, we all prefer yours," he said in a low voice.

Liberty laughed softly. "Well, I don't know the secret to her cheese grits, so don't go telling her that. She might withhold them, and there would be a riot."

He chuckled as I stood there, watching in silence.

Finally, I cleared my throat. "We need to get going."

Grinder glanced at me as if he'd forgotten I was there. "Where you taking her?" He seemed concerned.

This wasn't his fucking business.

"Doctor's appointment," Liberty offered when I didn't respond.

His eyes widened. "All right then. See you at church, Prez," he said to me, then walked into the kitchen.

We made it to the Charger without any more of my men stopping to chat with Liberty. Neither of us spoke as I pulled through the gate. I was annoyed, but I wasn't sure exactly why. I should be fucking relieved. She wasn't being difficult, and everyone seemed to like her being there. I wouldn't need to relocate her, which was something that had been in the back of my mind. I wasn't there full-time, like I once had been, and if Liberty decided to be the spoiled bitch she'd been with Selena, then I couldn't expect them all to deal with her.

Clearly, I'd been worried for nothing. She'd charmed the whole damn bunch, it seemed.

I glanced at her. She was wearing a hot-pink sundress that showed off her tan. She had a natural olive complexion, but she'd been out in the sun, and it had deepened. Her dark brown hair had some light streaks from the sun as well. It was almost as if she was glowing. Her face didn't appear as thin as it had when I left her here.

"How are you feeling?" I asked, breaking the silence.

My voice seemed to startle her. She jumped slightly and her eyes widened.

She licked her lips, then replied, "Good. Better actually. I haven't felt sick in the past four days. It's been a relief not to want to throw up when I smell bacon and sausage in the mornings."

Was that a good thing? How far along was she?

"How many, uh—how far along are you? I mean, like months or whatever."

A small frown crinkled her forehead slightly. "I'm not sure. This will be my first doctor's visit, but I have been reading some pregnancy information websites before I go to bed at night, and I know that you count by weeks, but the first week isn't actually when you conceived. It's the week of your period—or rather day one is the first day of your last period. I did the calculations, and I should be ten weeks tomorrow. That is, if I counted it right."

If she was two months, then there were only seven more to go. At least if she'd understood the website and it was a reputable one. She probably should have seen a doctor by now. I'd had to make some calls to get her an appointment with one of the best in the area.

"My Medicaid came through," she said, smiling. "I got the email two days ago." Then, she paused and bit her bottom lip. "But I don't think all doctors take it. Did you ask about this one?"

This doctor did not take Medicaid. She was one of the top OB-GYNs in Miami. However, I'd known that when I booked the appointment. I wasn't letting just anyone take care of her while she carried my kid.

"We won't be needing the Medicaid. I'm handling the bills," I told her.

"But this could get expensive. I mean, it will get expensive."

I glanced at her. "I've already gotten you on the insurance I have for my employees," I told her. "You don't need the Medicaid. Once the baby is born, I will have him or her put on my insurance. You can choose to use the Medicaid for yourself then if you want to."

She nodded and turned to look back out the window.

"It would probably be smart to have regular checkups after the baby is born. I've never had that before, but I am in my thirties now."

And there was the reminder of how irresponsible she was. As the mother of my kid, she needed to take better care of her health. I hoped like fuck they didn't find something wrong health-wise with her today that could affect the baby's health.

"You didn't see a doctor before this? So, you weren't on birth control?" I asked, feeling my annoyance creep back in.

"I went to the free clinic. They checked me and gave me birth control. But when I left Wallace, I didn't go get them refilled. I didn't think I'd need them …" She trailed off.

Well, maybe she hadn't been spreading her legs for random men. Just me. I still couldn't figure that one out. I was sixteen years older than her. She was a head turner. Men had to hit on her all the time. Why had she invited me into that motel room?

"I just assumed that a regular doctor that is getting paid does more of a checkup than the free clinic," she said. "I can't remember the last time I went to a regular doctor, so I don't know what they do at those."

I started to snap off at her and point out that if she'd let her mother help her, she'd have had all those things, just like Selena. I didn't though. There was no need for us to get into that. Her past was not my business. Getting along with her was my goal here.

Twenty-One
LIBERTY

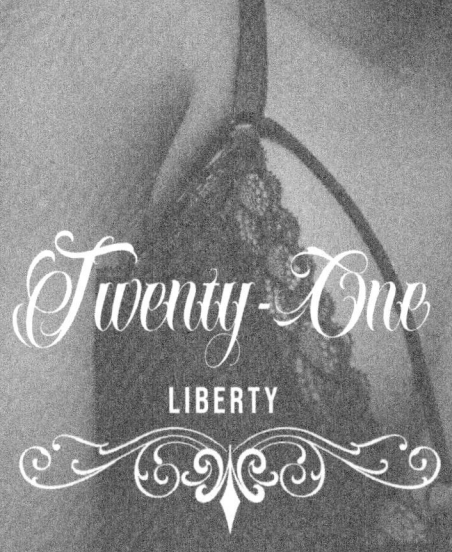

The doctor's office was nothing like what I was used to at the free clinic. The waiting room alone was fancy. Big, comfy leather sofas and chairs, elegant lamps, and side tables full of all kinds of magazines about pregnancy, babies, and parenting. There was even a little play area for toddlers.

Watching the other couples was a bit difficult. The dad would put his hand on the mom's stomach, and they'd whisper and laugh with each other. Excitement clear on their expressions.

Another mom who was very pregnant sat over near the toddler area while she watched her twin daughters play. They couldn't be more than two. I wondered how difficult that must be.

Liam said nothing as he sat down in one of the chairs across from the sofa I was on. We had walked in together, but our distance made a loud statement to anyone in the room that we weren't a couple.

"Liberty," a voice called out, and I looked over to see a nurse with a clipboard at the open door.

I stood up, and Liam did the same. He waited for me to go before he followed behind me.

"Liberty?" she asked.

"Yes," I replied.

"Right this way," she said, waving a hand for me to come through. "And you're the father?"

Liam gave her a small grin and nodded. The nurse blushed, and she fluttered her lashes as she gave him a flirty smile. Great. He was going to flirt with the nurses. I did my best to ignore it. He was a sexy man. Women were gonna look, and he sure wasn't mine, so I had no claim to him. It still stung to watch him respond to some stranger better than he did me.

"We will get your weight and check your vitals. However, you have to hold your bladder for now," she said. "If your husband would like, he can go wait in the room. It's that one right over there."

"He's not my husband," I blurted. I wanted that clear.

"Oh," she said, looking embarrassed, and then she flickered her gaze over to him with more interest. "I'm sorry. I shouldn't have assumed."

"It's fine," he told her. "And I'll go wait in the room. Thank you."

She watched him as he started down the hallway, and I cleared my throat to get her attention. The nurse's head snapped back to me, and she gave me an apologetic smile.

"Sorry, yes, let's see what your weight is."

Yes, let's. I rolled my eyes.

Once I was weighed and my heart rate and blood pressure were recorded, I was led to the examination room that Liam was already in. He was sitting in a chair with his right ankle propped on his left knee and a magazine open in his lap. He glanced up at me.

"It's the size of an apricot," he said.

The nurse giggled behind me. "Don't you love how they use food to give you the approximate size of the fetus?"

Liam smirked and closed the magazine, then placed it on the table beside him.

"You can go ahead and get on the table, and Dr. Savoy will be in here with you shortly," she said, then glanced over at Liam one more time before stepping out of the room.

Glad she was gone, I walked over and used the step stool to get onto the table.

"That magazine said you're not supposed to eat certain things. There was a list of them," he informed me.

I nodded. "Yep. I have a screenshot of that list on my phone. I read that a couple of weeks ago and saved it. Can't say I eat those things much anyway."

He studied me for a moment, then pulled his phone out of his pocket and turned his attention to sending a text.

"Seems like you've got Country aiming to please you," he said without looking up.

I didn't much care for his tone. Country had been so much help, and I'd never asked him for any of it.

"He offered to help. I didn't ask him."

Liam glanced up at me. "I'm sure he did." He dropped his gaze to my sundress, then went back to looking at his phone.

"What is that supposed to mean?" I asked him, feeling as if he'd accused me of something without using words.

"Nothing, Liberty. But some men are weak when it comes to a face like yours. Don't do anything that he will regret."

I stiffened. "What exactly are you insinuating, Liam?" I asked as my nails bit into my palms.

He ran a hand over his short beard. "Don't spread your legs for him. Not while you're carrying my kid."

My mouth dropped open. Had he really just said that? Did he think I was going to sleep around while I was pregnant? I started to say something when the door opened, and a petite older woman entered the room. She wore a pair of round glasses and had a businesslike smile on her face. She gave Liam a nod, but there was no flirty eyelash batting, and I decided I liked her already.

Her attention was fully on me. "I'm Dr. Savoy. It's a pleasure to meet you, Liberty. Your blood pressure and weight are both excellent. Nothing to be concerned about. Now, it says here that judging by your last period, you should be nine weeks and six days."

I nodded. "Yes."

"You are almost at the ten-week mark, and typically, I see a mother before then. I have the ultrasound room set up, and I'm going to personally take you in there. I would like to check things out myself, and seeing as"—she glanced at Liam—"you are my patient due to your family connections, you will remain a priority."

I looked at Liam, then back at the doctor. What did she mean, family connections? Was this someone he was related to, or was she referring to the family, as in the Mafia? I wasn't going to ask—at least not here.

"You can change into the hospital gown in the room. I have one waiting on you. Mr. Walsh is welcome to join you, or he can wait here while you change."

Liam was waiting on me to answer. Sure, he'd seen me naked, and his mouth had been on almost every part of my body, but things were different now. "I'd prefer to undress alone."

Dr. Savoy nodded and stepped back to wave a hand toward the door. "I'll take you to the ultrasound room, and then I'll come back and get Mr. Walsh when it is time."

I headed out the door without looking at him again.

Once I was undressed and in my open-back gown, I sat down on the table and waited. It was colder in here, and I had chill bumps break out on my arms and legs. Add that to the fact that I really needed to pee, and it was getting uncomfortable. There was a knock on the door, and then a moment later, Dr. Savoy stuck her head in.

"Ready?" she asked.

I nodded.

"I'll go get Mr. Walsh," she replied.

My nerves were building as I stared at the blank screen, where I assumed the ultrasound would be projected. What if something was wrong? What if there was no heartbeat? I hadn't thought much about these things before now, but the longer I sat here, the more worked up over it I seemed to get. I hadn't exactly wanted to get pregnant, but now that I was and I'd had time to grow attached to the idea of this baby, I wanted it.

The door opened, and in walked Dr. Savoy, followed by Liam.

I fisted my hands tightly in my lap. This was it. I'd know soon if everything was okay. She'd said I should have seen a doctor by now. What if my not coming in sooner harmed it in some way?

Closing my eyes, I took a deep breath.

"Everything's fine, Liberty," Dr. Savoy said, sensing my nerves. She patted my shoulder. "Lie back, and let's get this started before you get any more worked up. Try and relax." Her tone was gentle, and I focused on that, ignoring Liam's presence in the room.

"It is very normal to be nervous. Even a seasoned mom of three comes in here with a mix of excitement and anxiety," she assured me.

I nodded, lying back on the table.

The screen lit up, and she typed something in, then took a blanket and handed it to me. "Go ahead and cover yourself up. This is an internal probe since you are under twelve weeks pregnant. It gives us a better image. Your bladder should be full, and it isn't that comfortable, but bear with me. It won't be that long. Bend you knees and scoot toward me some."

"Okay," I replied, covering myself with the blanket, then bending my knees up like she'd instructed.

I watched the screen and tried to understand what I was seeing as the thing in her hand was inserted into me. She was right; it didn't feel great, but it wasn't painful. I had no idea what the picture was on the screen or how to tell what was the baby. I didn't much care for them calling it a fetus.

A sound came from the screen, and I stilled, glancing from the doctor back to the screen. It was a fast thumping sound.

Dr. Savoy smiled. "That's the heartbeat," she said.

I hadn't been prepared for the emotion that rushed into my chest as I sucked in a sob. Tears filled my eyes, making the screen blurry. The relief that came with that sound was overwhelming.

Dr. Savoy held out a tissue to me. I laughed and sniffled as I took it, then wiped at my face.

"Sorry," I said, then laughed again.

"Don't apologize. That is also a very normal reaction. It's a relief the first time you hear it. And your little one has a strong one. One hundred fifty beats per minute, to be exact."

Another small sob escaped me, followed by a laugh. A large warm hand slid over mine, and I stiffened, startled by the contact. I turned to look up at Liam as he stood beside me. His hand holding mine and his eyes fixed on the screen. I blinked and studied him. It was dark in here, but the light from the screen made his eyes appear glassy. The thought that he had gotten emotional only caused mine to fill with tears again as I turned to look back at the screen.

"Everything measures perfectly," Dr. Savoy told us. She used an arrow across the screen. "That right there is your baby."

I stared at it, trying to make it out but it was hard. The head I could see.

"This is the top of its head," she said, "and these are its legs. It's kicking away. Very active."

I watched in fascination as the little things I could now see were legs moved back and forth.

Liam's hand tightened on mine, and I pressed my lips together to keep from letting out another sob. I had been more hormonal lately. I'd cried over a picture of a mother holding her baby after birth that I'd seen while searching the pregnancy websites. But this was by far the most emotional I had been.

"Oh, and now, that is its arm. Looks like it's waving," she said, smiling at the screen and making notes as she clicked on certain things.

When the probe eased out of me, I wanted to beg her not to stop yet. I wasn't done looking at it. She handed me several photos, and I took them to see she had captured pictures of the head, legs, and arms.

"You and the baby are in excellent condition. I know you're ready to use the bathroom. Be sure to leave a urine sample. You can go in that room right there and do it. Once you're done, get dressed and meet me back in the examination room. I have some things to go over with you, and I'm going to give you a book that I like all my prenatal patients to read and keep for reference."

Liam had let go of my hand once the screen went off. I sat up and then handed him the photos to look at before hurrying to the bathroom. Getting a moment to myself, along with relieving my bladder, was needed.

I opened the bathroom door, then glanced back to see Liam looking at the photos in his hand with such intensity that my stupid eyes started stinging again.

Twenty-Two
LIAM

Sitting in the booth with a glass of whiskey in front of me, I wished like hell I had a cigarette. The shit with Diamond's death had been heavy. Blaise had just left with Huck and Gage. They'd traced it back to the Vipers and identified the man who had been here with her that night. The detectives assigned to the case were turning a blind eye to the family's interference. But they always did.

Tex walked up and sat down across from me. He'd been in Miami the past four days. I hadn't expected him to return until tomorrow.

I took a drink.

"You're back early," I said, setting the glass back on the table.

He sighed and leaned back. "Yeah, thought you might need me here. With the Viper shit. Saw Blaise and his men leaving."

I nodded. "Yeah. Per usual, my son-in-law found them before the cops."

Tex chuckled. "There is a reason why the Mafia is powerful."

I still hadn't spoken to Madeline about Liberty. Blaise had brought that up, too, and given me a deadline. I wanted to tell him to stay the fuck out of it, but I also respected that he didn't like keeping shit from my daughter.

"He demanded that I tell Madeline before Saturday, or he's doing it."

Tex raised an eyebrow. "About the baby?"

I nodded.

Tex smirked. "I wouldn't worry about it. From what I've witnessed this week, you let Madeline spend a little time with Liberty, and she'll be fucking tickled pink."

"What the fuck is that supposed to mean?"

He ran his thumb over his bottom lip as his expression bordered on amused. "You might not like your baby momma, but the club, she's got them all wrapped around her pretty little finger. Eating out of her hands. There might be a riot when the baby comes and you move her out of there."

I straightened in the booth and narrowed my eyes as I watched him fight back a smile. "You telling me she's flirting with my men down there and they are letting her?"

Tex shook his head. "Fuck no. The guys know better. Well, all but one," he said, then winced as if he'd not said it.

Her appointment had been a week ago, and it had taken me days after getting back here to get over the shit it had stirred in me. I hadn't wanted to leave. Seeing her getting all fucking emotional when the baby came up on that screen had mirrored my own unexpected response. For that moment when we were in there, watching our unborn child, I had felt connected to her in a way I'd never experienced with a soul in my life.

She had given me one of the ultrasound photos to keep and then thanked me for going with her and paying for it. I was so damn confused with how I felt that I didn't say much on the way back to the clubhouse. She went to show Nina and Goldie the pictures out at the pool, and I went to church. After that, most of us headed to Pepper's bar for some drinks.

Then, I had left and driven back here.

But every time I looked at that ultrasound picture, I remembered how seeing the baby and hearing its heartbeat had felt. With her hand in mine and the way she'd sobbed and laughed at the same time, looking at the screen. It was hard to see that woman as the one Selena seemed to know.

"Who's she flirting with?" I asked, feeling rage spark deep in my chest.

He shook his head. "She isn't flirting. I didn't say it was her. And he isn't either. Not really. But the boy is sunk. He can't take his eyes off her. From what I can see, she has no fucking clue."

My jaw was clenched so tightly that my molars ached. "Who?" I demanded.

Tex held up his hands. "Easy, Prez. I didn't come in here, meaning to stir up shit. No one has done a damn thing wrong. Liberty helps cook; she's making these fried pies and some chocolate pie that has fucking caramel in it regularly. She's got the back of the place looking like the damn botanical gardens, and everyone loves her."

"WHO?" I shouted, hating every word that was coming out of his mouth.

He took in a deep breath and muttered a curse. "If you care this much, why did you drop her off at the club?"

So I wouldn't fuck her every chance I got.

"Who?" I repeated.

He looked like he'd rather go eat a bucket of nails. "Country," he muttered. "But he's young. She's gorgeous and about his age. He knows she is carrying your baby, but you don't seem to give a shit about her. The guys talk about it. They can't understand why you'd drop her off like that."

I'd known that was who he was going to say. I stood up, taking my glass and drinking down the rest of it, then slammed it on the table.

"Come on, Prez. He's not done shit," Tex said. "And unless you gave your blessing, he won't."

I wasn't giving my fucking blessing. I couldn't even leave her at the goddamn Sanctuary with my people and know she was safe. My own men were lusting over her. Fuck!

"Where are you going?" Tex called out as I stalked toward the back door. "Don't kill him for doing nothing!"

I wasn't killing anyone. I was going to get what belonged to me. Guessed the only place I could be sure she was safe was my house. The idea of her being there didn't seem to bother me so much anymore. She wouldn't be around horny men. I'd stay here at the club. No temptation. We'd be fine.

Drifter was coming inside as I reached the door.

"Whoa," he said, stepping out of my way. "Who pissed you off?"

That was a list I didn't have time to give him.

I shook my head and stormed out the door. "I'll be back tonight late."

"All right," he drawled.

Unlocking my car, I climbed inside. I was doing this to save Country's ass. She'd only been there two weeks, and if he was this far gone already, then he'd do something stupid within a month. I knew her appeal. I just hadn't realized she'd still have that pull on a man once she was pregnant. I'd underestimated her.

"Hearts live by being wounded."
—Oscar Wilde

Twenty-Three

LIBERTY

Nina, Goldie, and Dolly had insisted that I join them at the pool today. They had explained that when Dolly was here during the summer, they liked to fit in at least one margarita day.

I was glad I'd decided to do this with them. The cool water felt amazing in this summer heat.

The only bathing suit I owned was a bright blue bikini that no longer held my boobs. Nina had given me one of hers, and although it might as well be a thong, it did cover my boobs better. Goldie had made the point that these men saw strippers and owned a porn production company. The bikini I had on was way more fabric than they were used to.

The small bump now showing up on my stomach excited me, and I doubted any of the men wanted to look at a pregnant woman in a bikini. Not when Dolly was lying out, looking all curvy and gorgeous. Although, after watching Micah with her, I doubted anyone was brave enough to look her way. He had already come out here twice to reapply sunblock on her and whisper things in her ear that made her blush. I was sure it was my crazy hormones, but I'd never been so envious in my life.

I hadn't heard a peep from Liam since he'd dropped me off after the doctor's appointment a week ago. Not that I was surprised, but I'd thought that maybe something might have changed when he held my hand. Nothing, in fact, had changed at all. Getting my hopes up for anything with that man was just gonna lead to heartbreak.

When he had left me here, I'd never felt so unwanted and alone. But that wasn't the case anymore. It was like a big family here. Granted, it was an odd one, where it was possible you might walk into the main den and catch a naked woman bouncing on a man's lap while another guy stood, watching and getting himself off. Yep, I had actually seen that happen.

Lying back on the lounge chair, I soaked in the warmth as my body dried from my latest dip to cool off.

"I'm going in to make more margaritas," Goldie said. "Do you want me to make you another virgin, Liberty?" she asked.

I shook my head. "I'm good with my water, but thank you," I said, shading my eyes to look at her.

She grabbed the empty pitcher to go inside when I noticed Micah and Country walking in this direction. Micah was probably coming to coat Dolly up again. The girl was not going to get anywhere close to burned.

"Micah," Dolly said, seeing him. "You were just here less than an hour ago. I do not need more sunblock."

Micah stopped beside her and leaned down to touch her lips reverently. "I miss you inside, Tink. The bedroom is real lonely," he told her in a husky voice.

She sat up and swung her bare feet over the side to slip on her flip-flops. Micah Abe was gorgeous. I couldn't say I blamed her. I'd be jumping up and going with him too.

Nina was reading a book in the shade, so I closed my eyes again. I might even doze off. I never burned, so the fact that I didn't have my own sunblock applier to check on me was not an issue.

A splash of cold water ended my thoughts of slumber with a start. It wasn't a lot, but it was shocking with my skin warming up like it was. I squealed as my eyes flew open to see Country standing over me, grinning.

"You looked like you needed cooling down," he said.

I laughed at the water droplets now coating me.

"Figured you weren't in danger of getting a sunburn, but you might be overheated," he teased.

"Yes, well, perhaps you should prepare me before you cool me off," I replied.

He reached over and picked up my water bottle. "Probably need to hydrate," he said. "Need me to get you some more ice?"

I sat up and took the bottle. He was right. If I was going to stay out in this heat, I should drink more.

I shook my head. "This is fine."

"Country!" a familiar deep voice barked, causing me to stiffen in recognition.

Country's eyes widened, and his tanned face paled before he turned around. "Prez," he replied.

I glanced at Nina, who was no longer reading, but shifting her gaze from Liam to Country with concern etched in her brow. Something was wrong. I stood up beside him, and Country immediately began walking toward Liam.

Liam's glare went from Country to me, and even from a distance, I could see the way his jaw clenched as his eyes narrowed. He was pissed. What was wrong?

He said something to Country, who nodded his head and went toward the building, but Liam began stalking in my direction. I stood there, unsure of what was about to happen and why he was here. I didn't have another doctor's appointment for three more weeks. I hadn't expected to see him until then.

His gaze traveled down my body and stopped at my stomach briefly before snapping back up to my face.

"You not got something more than that to wear out here?" he bit out.

I glanced over at Nina, who looked more put out than worried. Her eyes met mine, and she stood up. Was she going to leave me out here with him?

"I, uh, well, no," I stammered. Hearing my voice sound so weak and timid made me feel pathetic. Why did I let him do this to me?

I straightened my shoulders. He wasn't going to make me cower.

His eyes dropped back down to my stomach. It wasn't big, but there was a definite bump compared to how it had been before. His nostrils flared, and I felt a small shiver as he kept looking at it.

"I don't like you displaying yourself," he said through clenched teeth, finally tearing his eyes off my bump and looking at me.

"It's more than the strippers wear at your clubs," I said, using Nina's words, lifting my chin defiantly.

He leaned closer to me. "You're not one of my goddamn strippers. You're the mother of my child, and I don't want your body on fucking display!" he ground out.

"I gave her that bikini, Prez. She wouldn't come out here because her boobs were too big for the one she owned," Nina said, coming up beside us.

Liam cut his eyes at her for a moment, and then they were right back on me. "Go pack your things," he ordered.

"What?" I asked, panicked.

I had just taken up for myself. He couldn't make me leave for that. I didn't want to be stuck back at the bedroom at the club. I liked it here. I wasn't alone here.

"You heard me, Liberty."

"Prez, it was just a swim. No one has even seen her but us," Nina said in a pleading tone.

"Country saw her," he bit out.

"But, Prez, she—" Nina started but was cut off.

"This is not up for fucking debate!"

Her eyes flared brightly, and she glared at him. "If you hadn't left her here, then no one would have had a chance to go sniffin'. Remember that!" she shot back at him, then turned and headed for the clubhouse.

Liam's attention was fully on me. "Sniffin'? How much sniffin' has he done, Liberty?"

I shook my head, worried about Country. "Nothing. None. He's my friend!"

Liam smirked, but he looked cold and deadly. "No, Liberty, he isn't. He's a man. You're a hot piece of ass. He's not your goddamn friend. You aren't that naive."

I crossed my arms over my chest defensively. "I've made friends here. I'm not causing problems. I don't want to go back to your strip-club bedroom. It's loud there."

He cracked his jaw, and his eyes were back on my stomach again. "You're not going to the club. You're going to my house."

His house. I blinked, not sure I'd heard him correctly. He was taking me to his house.

"In Ocala?" I asked, suddenly worried he had one here in Miami and he was gonna dump me there and leave me alone.

He nodded.

"Oh," I replied.

Did I want that? To live in his house with him? I felt the tingle between my legs. I knew my body wanted that. Lately, I'd found myself getting easily turned on. I pleasured myself in bed every night, remembering the day in his office before he turned cold and brought me here.

"Go pack your shit," he said again. "I'll be up to get it soon. And get some goddamn clothes on." His gaze snapped back up to my face.

"Okay," I whispered.

I shouldn't let him talk to me like this. I didn't deserve it. I had done all I could to be helpful while I was here. But he was taking me to his house, and I wanted to go. That man who had held my hand in the ultrasound room—I liked him. A lot. A large portion of me clung to that glimpse of him and ached for it. Even knowing it was stupid to do it.

He stepped back, and I started to walk off.

"Wait," he said, stopping me.

I turned back around to see him taking off his vest. I stood there as he held it out to me.

"Put this on. Don't parade around in front of anyone like that. Cover up."

I reached out and took the vest, glancing at it, then back at him. "I'm still a little damp."

He scowled. "I don't give a fuck. Put it on."

I slid an arm in one large hole, then the other. It swallowed me. Taking the sides, I held them together so that my body was no longer visible.

He nodded his head once, but said nothing. His gaze was locked on his vest as the veins in his neck stood out as he flexed. The tension was coming off him in waves, making me feel jittery. I turned and hurried for the door, needing to get away from him.

When I reached the door, I didn't look back to see if he was following me, but went in and started for the stairs.

Jars, Nina's husband, came stalking out of the kitchen when his eyes met mine. He stilled, taking in the vest, and the grim look on his face faded. I gave him a small wave and kept going. I couldn't get to the room and out of this bikini fast enough. However, the smell of leather, cigarettes, and Liam wrapped around me was addictive. I wished I didn't have to take the vest off.

Twenty-Four

LIAM

She hadn't made it to the door before I was headed after her. Seeing her walk away, wrapped in my cut, and thinking about what was underneath made me snap. She had a small bump on her once-flat stomach. I hadn't expected that, but I hadn't seen her naked in over two weeks. Seemed her body was changing in more ways than her growing bigger tits. The sight of her stomach had unleashed some territorial monster inside me. I'd never felt it before, but I knew no one was safe as long as she was in that fucking bikini.

When I jerked open the door, my eyes locked on Jars. His gaze narrowed when he saw me. Nina must have told him about how I'd spoken to her. She should have stayed out of my shit.

"She's wearing your cut," he said.

I nodded. She was. Just like the back of my bike. She was the only female to ride there and now the only one to have my cut on her body. I knew she had no fucking clue the claim that came with that, but I didn't think it was wise for her to. Just because I wasn't going to be able to keep my hands off her and my cock out of her cunt didn't mean we were going to be what that cut signified.

I stalked past Jars and took the stairs two at a time. I turned the knob to find it locked. Not wanting to wait on her to answer, I went into the library next door and took my extra key from my office desk.

Sticking it into the door, I turned and swung it open.

Liberty gasped, and her arms went to her bare breasts, but her stomach and pussy remained uncovered. Slamming the door behind me, I took in the sight of her. She was breathing hard as she watched me. Her eyes were wide, but there was no fear in her honey-brown depths. What I did see only made my cock twitch. She wanted me.

Her arms fell to her sides as I closed the distance between us, and she stood there, waiting. Reaching out, I fondled her tits that just seemed to keep growing, then moved one palm down to her small, rounded belly. She sucked in a breath as I felt the hard bump, covered by her silky-smooth, sun-kissed skin. That was mine inside there. The doctor had said it was perfect. Healthy. I felt a tug in my chest, and I lifted my eyes to see her watching me with her bottom lip clasped firmly between her teeth.

She was so fucking gorgeous; it was painful. Young, beautiful, and a complete disaster. We weren't a fit. I was too old for a relationship with someone her age. I didn't know if she'd be a good mother or not. She'd cried in the ultrasound room, but then that could have just been hormones. Those got fucked up when a woman was pregnant.

Her body trembled, and my hand started moving down as if it had a mind of its own. Seemed it and my cock were in one accord. She opened her legs wider just as my hand slid over her slick mound. When my fingers met the saturated lips of her pussy, I wanted to growl like a damn animal. Damn, she was soaking wet. Almost dripping.

"You always this fucking wet?" I asked her. "Or is it just for me?"

She let out an uneven breath. "Lately"—she gasped as I pressed a finger into her—"I seem to be aroused easily, but, no, when I pleasure myself at night, I'm never this wet. I think"—she let out a small cry when two fingers sank deep into her and grabbed on to my arm for balance—"this is just for you."

I could feel my pulse in my damn dick. I wrapped my other arm around her and began to do with my fingers what I was going to do to her with my dick. "You telling me you're horny and finger-fucking yourself?"

She nodded, her eyes hooded as her head fell back, causing the long locks to cascade behind her.

"You sure it's not some other man getting you worked up?" I asked, knowing I'd kill Country if it was. No one in this club could protect him.

She shook her head. "No, I read about it. It's the pregnancy. It can do this."

Jesus Christ. Being pregnant made her horny, and I was taking her to my house. Was there a limit to how much she could be fucked? Because I wasn't sure I could control myself if she was walking around like this all the time.

"When you stick those pretty fingers inside this wet cunt, what are you thinking about?" I asked her, rubbing her clit with my thumb, and a gush of her wetness soaked my hand. God, when she did those little squirts, it made me insane.

"Your office," she panted, lifting her hips to get more of my fingers.

Fuck.

"Get on the bed on all fours. I've missed that ass," I ordered, taking my fingers from her and pulling off my shirt.

She hurried to the bed and crawled up onto it. I inhaled and realized the entire room smelled like her. Would my house be like this too? Was I going to have her scent all over it?

Her ass was in my direct view as I unfastened my jeans. I decided I didn't give a fuck. The house might smell like her fucking pussy if she was gonna be like this. Needy and compliant. I hurried to strip the rest of my things off and watched as she wiggled that plump ass in the air for me.

Climbing on behind her, I covered both her cheeks with my hands and spread them open to bury my face in between and lick. Her moans went straight to my rigid dick, and it jerked at the sound of it. There would be time for this later. I gave the area between her legs one last long lick, then went up on my knees behind her and slid inside, the heavenly slick walls squeezing my cock.

"AH! GOD! YES!" she cried out, throwing her head back.

I grabbed her hair in my hand and held it at that angle. "This what you needed?" My balls were already tingling. What the hell was she doing to me?

"Yes! Please! Oh, yes! Please, Liam, fuck me deep!" she begged.

As I kept my hold on her hair, my other hand gripped one side of her ass, and I slammed into her hard several times while she screamed out my name. The first hot squirt on my cock dripped down my balls. She'd done that in the motel that first time. I had almost shot my load right then. She hadn't done it over and over, like she was doing now. If this was a side effect of pregnancy, then I might need to be locked up to be kept away from knocking her up a second time.

I let go of her hair to grab on to her hips and pound her cunt.

"Oh! YES! Liam! I love how you stretch me," she moaned.

"You keep talking with that dirty mouth, and this is gonna be over sooner than either of us wants," I warned her, then landed a loud smack on her jiggling ass.

Her body bowed and jerked as she unleashed the hardest ejaculation yet. Fucking hell. My name tore from her lips just as I began to shoot my thick load into her. I trembled as it kept going much longer than it normally did.

When I stilled, her arms gave out, and she laid her head on the mattress with her bottom still up in the air and me buried inside her. I panted as I stared down at her. That was by far the most phenomenal fuck of my life, and I'd had sex with pros who did it on camera for a living.

Nothing came close to comparing to this.

I slid out of her, and she sank onto the bed and rolled over to her side with a deep, sated sigh. My eyes immediately went to the bump. Just looking at it and knowing I'd put that there, that it was mine, made me want to beat on my chest like a caveman. I didn't want to claim this woman. But right now, while she carried my child, I was gonna enjoy every inch of this body.

She turned her head and looked up at me. "You have no idea how much I needed that."

A smirk touched my lips. The satisfied look on her face as she smiled up at me had me wanting to grab my cut and wrap it around her while she was like this. Naked, filled with my cum, and on my bed.

That was a fantasy that was too dangerous to dwell on though. I'd have to control it. Remember what I knew about her, and that with our age difference, there would never be a future for us.

I moved off the bed and grabbed my jeans. "Get dressed," I told her, knowing if we stayed like this much longer, there would be a round two.

We'd been loud. I knew she wasn't aware that her screams had been heard by others. I'd allowed it because they all needed to know whose cunt this was.

She started to get up, and my gaze went to her pussy.

"Don't clean it up. Put your panties on like that. I want my cum leaking out of you the entire ride there."

Heat flared in her eyes as her face flushed, and then she shivered.

Yeah, if this was how she was going to react, then I might fuck her to death. I hoped to God I was able to set boundaries. If she had any idea how little control I had over myself when it came to wanting her, she could use it on me whenever she wanted. I'd have her bent over the first available object with my head between her legs.

"Between me and you, I'm pretty messy," she said, licking her bottom lip.

My eyes zeroed in on those lips, and I wondered how good that mouth was at taking a cock. Having mine buried in it while she looked up at me with those eyes was suddenly all I could think about.

She lowered her hand, and I tore my eyes off her lips to see her slip it between her legs. My mouth fell slightly open as she then lifted it for me to see the mix of our release coating them.

"See? This is gonna make a wet spot on my shorts."

I swallowed hard as my dick began to come back to life. "Wear a sundress then," I told her. "That way, you can open your legs and let me play on the drive home."

She sucked in a breath, causing her boobs to bounce, then took those coated fingers and slipped them between her lips.

Mother of God.

Twenty-Five

LIBERTY

Slowly opening my eyes, I was disoriented for a moment, then remembered I was in Liam's car. It was dark out, and we were stopped.

Liam turned off the ignition. "We're here," he said, his voice slightly husky.

I'd slept the entire ride? I hadn't meant to go to sleep, but when I had sat down, I couldn't hold my eyes open.

"Wait there," he told me. "I need to go turn on the lights."

I nodded, trying to make out the house in front of us. There was a porch. It looked almost like it might wrap around. A large oak tree was to the far right, and I could tell there was a second story.

The exterior lights came on, and I sucked in a breath. Liam had a farmhouse, complete with a porch swing. I hadn't expected this. It was a cream color with white trim. The front door opened, and a Great Dane, who I knew must be Ozzy, came barreling down the stairs. I opened my door just as he went to the tree to relieve himself.

"I believe I told you about him," Liam said, walking toward me.

"He's gorgeous," I replied as Ozzy finished and started toward me, his eyes on me.

I didn't need to bend down to greet him. He was almost at my waist.

"Hello, Ozzy," I said as he sniffed between my legs.

My eyes shot up to Liam, who was smirking. Ozzy stilled, and he rubbed his nose against my stomach. Could he tell I was pregnant?

"Ozzy, this is Liberty. She's going to be a guest for a while," Liam told him, then walked over to the trunk to get my things.

The dog studied me, and then his nose went back to my crotch.

I laughed, backing up. "Let's not do that," I told him.

"Yes, Oz. I fucked her. You got a sniff. Now, stop," he said as he pulled out a suitcase.

My panties felt more sticky than anything now. I felt my body flush, however, hearing Liam talk about what we'd done. I wished I hadn't gone to sleep. The thought of him touching me on the drive here had been exciting. Leave it to my pregnant body to decide I needed rest.

"You slept through the security gate, but the house has an electric gate around the property, and it requires a password to get in. The password changes every week. When you are inside here, you're safe. Plus, Ozzy hears everything. Come on," Liam said as he carried my suitcases toward the house.

I followed behind him, and Ozzy stayed at my side.

There was a large dog bed on the front porch, and a swing sat to the right. From here, I was pretty sure the porch wrapped around the house. Liam walked inside and flipped on the interior light. The entryway had a hardwood floor and exposed wooden beams on the ceiling, and the walls were a warm blue. Ozzy's paws clicked on the wooden floor as he came inside and moved to my side again. I ran my hand over his head.

"Stairs are this way. Only bedroom on this floor is mine. The others are upstairs," he told me as he went toward the stairs.

We wouldn't be sleeping in the same bed, it seemed. I tried not to feel disappointment. Not once had he acted as if that was what he wanted to do. I'd kind of assumed he wouldn't put me in his room, but I'd enjoyed being surrounded by his things at the clubhouse.

He turned left when we reached the top of the stairs and then made another left turn into a bedroom. It was big with a queen-size bed, dresser, chair and ottoman in the corner, and a floor lamp beside it. The door to the left was open, and I could see a bathroom through there.

"This is the guest room. There are three other rooms. One belongs to my grandsons, one is a home office, and the other simply has a bed. I just keep the door shut," he said, setting my suitcases down. "That door is the closet. There should be plenty of hangers for your things. If not, let me know. I have more. The bathroom is there, and it's stocked with whatever you need."

I scanned the room, then turned back to him. "This is nice. I didn't expect your house to look like this," I admitted.

He cocked an eyebrow. "What did you expect? Stripper poles and concrete floors?"

I shrugged, pursing my lips to keep from laughing.

He smirked. "This is where my grandkids come to visit. It's my peace away from all the other crazy in my life."

That made sense. I guessed I just hadn't seen him that way or realized there was this side to him that existed.

"I'll order us something to eat. Get cleaned up if you'd like. Ozzy might stop trying to get his face in your crotch if you do," he said with a curl to his lips.

"Okay," I replied.

"Pizza good with you?" he asked as he turned and headed for the door.

"Yeah," I replied.

"Anything you don't like on it?"

I shrugged. "Lately, I've had a thing for cheese. Lots of it."

"Extra-cheese pizza. Got it," he said with a nod. "Ozzy," he called.

The dog looked at me as if he didn't want to go, but turned and followed Liam out of the room.

Once the door closed, I stood there, staring at it. I was in Liam's house. We'd had incredible sex. He hadn't left me hours away from him. These were all good signs. Maybe he'd gotten jealous of Country. That was a positive. If he felt jealousy, then he could feel more. This was my chance to win him over. But that would mean opening myself up to future pain. What if I let this thing I felt for him grow and he never felt anything?

Placing a hand on my stomach, I knew this was a chance I owed our baby. It wasn't just about me. Not everyone fell in love easy. If I had allowed myself to admit how I felt about him, how he made me feel, then I knew it would become more. Because the guy in the bar that night, the one who had taken me back to my motel room, and the man who had held my hand at the ultrasound—that man made me feel deeper than anyone ever had.

Ozzy greeted me the moment I hit the bottom step on the staircase.

Grinning, I gave his head a pat. "I don't know my way around. Want to lead me to Liam?"

I wasn't really surprised when he turned and started walking, then glanced back at me to make sure I was following. Of course Liam would have a smart dog. Ozzy led me across the foyer and then turned right down a short hallway before turning through an arched doorway. The large room held a massive fireplace at its center, a brown leather sectional, rustic-style coffee table and end tables, and a pool table. The flat screen TV hung on the far-right wall.

Liam was sitting on the sofa, and two boxes of pizza were on the large, sturdy wooden table in front of him. There was a bottle of water and a glass of what looked like whiskey on coasters on either side of the boxes.

The television was a sports channel, but they were talking about horse racing. I found that odd—at least for Liam. He didn't strike me as a gambling kinda man or one who was interested in horses. When his gaze swung over to meet mine, it drifted down my body. The pink polka-dot boxer shorts and tank top were my usual loungewear. He paused a moment at my feet, then motioned with his hand for me to come to the sofa.

"Come eat," he said simply.

Ozzy padded beside me, and when I sat down across from the pizzas, he made himself comfortable at my feet.

"Didn't know what you'd want to drink. I grabbed you a water because I honestly don't have much else but beer or whiskey. There was some orange juice, but the expiration date is questionable."

Smiling, I reached for the bottle of water. "This is perfect. Thank you."

He opened the boxes. The sight of the cheese pizza made my mouth water. Liam leaned forward and took a piece, then placed it on a paper plate and handed it to me before getting a slice from what looked like a meat lovers pizza.

Shifting my attention back to the television, I took a bite of the greasy cheesy goodness and sighed with pleasure. This was perfect.

"Best pizza in town," he said beside me.

I finished chewing, then glanced at him. "It's so good."

He smirked, then took a bite of his while watching the large screen.

We ate in silence for a few minutes. This was nice. It had been a while since I'd had a meal without a lot of people talking and almost-naked females walking around. I did miss my new friends, but being here with Liam was much better.

"I wouldn't have pegged you for a horse-racing guy," I said after I finished my slice.

"I'm not. I don't gamble, and I've never much cared about horses. But my daughter married into that world. I like to see how their horses are doing," he said.

I had lived here most of my life and I'd heard about Hughes Farm being the biggest racehorse stables in the southeast. Men had talked about betting on one of their horses at Abernathy's many times. The connection just hadn't clicked.

"They have horses in this one?"

"This is a recap. Races that were held today. They aren't major ones, but my grandson has his first horse in one of them. He came in second, and I was hoping they'd show him."

His grandson had a racehorse! I watched the screen as the announcers continued to talk and show clips from different races, finding myself fully invested.

"How old is your grandson?" I asked.

"Cree is five. Eli is ten months," he replied, not taking his eyes off the screen. "There, that one." There was a trace of pride in his voice. "Demigod."

The announcers began talking about Demigod and his owner being Garrett Hughes's grandson and Blaise Hughes's oldest son. They chuckled about having yet another Hughes take over the racing world and watching the first of many Cree Hughes's horses on the track.

I glanced over at Liam, who was smiling as he listened.

"Did he name the horse?" I asked.

Liam nodded. "Yeah. His mom has been reading him some kids book series about Greek gods and their kids or something like that. I don't know exactly. But he's very into it."

I set the empty plate down and curled my feet up under me as I leaned back on the soft leather.

Liam's eyes moved from the television to my legs before looking at me. "You're full?"

I nodded. "Yes, but I'm a fan of leftover pizza."

His eyes dropped back to my bare legs. "Are you cold? Need a blanket?"

I shook my head. "I'm fine. Thank you."

He seemed appeased, then took another slice from the meat lovers box. I scanned the room. There were very few personal things or decorations. There was a wall with several frames that hung in a fashion that I doubted Liam had done himself. Not that a man couldn't decorate, but this was Liam.

I studied the photographs, realizing most were of one little boy, who I assumed was Cree. There were two with the boy and a baby. My eyes stopped on one that was an older photo. Faded with time. Two teenage boys leaning against the front of Liam's car. One was grinning with a cigarette clenched between his teeth. Then, there was Liam. Even without the beard, I could tell it was him. His arms were crossed over his chest, but a beer bottle hung from one of his hands. They were both shirtless and wearing jeans. He was tattooed, even back then. Not as many as he had now, but they were there.

"How old were you in that photo?" I asked.

He turned to look in the direction I was studying. "Seventeen," he replied.

"Who is the other guy?" I asked, wondering if it was one of the men at the clubhouse I'd gotten to know.

"Tulsa. He was my best friend. We grew up together," he said, turning his attention back to the television. "You met his son, Micah."

I remembered Country telling me about Tulsa, but I didn't dare mention it. I also knew his best friend was dead.

"He was shot sixteen years ago next week," he added, his tone taking on a darker note. As if the thought of it still caused an ache. I knew it did. Although time had helped the pain of losing those I loved, it was never something that went away completely.

I slid my hand over and covered his. He tensed, and I almost drew my hand away, but he turned to look at me. It wasn't sadness that I saw. I shivered slightly as his gaze dropped to my mouth, then my breasts.

"You walk around here in tops like that and no bra, Liberty, you're gonna get fucked." There was a warning in his voice.

"I think I mentioned that lately, I want, uh, it, all the time," I replied, licking my lips.

He inhaled sharply through his nose, then turned his hand over, threading his fingers through mine before standing up and taking me with him. "Damn dog seems to be too interested in your scent. Gonna need to take this to the bedroom and shut him out," he said, pulling me to his body.

He let go of my hand and ran both of his over my stomach. "Fuck, I like that," he murmured. He gripped my waist and turned me around, facing away from him, then gently pushed me forward. "Right through there," he said, leading me to the door on the wall opposite the television.

"Stay," Liam told Ozzy firmly when he stood to walk beside me.

When I stopped at the closed door, he reached around me and opened it with one hand while gripping my hip with the other. Not letting go of me, he walked us inside, his body pressed against my back.

The scent hit me, reminding me of how his suite at the clubhouse had smelled. It was pure Liam. I inhaled as my eyes scanned the room, but my shirt was being pulled over my head before I saw more than the large wood-framed bed.

Liam palmed my breasts, and his hot breath against my neck caused me to shiver. He kissed and licked as he worked his way down to my shoulder, then back up to just below my ear. His hands fondled my boobs, rolling each nipple between his thumb and forefinger.

"You always smell so damn good," he murmured.

My head fell back against his chest, and I closed my eyes as pleasure pooled between my legs. He slid his hands down to my stomach and held it for a moment while he nibbled on my earlobe, then moved one hand under the front of my boxer shorts that no longer hung as loosely on my hips as they once had.

I sucked in a breath and opened my eyes to watch his tanned hand move under my panties before he eased a finger between my wet, swollen lips.

"Jesus, baby," his deep voice said, his mouth so close to my ear that I broke out in goose bumps. "Get these off," he growled, then stepped back, taking my boxers and panties down with one hard tug until they were at my ankles.

I stepped out of them and kicked them to the side.

His hands cupped my butt. "I want you on my face," he told me, then shoved me toward the bed.

I glanced back at him as he pulled his shirt off and tossed it aside, then began working on his jeans. The hunger in his gaze as he lifted his chin, nodding toward the bed, sent another wave of excitement through me.

"Climb on and let me watch your ass," he ordered. "Then, you're gonna ride my mouth."

I licked my bottom lip. "What?" My breathing quickened.

"You're gonna straddle my head and put that dripping wet pussy on my mouth and ride it."

I nodded, ready to do whatever he asked of me. However, when he stood there, completely naked, I was distracted by every defined muscle, the V beneath his abs, his tattoos, which only added to every impressive inch of him, and I wanted to run my hands over each ripple.

He moved toward me, and my eyes dropped to the long, thick erection, making my mouth water.

"Climb on the bed," he said, turning me around, then landing a slap onto my bottom. "I'll have my cock in your mouth soon enough, making you gag on it."

Okay. Wow. I'd never really wanted to give Wallace a blow job, but I wanted Liam's cock in my mouth.

Turning from him, I lifted a knee and crawled up onto the mattress, aware that he was watching me. A slight quiver between my legs caused me to pause, and I felt a dampness on my inner thighs. I heard him mutter a curse, and then the bed dipped as he moved onto it. I waited while he lay down on his back near the middle, then grabbed my thigh and pulled me to him.

"The next time that pussy comes, it's gonna be on my face."

Opening my thighs, I placed a knee on each side of his head, then stared down at him. He grabbed the top of my thighs and brought me down until his tongue was running along the sensitive folds.

Crying out, I grabbed the headboard to steady myself as he pressed me down further until his nose was bumping my clit. Rocking my hips, growing more desperate for him. His beard scratched my skin, and the thought of it getting wet from my arousal caused another gush to release from deep inside me.

"That feels so good," I moaned, throwing my head back and closing my eyes.

His deep growl of approval vibrated between my legs, sending tingles throughout my body. My grip tightened as I drew closer to the orgasm I so desperately craved. Liam flattened his tongue, and I pressed against it. That sent me falling over the edge.

"YES! Oh God! Liam!" I shouted as my body began to jerk.

His fingers dug into my thighs as he held me there and continued to use his tongue, lapping up my release. When I stopped moving, his hands slid up to my hips, and he pushed me off him and onto my back.

Grabbing my right leg, he draped it over his shoulder and plunged into me hard.

"FUCK!" he roared, clenching his teeth with his eyes closed.

I watched the veins in his neck stand out and his muscular shoulders and arms flex while he held still, his cock fully sheathed inside me.

Already needy for more, I lifted my hips, and his hazel eyes snapped open and locked on me.

"Don't do that," he warned. "I'm too close. This creaming pussy, clenching me so damn tight after you just rubbed it all over my face, has me ready to explode."

I wiggled my hips, and his eyes flared. Then, his hand gripped my neck. Gasping, I stared up at him as he squeezed it. Not so tight that I couldn't breathe, but it wasn't exactly gentle.

"Keep still, Liberty," he growled, his voice sounding more like an animal than a man.

A whimper broke free as trepidation and a carnal fervor began to spread through me, warring for which one was stronger even though both seemed to feed off the other.

"That's it." He released my neck and ran a finger down my cheek. "Good girl."

I tried to stay still as he continued tracing a path over my collarbone, my breast, circling my nipple, before stopping at my stomach.

"Shouldn't make me so damn crazed," he said, staring at my bump. "But I can't help it. Every time I think about my seed inside you, that your sexy little body is growing a part of me, I get territorial. I want to mark what's mine."

Another small sound escaped my lips. I was going to come without him even moving. Just from listening to the deep, husky sound of his voice as he stretched me.

His hand locked down on my throat again, and then he began to ease out slowly before thrusting back inside.

"Please, Liam, don't stop," I begged.

Letting go of my neck he ran his hand up the leg that he had over his shoulder, then moved it off, pressing my thighs open. He lifted his hips up, then slammed back down. I bucked off the mattress, feeling so close to that peak and aching for it.

"This horny pussy needs fucked hard," he said, and I nodded frantically.

I almost wept at the gleam in his eyes, thinking he was going to continue the torture of holding me right out on the edge. But a dark snarl tore from him, and he once again clamped down on my throat before giving me what I'd been desperate for.

With each slap of our bodies, I could hear the wetness I kept leaking.

"Goddamn, that's a greedy cunt," he said with a grunt.

"YES!" I said with a cry, grabbing handfuls of the cover beneath me as he pounded into me like a man possessed.

The headboard thumped loudly against the wall.

"Give it to me," he panted. "Let me feel it."

The frenzy flaring inside me surged as a spray of warmth released, and I clawed at Liam's arms, arching into him and shuddering.

"GAH! FUCK!" tore from deep in his chest as he pumped three times while spurts of heat filled me.

I was shaking as I fell back onto the mattress. It was hard to catch my breath, but I kept my eyes open and watched him. A tremor ran over him, and his gaze lingered on our connected bodies before moving up to meet mine.

We stayed there for a moment. Not moving.

Finally, he let out a long breath and slid out of me. "Stay here. I'll get something to clean you up," he said as he started to move.

Reaching out, I grabbed his arm to stop him. "No. Don't," I told him.

He shifted, then rolled over beside me, and I turned on my side, pressing my back against his chest. His arm came over me, and he laid his palm over my stomach.

"How's your throat?" he asked.

I smiled softly. "Fine."

"I didn't squeeze too hard?"

I shook my head. "No."

He ran his nose over the side of my head, nuzzling me. "It's your fault. You've got a dirty mouth."

I let out a laugh. "You're one to talk about dirty mouths."

He made a low humming sound. "Yeah, but when words like that come out of your pretty mouth, it seems to be a trigger for me. I can't fuck you hard enough."

I pressed closer against his chest, soaking in the warmth of his body. This was what I had been aching for. I'd wanted this connection with him. I wasn't an affectionate person—or at least that was a complaint Wallace had often had with me. I'd feared Abilene had managed to break me. Take away any sense of giving and accepting another's affection.

But I knew now that wasn't the case. Because there was nowhere I'd rather be than right here. Wrapped up in Liam's arms, safe in his bed. Wanted.

Closing my eyes, I drifted off, peaceful, and it felt perfect.

Twenty-Six

LIBERTY

I let out a squeak, startled when I opened my eyes to see a pair of baby-blue ones staring back at me. Ozzy tilted his head to the side, but didn't seem to be bothered by my response to him being in my face. Grinning, I reached over and ran my hand over his head.

"Good morning to you too," I said.

His coat was a pale gray with darker splotches. I'd never seen a Great Dane with this coloring, but then he might be the first one I had been this close to.

I sat up and glanced over at the rest of the empty bed. I touched the pillow where Liam's head imprint was, and it felt cool. He'd been up for a while, it seemed. A smile tugged on my lips as I thought about last night. A warm feeling settled in my chest, and I moved to swing my legs over the side of the bed.

Ozzy backed up to give me some room, and I noticed a large dog bed on the floor beside me. That hadn't been there last night. Had Liam put Ozzy's bed beside me when he let him in last night? I had slept through the night, not waking up once, which was rare. Since being pregnant, I had found I needed to pee several times a night.

My bladder wasn't exactly thrilled with me either. I stood up and headed to the bathroom when I noticed two keys and a note on the bedside table.

I moved the keys and picked up the piece of notebook paper. Liam's neat, masculine handwriting was something I was familiar with after working on his files at the strip club.

Liberty,

The blue key is the house key. The one on the chain is the car key. I added your number to my cell, and I put mine in yours. You really should put a lock code on your phone.

I'll be at the club most of the day, but I have a couple of meetings elsewhere. Text if you need something or have questions.

I left money on the counter in the kitchen. You're going to want to go get some groceries. You'll find I don't keep much here. And the gate code is 138265.

Liam

I held the paper and reread it, looking for something that felt as warm and happy as I had felt when I woke up in his bed. But there was nothing. It was almost businesslike. Perhaps I was reading too much into it. He'd left me the key to his car. That hadn't been expected. He had to trust me to just leave me alone at his house with the key to his car. It was more than he'd thought of me before he dropped me off at the clubhouse.

I looked down at Ozzy, who was still watching me. "I'm being an emotional female, aren't I?"

Ozzy didn't respond.

Laying the note back on the table, I went to his bathroom and relieved my bladder, then dressed in my discarded clothing. Picking up the keys and my note, I made my way to the room I'd been given. I wanted to shower in Liam's so that I could smell like his body wash or soap. But he'd given me a room and bathroom. Until he changed his mind about our sleeping arrangements, I didn't want to assume I could use his things.

I set down my items on the dresser in the bedroom that was to be mine for now. I went to get my suitcases and laid them out on the bed. I'd lived out of them at the clubhouse, but there was an empty closet here that Liam had told me to use. It would be nice to have my things out so I could see them.

Going over to the closet I opened the door to get out hangers, only to find this was more like a small room. Reaching around inside to find the light switch, I turned it on and stared in awe at the two long walls with double poles to hang things. The far back wall had a built-in floor-to-ceiling mirror and counters on each side with drawers beneath.

"Holy smokes, Ozzy," I whispered, walking in and looking around.

When I turned to look back at the door, I realized there were small square slots for shoes covering the side of the wall that the light switch wasn't on. I counted them. Fifty. Who needed fifty shoes?

I took several hangers and started working on getting my things put away. Ozzy followed me back and forth until he decided to just sit down beside the closet door. It didn't take very long until I had all my clothes placed neatly inside. Standing there, I looked at my things, which barely took up any space, making me chuckle.

"Don't judge, Ozzy," I told him, turning and heading for the bathroom. "When a girl moves around as much as I do, you don't want to own too many things."

I walked over to a tall square basket and picked up one of the rolled-up white towels inside it. I ran my hand over it. "Soft, fluffy towels," I said, then cut my eyes to Ozzy. "These are shockingly luxurious for Liam, don't you think?"

Placing the towel beside the shower, I began to undress while I planned out the day. I would get ready, then check out his kitchen, and make a grocery list. I could cook a meal for tonight. He must not cook for himself if he didn't keep much food here.

Ozzy settled himself on the floor and rested his chin on his paws as I stepped into the shower. He was clearly a social dog. I wondered how often he was left here alone. That thought bothered me. I peeked out at him from the shower door. He lifted his head.

"We will go outside and play later. I can toss you a stick or ball. Okay?" I told him, then went to stand under the warm spray.

I started imagining a swing set out back and pushing a little one. I couldn't decide if I wanted a boy or girl. The idea of having either made me smile. I pictured Ozzy running around in the yard while our baby giggled, watching him.

Happiness was starting to seep in, and I'd always been scared to trust it. In my past, happy things were fleeting, if they came at all. But I'd woken up in Liam's bed this morning. He had moved me into his house.

Maybe this time, it was okay to just let go of my control and have some faith.

Twenty-Seven

LIAM

"I'm assuming you didn't get a cat," Tex said as he sat down in one of the chairs across from my desk.

My gaze shifted to the scratch marks showing from underneath the short sleeves of my shirt, then back to Tex.

"Did you get the liquor order straightened out?" I asked him, ignoring his comment.

I didn't want to discuss where the marks had come from. I'd been having a hard enough time with getting Liberty out of my head all day. The reasons why it was a bad thing that I'd let her sleep in my bed with me last night being first and foremost.

"Ah, come on. I've given you all fucking morning. I even waited until midafternoon for you to tell me you'd moved that hot, sexy, young baby momma into your house," he complained.

Shit. You'd think bikers wouldn't gossip like a bunch of old ladies.

"Who told you that?" I asked. This wasn't something I wanted getting out. I was struggling with it enough as it was. Once Madeline found out—fuck. I didn't want to think about her reaction.

Tex gave me a pointed look. "You really have to ask that?"

"Micah," I sighed.

Should have known the fucker couldn't keep his mouth shut. If I hadn't raised the bastard, I'd have beaten him within an inch of his life years ago.

Tex nodded, then gave me a sly grin. "Since the cat's out of the bag," he said, then wiggled his eyebrows.

I glared at him, not finding his pun humorous in the least.

"Tell me you got her home last night, got those tits and that ass naked, worshipped them, then fucked the hell out of her," he said. "I mean, you did something, obviously. I doubt those claw marks were an accident."

"No one is to know," I told him through clenched teeth. "I don't want people knowing she's in my house. It's bad enough that I knocked her up."

Tex frowned. "What's so bad about it? She's gorgeous with big tits and a bouncy, round ass, and you get to tap that whenever you want. I'm struggling to find the problem."

He needed to stop talking about her body. I didn't like it, and again, that was another fucking problem I couldn't control.

"I've told you already. She's sixteen years younger than me. She was a bartender without a car and living in a goddamn motel, and I fucked her hours after meeting her. Not once either. Several times. What do you think Madeline is going to think when she finds this out? She was so excited about the doctor. Wanted us to come over for dinner. You think she's gonna want a homeless bartender who is only six years older than her to come over for dinner? What about the boys? I'm about to give them an aunt or uncle who is younger than they are." I ran a hand over my head and sighed.

Telling him that all I could think about was her dirty mouth, and her soaking wet cunt wasn't happening. I had to get a handle on it and set some line that wouldn't be crossed.

The whole thing with her in the bikini and Country drooling all over her had set me off. Then, when I saw her stomach wasn't flat anymore, I lost my damn mind. The word *MINE* roared in my head so loudly that I almost shouted it. Thank fuck I hadn't.

Having her all curled up against me in bed, smelling like heaven, while my hand held one of her big, swollen tits when I opened my eyes this morning hadn't helped. I shouldn't have let her stay in my room. It had been a mistake. The ice-cold shower I took didn't ease much, considering when I got out, she was still lying in my bed, naked.

I'd had to get the hell out of that house before I climbed on top of her and she woke up with my dick buried inside her. I wasn't sure I could go back. At least not today.

"Why are you concerned about what Madeline thinks? She didn't care that you didn't approve of her choice in a husband. She's your daughter, but, man, Liberty is carrying your other kid."

I shook my head. "I'm too old for this. A relationship with a woman that young. She might be thirty-one, but she's got herself as pulled together as much as a sorority girl does. Hell, at least sorority girls are in college, getting a degree. She didn't even do that. I need someone mature."

Tex chuckled. "When did you start thinking like some old grandpa? You've got a smoking hot piece of young ass. Sure, she might be a mess, and, hell, maybe she's a little crazy even, but who the fuck cares? She's got your baby up in her; she's sleeping in your bed, spreading those sweet thighs for you. Dude, snap out of it," he said, then stood up.

Dammit! I didn't need a reminder about her fucking spread thighs.

My phone started ringing, and I looked down to see Selena's name lighting up the screen. Just what I needed right now. To deal with this. I'd been dodging her the best I could, but she didn't seem to give up easily.

"Probably want to cut that shit loose," Tex said. "Good luck with that." he added with a nod, then turned to leave the office.

I waited until the door closed, then hit Answer and leaned back in my chair, dreading this.

"Selena," I said in greeting.

"Liam," she replied, sounding happy to hear my voice. "I thought I'd give you a call since I hadn't heard back from you after my last text message. I've been worried about you. I hope everything is okay."

I tilted my head back and stared at the ceiling. This was going to be annoyingly dramatic. I had thought our casual dating was going well. No attachment on her part. I'd figured out that I was wrong. Women got attached even when they claimed they weren't. Another reason I couldn't keep fucking Liberty. She would get attached.

"I've had some personal stuff going on, Selena. Right now, dating just isn't something I can fit into my life. I'm sorry I've not gotten back to you. Things have been busy, and I've had a lot of distractions. I'm not in a headspace to date," I said, ripping off the Band-Aid and getting it out there.

"Oh," she replied, disappointment in her tone. "I-I hope I wasn't being pushy. I just—I mean, I was having a good time.

I thought you were too. We don't have to date, but we could just see each other as friends when you have time. I could bring dinner over to your place if you're too tired to come over here. I'd love to see your house. Meet Oscar."

Her hopefulness made me feel like shit. Even if she'd just called my dog by the wrong name.

"That's not a good idea," I told her, leaving out that her sister was living in my house. She probably didn't need to hear that from me.

"Everyone needs a helping hand from a friend. You're obviously going through a tough time, Liam. I want to help you. I'm not trying to make this into anything more."

How many times was I going to have to tell this woman no? Probably until I admit the truth—or at least part of it. No woman would want to be friends and hang out when I had a baby momma living under my roof.

"I didn't want to have to tell you this. I'm not proud of it, but I'm taking responsibility for my actions," I said, prepping myself for whatever reaction I was about to get. "I had a one-night stand with a bartender I met one night before you and I went on our first date. She got pregnant. I'm dealing with that and making sure she's taken care of." I stopped, hoping this would end it, that she'd be appalled and hang up on me.

"Are you sure it's yours? If she had a one-night stand with you, then—"

"It's mine. I had a paternity test done," I interrupted before she could continue on about it anymore.

"Oh. I see. Well …" She paused, and I waited for her to say *goodbye* or *have a nice life* or maybe *fuck you* before hanging up.

Then, I heard the sniffling, and I dropped my head into my hand. Fucking hell, she was going to cry. A sob came over the line. Was she seriously crying over this?

"I'm sorry. I just—it's the anniversary of my mom's death. I'm struggling. Not having family to talk to. I just needed someone, and you were the only one I could think of that I wanted to talk to. I know you've got all this on you, and I don't want to dump my stuff on you too."

I'd left Liberty at home this morning and not texted or called her all day. Was she struggling with this? I knew she hadn't gone to the funeral, but maybe it was for reasons I didn't know. Like facing it was too much. She'd been younger than Selena. She might not have been ready to accept her death. Was she crying at home alone too?

"Again, I'm sorry for bothering you," she said after another sob.

I realized I hadn't responded earlier and cleared my throat.

"I'm, uh, sorry. I know that must be tough," I replied.

She sniffled, then let out a breathy laugh. "I don't suppose you could find a couple of hours to maybe come over to help me eat a carton of ice cream and let me borrow your shoulder to cry on for a little bit?"

I did feel bad for her, but I wouldn't be going to her house ever again.

"I can't, Selena. I'm sorry. I need to get back to work. I do wish you all the best, and I hope tomorrow is a better day for you," I told her. "Goodbye."

My thumb hit the End button, and I stared at the screen, wondering if I should check on Liberty. But if she was sad, I'd want to go comfort her, and then I'd want to fuck her. She didn't need that, and I didn't need to be the one she cried on.

It would only make her grow dependent on me. Start getting feelings.

I'd just had a taste of what a woman who had started wanting shit and a future was like when I tried to shake her loose. That shit wasn't easy with someone you could just shut out. It would be even harder with Liberty if she started wanting more with me. She would be in my life for the next eighteen or nineteen years. We were gonna have to raise a kid together. We needed to get along.

Twenty-Eight
LIBERTY

Ozzy came racing back to me with the stick in his mouth. I tried my best to smile for him despite the knot in my chest that had been there since last night, when I'd realized Liam wasn't coming home. I didn't have an appetite by that point and wrapped up all the food that I'd made for dinner, then put it in the fridge. I had managed to eat some for lunch today. I'd not wanted anything at breakfast.

My phone dinged, alerting me of a text, and I pulled it out of my pocket, hoping it was Liam with a very good excuse.

> **Unknown Number:** It's Wallace. You keep blocking me. Until you talk to me, Liberty, I'm going to keep texting you and calling. I'll get new numbers. I need you to give me a chance. I can fix this. I can fix us. I love you. Please, baby, I am begging you. Talk to me.

I read the text, and my mood plummeted more. He wasn't going to stop, apparently. He wanted me to talk to him, so I'd respond.

> **Me:** Please stop trying to contact me. I am pregnant. It's not yours. I had a paternity test done. I'm living with the father. What we had is done. It's over.

I hit Send. Then went to block the number. That should fix that. Wallace would not keep on pursuing me once he knew I was pregnant. If only Liam wanted to text me as badly as Wallace wanted to.

Ozzy dropped the stick at my feet, and I stuck my phone back in my pocket, then bent down to pat his head, praising him before I picked it up to toss it again. We'd been doing this for thirty minutes, but he didn't seem to grow tired of it. At least I had him for company. He rarely left my side. Ozzy might be the best relationship I'd ever had. When Liam moved me out after the baby was born, I wondered if he'd let me take Ozzy.

I'd woken up this morning to Ozzy staring at me again as he stood beside my bed. When I had gone to sleep last night, he had lain down on the floor beside my bed. I had told him to go to his bed, but he had just looked at me, then put his head back down on the rug.

When I couldn't find his food this morning because Liam hadn't told me where that was, he had gone over to the cabinet it was kept in and barked once. I filled his bowl to the top. There were no directions on how much I was to give him, but since he was massive, I'd figured he required a large portion.

"He'll keep you out here for hours, throwing that, if you let him," Liam called out.

I immediately felt joy at the sound of his voice until I remembered he'd been gone since yesterday morning and it was almost time to eat dinner.

"It seems that way," I replied, barely glancing at him.

If he thought he was going to leave me here like this all the time, then he had another thing coming. I'd go get a job. I needed one anyway. I wasn't going to just stay here like some kept woman, waiting for her man to give her the time of day.

Ozzy was back with the stick, and he dropped it, then ran over to greet Liam. Traitor. No, that wasn't fair. Liam was his owner. He loved him and was happy to see him. I would be, too, if he wasn't a jackass. He could have at least texted me. I had spent three hours on that meal last night, trying to make something he'd enjoy. Silly me had even set the table and put on one of my nice sundresses.

Never again.

I couldn't stand out in the backyard and pout like a baby. Swallowing my hurt feelings, I headed in their direction as Liam gave Ozzy some love. I was almost there when Ozzy spotted me and left Liam to run back over and stand beside me. I got a tiny sliver of enjoyment from that, but kept my face neutral.

"Car drive okay for you?" he asked. "I see you took it out."

"I went grocery shopping yesterday with the money you'd left," I told him. I'd spent most of it on the dinner last night. I needed to take some of my money and go buy healthy items for me to have on hand to eat, but today, I'd been in a funk.

"Good. I hoped you would," he replied.

I started to walk on past him and go into the house. Unless he wanted to explain where he'd been and why he hadn't called, then I had nothing more to say.

"How were you yesterday? I thought about calling, but I didn't know if you wanted to talk or if you just wanted to be alone."

I paused. Talk about what? Us having sex in his bed and me sleeping in it?

I turned back around to look at him. The serious expression on his face confused me.

"I'm not sure what you are asking me."

He appeared slightly annoyed by my response. Well, I'd left slightly annoyed behind sometime yesterday evening when he hadn't shown up.

"Selena called me yesterday."

Oh. Had he told her about the pregnancy? Had she said she was going to call me?

I shrugged. "Okay, and?"

His expression immediately hardened, and his mouth drew into a tight line. Did he want me to tell her? What was I not getting here?

"The anniversary of your mom's death ring a bell? Selena was pretty torn up about it. Wanted me to come over so she'd have someone to talk to. That's not something I can do for her, considering our situation, but I figured you're her sister, so you'd want to at least talk to her. I was trying to understand why you hadn't gone to the funeral and give you the benefit of the doubt, but you can see how this makes me judge your character."

My mom? Had yesterday been Abilene's death anniversary? I hadn't cared enough to remember the date. But why had he called that woman my mom? Evil stepmother and my mom were not the same thing. Was he with Selena yesterday? Was that why he hadn't come home?

He was giving me a disapproving look, like he had a right to judge me. Yet he'd gone to Selena to comfort her and was lying about it.

"I'm sorry, Liam. But seeing as how my mother died on February 15, 1999, I don't know what you're talking about," I snapped as pain, anger, betrayal all grew where, for a moment two nights ago, joy had been. But that was always fleeting, wasn't it?

He narrowed his eyes. "You are aware I dated Selena. She wouldn't lie about her mother's death. She doesn't have a reason to."

I just stood there and stared at him. Selena wouldn't lie. But I would? My hands were trembling at my sides, and I fisted them until I could feel my nails digging into my palms.

"Is it because she has an education? Because she's a doctor? Or maybe because she's got her own house and a car? She makes a lot of money? Is that why you don't question anything she's told you? My being a bartender without a car and anywhere to live makes me a liar? I can see where that makes complete sense, Liam. Did you get a college education to be the president of a motorcycle club and own strip clubs? Tell me, what degree does one get for that?" My voice had gone from a sarcastic snarl to a shout.

Tears burned my eyes, and I refused to cry in front of him. Turning, I ran the rest of the way until I was inside the house and headed up to my bedroom.

I should have stayed in Miami. They liked me there. No one accused me of lying or talked down to me. My chest didn't feel like someone had punched their fist through it when I was there.

For almost eight years, I had lived in a house where I'd been beaten down, and when I was kicked out the door at eighteen, I'd sworn I'd never let that happen to me again.

Ozzy appeared at my side just as I opened the door to the bedroom, and I sighed, looking down at him. He probably thought we were playing chase. I let him follow me in before I closed the door. The first tear fell, and I let the rest go.

I had refused to cry over Liam ignoring me on a night that I had believed was going to be the beginning of something for us. But this accusation was too much. He had taken my already-wounded feelings and shown me just how much power he had over my emotions.

He had never asked me about my childhood or my parents. My past hadn't seemed important to him. He thought he knew it all because of the things Selena had told him. He'd had no desire to find out from me. While Country had asked me all about my life, growing up. He knew more about me than the father of my child.

I dropped my head into my hands and let out a small sob.

Ozzy whimpered beside me, but I couldn't reassure him. I needed to cry.

Twenty-Nine

LIAM

I stood at her door, listening to the sound of her sobbing. That wasn't what I'd meant to do. It had all come out wrong, and I'd gotten so fucking pissed that she hadn't seemed to give a shit about the death of her mother. Her not going to her mom's funeral or grieving with her sister had seemed so unlike the woman I was getting to know. All the things Selena had claimed Liberty was didn't match up to the friendly, charming person that she appeared to be.

My club adored her. All of them. Hell, Nina had teared up and hugged her tightly when we left. Then, there was Ozzy. He was in there with her now. Until Liberty, he'd never left my side for anyone other than Cree. Dogs were supposed to be better judges of character than humans.

The only factor here was Selena. Yeah, I had believed what she'd said because she was a well-respected doctor. She had it all, and Liberty didn't. Wouldn't an older sister tell the truth about her younger sibling? It seemed to me there had to be a lot of hurt caused by Liberty for Selena to dislike her so much.

Shit just didn't make sense.

Listening to Liberty's cries, however, was more than I could handle. I wanted her to stop. I liked it when she was smiling and laughing. This was brutal, and my own damn chest felt as if someone were stabbing me with each heartbreaking sound.

I started to knock, then changed my mind and turned the knob.

Pushing the door open, I took a step inside, then saw her on the bed, her face red and splotchy, lashes spiky from the tears. Her eyes lifted to meet mine, and she wiped at her cheeks with both hands, as if trying to hide the fact that she had been crying from me.

A deep growl snapped my attention from her, and I saw Ozzy standing at the corner of the bed, looking at me with disapproval. He'd never growled at me. That didn't ease the way I was feeling. He was protecting her, which meant he trusted her over me.

I looked back at her as she crossed her arms over her chest, her eyes shifting toward the far wall and glaring at it. The tight line she was trying to make with her mouth didn't mask the quivering of her bottom lip.

Dammit. What had I gotten wrong?

"You're right," I told her, but she didn't stop glaring at the bare wall. "I don't have a college education. I barely finished high school. The men I am closest to, the brothers I trust, none of them went to college. Hell, a few have even been in jail at some point."

She sucked in her bottom lip to stop the tiny trembling it had been doing.

"I made a lot of unfair assumptions about you. Before I knew you were also the sexy bartender who I took to her motel room and had unbelievably spectacular sex with, you were just Selena's sister, and she told me things about you that I took at face value. I saw no reason she'd lie about it. But I shouldn't have labeled you like I did. I'm sorry."

I stopped when her eyes finally swung back to me. The pretty honey-brown color shone with more unshed tears.

The urge to go to her and pull her into my arms and kiss away all that sadness was really fucking strong, but I had more to say. She deserved it.

"I'm an asshole. Even my dog seems to be smarter than me," I said, motioning to Ozzy, who was now standing between us like he was ready to protect her at all costs. "Liberty, would you please tell me about your parents? Why you didn't go to college like Selena did. Why you and Selena aren't close. I want to hear it all from you. Not because I believe what she said. I don't. Not anymore at least. But I want to know about you. You're going to be the mother of my child, and I'd like us to respect each other. And I know I have to earn that from you, and I've done a piss-poor job so far of earning any respect, but I'm changing that. Starting right now."

A single tear ran down her face, and she sniffed, uncrossing her arms and reaching up to wipe it away. Right now, she looked so young, but then she was, especially compared to me. There was also a lot of sadness in her eyes, and I would do just about anything to make that shit go away.

She lifted her chin, and her eyes met mine again. "Until I was seven years old, I lived in Charleston. My mom, dad, and I lived across the street from his mother, Mama D. It was perfect. Then, my Mama D got sick and passed away when I was six years old. It was hard on us all, but my dad struggled with it. Seven months later, my momma was in a car accident that killed her on impact. Nothing was the same after that." She paused and sucked in air, then dropped her gaze to her hands.

"When my dad was in college, before he met my mom, he had a girlfriend, Abilene, that he got pregnant. They'd been broken up when she told him about it, but then she told him that she'd aborted it. After Mom died, that ex-girlfriend contacted him through Facebook. She hadn't gotten an abortion, and her daughter wanted to meet her father." Liberty let out a deep sigh.

"He packed us up, and we moved to Ocala so he could be near his other daughter. He wanted me to have a sister, and I think he truly believed Abilene would help ease the void in my life that Mom and Mama D had left." A laugh that wasn't from humor but sounded more seeped in pain came from her. "That wasn't the case. Abilene hated me. Selena tolerated me, but she blamed me that our father had been with me and my mom. He hadn't known about her. It was never his fault, but instead of blaming her mother, Selena pinned that hurt on me.

"When I was ten, my dad was in the hospital after having a heart attack. As soon as she heard, Abilene went and checked Selena out of school, then rushed to see him. They were with him when he died." She shrugged. "My school was right next to Selena's, but Abilene didn't think to get me. So, I never made it to the hospital to see him before he was gone. And that was the first day of eight years in hell."

Anger built inside me with each word she spoke. However, I wasn't sure who I was angrier with—me or Selena or the bitch Abilene. I took a step toward her, and Ozzy growled again.

"The week following my dad's funeral, Abilene moved me from my bedroom to one in the basement. It was the only finished part of the basement. The rest was one open area with a washer and dryer, but nothing else. I was given a twin mattress on the floor as my bed. Selena took my bedroom, along with my furniture. Which happened to be furniture I'd picked out with my mom on the last birthday I had with her." She sniffled and rubbed her face again, and then her stare hardened.

"So, no, I didn't go to Abilene's funeral. I didn't even send flowers. I had shots of tequila with some friends instead. Not one day in that woman's life had she been even remotely kind to me.

"While Selena had big, extravagant birthday parties, neither of them ever acknowledged my birthday. The money my father had left behind for my college education was used for Selena's. I tried to get loans, keep a job, go to college. It was too hard. I couldn't afford it, and after almost two years, I stopped trying.

"As for a car, Selena was given a brand-new one on her sixteenth birthday and another one on her high school graduation. I rode the bus to school until I started having friends who had cars. I wasn't able to get a driver's license until I was eighteen because my guardian wouldn't take me to get one.

"I could sit here and tell you one story after another about things she did to me, that both of them did, but I try not to think about it. I learned a long time ago that dwelling on the pain they'd caused makes me bitter, and I don't want to be that person."

I stood there, trying to find a way past the guilt, shame, and horror of what all I'd said to her. How I'd treated her clawed at my fucking soul. Words were lodged in my throat. I couldn't think of an apology that was good enough.

She took a deep breath and shrugged with a beautiful yet sad smile on her face. "That's my story, Liam. Thanks for asking."

Fuck. I wished she'd just thrown a brick at my chest instead.

"I can't ..." I started, then shook my head. My voice was hoarse.

Unfamiliar emotion I didn't know how to process worked its way through me, and I was lost on how to maneuver around it. Trying again, I took another step toward her, and it seemed Ozzy was trusting me to go near her now.

"There isn't a sufficient apology that would make up for what I said and how I treated you. But I am sorry, Liberty. Real damn sorry."

She nodded, her smile softening. "I can see that. You aren't looking at me like I'm something you wish you weren't stuck with anymore."

I winced. Had I done that? I hadn't realized it.

"I should have come back last night. I should have called or texted."

She dropped her gaze to her lap again. "Selena called, and she's hard for you to turn down," she said, trying to sound flippant.

"I told you I didn't go to Selena's. I was at the club all night."

She glanced back up at me. "You didn't?" she asked, sounding relieved.

I shook my head. "No. I wouldn't do that. I didn't want to do that. I wanted to come back here and fuck you again. I'd thought about it all damn day. But we can't do that and get this all confused."

She bit her bottom lip for a moment. Her tears had dried up. My eyes drifted down to the tube top she was wearing. It was bright blue and didn't cover all of her stomach. It looked like her tits were in danger of popping out from the top at any moment.

"I don't know," she said softly. "We are having a baby together. It would help if we liked each other. Not a relationship or anything. I know you don't want that, but while my body is dealing with all these pregnancy symptoms, it seems you'd be the best option to help me with them. It doesn't have to be more than that."

I stared at her. She seemed nervous as she waited on me to respond. I'd just sent her running to her room, crying, like a bastard. Was she really suggesting we fuck while she was pregnant? Could I trust that she wouldn't get some emotional attachment to me?

Bigger question was, did I want her to not get attached because the idea of her forming a deeper need for me caused me to have a greedy craving for it? For her to want me. Rely on me. No matter how foolish that was, it was there, raising its head in all its possessive glory.

"Are you saying that we can fuck, that your cunt is mine to take care of, and we can live in this house together while I make sure you have everything you need, and when this ends with us sexually, we can still be friends? Raise a kid together without any bitterness or regret in our relationship?"

She nodded, her eyes no longer red-rimmed, but guarded. As if she didn't believe I'd agree. Right now, I wanted to strip her bottoms off and bury my face between her legs until she came on my tongue several times. I didn't want the memory of her tears and broken sobs. But she needed to know I respected her too.

"I'd kill anyone else that touched you," I admitted. "If pregnancy makes your pussy needy, then I'm the only one allowed to take care of it. The one thing between us that has never been an issue is sex. You are without a doubt the best fuck of my life. But for us to end up as friends, we need to also build a foundation."

"Okay," she replied. "We could start with having dinner together."

"You hungry, darlin'?" I asked, an amused grin curling the corners of my mouth.

She lifted a shoulder. "A little. Are you?"

"I'll order us something. What do you want?" I asked.

She turned and slid off the bed, causing Ozzy to hurry to her side. "No need to order anything. I made dinner last night. It's all in the refrigerator. I just need to heat it up."

More fucking guilt settled on my chest as she walked toward me. She'd made dinner. I hadn't come home. Damn, I had to find a balance. A way to make it up to her, but not … let myself fall for her while keeping that smile on her face. She'd had enough heartbreak in her life, and I didn't want to be another one.

"I'm sorry I didn't come home last night," I said when she reached me.

She smiled. "I guess I'll forgive you. But only if you love my chicken potpie and corn fritters."

"That's what you cooked last night? Homemade?" I asked, surprised.

She looked at me as if I had asked a crazy question. "Of course it's homemade."

If her cooking was as fantastic as her cunt, I might be fucked, both literally and figuratively.

Thirty

LIBERTY

When my eyes opened, there weren't a pair of blue ones staring back at me, but there was a heavy arm around me, cupping my breast, and a hard, warm body pressed to my back. He was still here. Pressing my lips together to try and not act like a giddy idiot, I enjoyed the moment. The sunshine coming through the wooden blinds told me it wasn't early. We had slept in. But then we'd been up late. Sex in the shower, then again in the bed. I must have fallen asleep right after because I just remembered the sated feeling from the fifth orgasm he'd given me.

His hand squeezed my boob as he placed a kiss to my head. "Mornin'," he mumbled huskily.

I scooted closer to him.

"Mmm, keep wiggling that ass, and you'll get fucked," he warned, then pressed his hard length against my bottom.

"I need to pee first," I admitted.

He groaned and held me tighter, pinching my nipple. "Don't get up yet," he said. "This feels good."

I had told him I could do this without getting attached, but the way my heart was soaring, I knew I'd lied. I was already attached. It was the only reason his words had been able to hurt me. He didn't know that though. It was a secret I had to keep if I wanted this.

"Where's Ozzy?" I asked.

"I put him outside the room about an hour ago," he said, rocking his hips so that his erection rubbed between the cheeks of my butt. "He keeps pulling his bed over to lie beside you at night. Seems you stole my dog."

I giggled, then gasped as his hand slid down my stomach, stopping right above my mound.

"I thought maybe the horny fucker smelled your aroused pussy, and that was what had him staying by your side. But I believe it's this," he said, caressing my stomach. "He can tell you're pregnant."

His fingers brushed down close to my clit.

"You think?" I asked in a breathy tone.

"Mmhmm," he replied, then kissed my ear. "Sure you need to pee? Because I'm about to play with my favorite wet toy."

As much as I didn't want to stop this, I also wasn't sure I could survive the humiliation if I peed on him.

"I should probably go pee first," I reminded him.

He licked just below my ear. "If you're sure."

I was already panting, so I just nodded.

His arm lifted from me, and he rolled onto his back. "All right."

Hating my stupid bladder, I sat up and hurried to the bathroom.

"Goddamn, that's a juicy ass."

The raspy tone of his voice sent a shiver through me. A grin spread across my face as I saw the way our clothing had been tossed around the bathroom last night when we got in here. Liam had been impatient to get me naked. I had barely gotten in the shower when he hooked my leg over his arm and slammed into me.

I finished relieving myself, wanting to be back in the bed with him. This was the morning I'd wanted since sleeping in his bed the first night. On my way back to him, I glanced at myself in the mirror. Seeing the small changes in my body was exciting. Knowing it was Liam's baby inside me, causing this, made it seem even more special.

When I walked back into the room, he was on his side, facing me. His eyes drifted down my body, and I loved how heated they got. He didn't love me, but he did love having sex with me.

He lifted the covers for me to climb back in beside him. I started to turn my back to him, but he grabbed my waist.

"I want those titties pressed against my chest," he said, tugging me close to him, then taking my leg and laying it over his hip so that his cock was pushing against my opening. His hand slid down and cupped my bottom. "That's even better," he said, holding me.

I ran my fingers over the tattoos on his biceps. Trailing the tips of my nails over the designs.

The swollen head of his erection jerked, sliding against the slickness.

"That's it. Drip that sweet cream all over my dick," he drawled, running his finger in between my butt cheeks. "Naughty little girl wants my cock all the time. I was gonna give you a break this morning. Thought you might be sore. But look how wet you are already."

I was gripping his arm now, my lips slightly parted as my breath came in heavy.

His lips trailed down the side of my face. "Tell me what you want," he whispered against my skin. "You want me buried inside you? Is that what you need?"

I nodded, moving my hips so that I felt him right outside my hole.

He made a tsking sound, and then his hand landed with a firm swat on my bottom. "Use your words. I want to hear that dirty mouth tell me what you want."

"Fuck me," I begged. "Please, Liam. I need you to fuck me."

A deep, pleased-sounding growl rippled inside his chest as he grabbed my thigh, pulling me on top of him while he rolled onto his back. I placed both my hands on his chest and stared down at him while my hair fell in a curtain around my face, brushing just past my nipples.

"Take it then. Ride my cock," he ordered, gripping my hips.

His gaze dropped to my boobs, and I felt him twitch inside me.

Lifting my bottom up, then sliding back down on him, I moaned with pleasure. "You're so deep."

He brushed my hair back from my right breast, then leaned up to lick it. "Fuck me, baby. I want to see these titties bounce."

Leaning back, I placed my hands on his upper thighs for balance and began to move up and down. Liam's gaze was locked on my breasts. The pulsing pleasure sent a warm release through me, and the added wetness made a sound every time I sank back down on him.

"Sexiest fucking thing I've ever seen," he swore, running his hands over my stomach, then my chest. "Listen to that leaking pussy making a mess."

A whimper came from me, and I fell forward, grabbing on to his shoulders as a tremor shook me. His hot mouth closed around one of my nipples and began to suck.

I was almost there.

"Suck harder," I pleaded. "Bite me, Liam. I'm so close. I'm gonna come," I cried out as a warning tingle made my body tense up.

Liam's teeth clamped down, and the climax erupted from me. I screamed his name, bucking wildly, wanting to prolong the moment.

"FUCK! Your cunt is pumping my cock," he growled, taking my bottom and slamming me down on him faster.

Then, in one quick move, he flipped me over onto my back, spreading my legs wide open while holding each bent knee.

"GOD! This pussy drives me crazy. Gushing all over my dick, needing it. Is this what you wanted? Hmm?"

"Yes," I gasped as my body began to tremble at the promise of another release. I threw my head back and lifted my hips. "That's it! Fuck me," I panted, needing more. "Fuck me!"

"Fuuuck!" he roared as his body convulsed.

My own shout filled the room as a spray came from my opening, and I began to jerk beneath him, unable to contain the jolts going through me.

"Holy fuck," he ground out, still pumping inside me. "That's a magical pussy."

I opened my eyes to see him looking down at where he was moving slowly inside me now. A giggle bubbled up, and I let it out.

He lifted his eyes to mine, and then a slow grin spread across his face.

"Magical?" I asked him, still feeling blissed out.

"You heard me. It's using its powers to get me addicted to it."

He looked back down at us and slid out of me slowly, then reached down and used his fingers to open me up. A pleased, almost-feral gleam came over his eyes.

"What are you doing?" I asked.

"Enjoying the sight of my load leaking out of you," he hissed, then licked his bottom lip. Then, he took a finger and ran it around my entrance before sticking it inside. "I want it in there for now. That way, your panties will be sticky with my cum all day. And you'll remember who takes care of it."

I didn't need a reminder, but I smiled at his words. Liam Walsh was claiming me even if he didn't realize it yet.

"Probably need to get dressed," he said as he moved to get out of bed.

"You're leaving?" I asked, already feeling the high from what we'd just experienced vanish. My eyes fell to his bare butt and the way it flexed, along with his thighs, as he walked.

"Yeah, but I was talking about you," he replied, sauntering toward the bathroom.

"Me? I need to get dressed?" I asked, a little distracted by the view.

He stopped just inside the door and glanced back at me. "I can't take you like that to go shopping for flowers and shit."

I sat up quickly. "Flowers?"

He nodded. "You've seen my yard. Needs some work. Figure you'd already started fixing it up in your head."

I swung my legs off the bed and stared at him as a smile stretched across my face so big that it hurt. "You're serious?!" I squealed.

"Why would I lie about that? Now, get some clothes on before I forget what we are doing and we end up back in that bed."

Jumping up, I ran to him and threw my arms around his neck. Yes, I had thought about all the flower beds and shrubbery that would dress the already-beautiful house up, but I hadn't wanted to mention it. He had seemed put off by my doing it at the clubhouse.

"Thank you!" I said, pressing a kiss to his bearded jaw.

"You want to buy flowers, darlin', you need to stop pressing your body on me," he warned as one of his hands ran down my back.

Biting my lip, I stepped back, letting him go. "I'll go get on some clothes."

I caught his smirk before I turned to hurry to my bedroom and get ready. When the door opened, Ozzy came barreling in, almost knocking me over.

"Oz! Watch it!" Liam scolded him.

I bent over to pet him, feeling bad he'd been locked out for so long.

"Clothes, Liberty. Not a view of your ass stuck up in the air."

Liam's reminder sounded stern, but I grinned as I stood up and walked out the door with a slight swing of my hips just because I knew he was watching.

Ozzy fell into step beside me.

"You'd better be glad you have such a great ass, you dog thief," Liam called out.

I laughed all the way to my room.

Thirty-One

LIAM

One rap on my office door, and it swung open. I had spent over an hour trying to figure out how Liberty had done that paperless bill filing. I should have had her show me. Expecting to see Tex or Drifter walk in, I turned to see Madeline instead. The happiness I felt at the sight of her vanished when I saw the expression on her face.

"Hello, Liam," she said, walking inside and closing the door behind her.

She had been calling me Dad more and more lately. Being addressed as Liam meant the stern expression on her face was because of me. It didn't take me asking her to know why. Saturday had come and gone without my telling her about Liberty. I'd been a little distracted with Liberty in my bed. Blaise sure didn't give any leeway.

I stood up and walked around the desk. I didn't like the formal feeling of talking to her with my office desk between us. She wasn't business. She was my family.

"By your tone of voice, I'm taking it that Blaise told you about Liberty," I said.

She tilted her head slightly to the left and crossed her arms over her chest. "Yes. My husband did tell me that my father was going to have another child. Why is it that my husband had to tell me? Why didn't you tell me? This is kind of big news. Something that I should have heard from you."

I really hadn't wanted it to happen this way. She was angry and probably hurt. Disappointed in me. A host of shit that I hadn't even thought of yet.

I motioned at the chair. "Have a seat. Let me explain," I said.

She moved over and sat down, crossing her legs. "I'm listening."

There was no way to make this sound good. I couldn't sugarcoat it.

Sighing, I sat in the chair across from her and leaned back.

"A little over two months ago, I stopped at a bar on my way back from Miami. I was on my Harley, and the rain got too heavy. Anyway, the bartender was attractive. She made me laugh. I enjoyed talking to her. Her boss sent her home early, but she didn't have a ride. I gave her one. She was living in a motel because she and her boyfriend had broken up due to his cheating on her a few weeks prior and they'd been living together." I paused.

How was I supposed to explain this? *A sexy-as-fuck woman invited me in, and I kissed her, then peeled her tank top off.*

"You had sex with her," Madeline said. "Got that part. Continue."

I nodded. "Yeah. Well, I left before she woke up. Figured I'd not see her again. She was young. Too young for me to be messing with. And I had my first date with the doctor lined up."

"You're aware my father-in-law is married to a much younger woman, and we are very close."

I shook my head. "Fawn isn't as young as Liberty."

Madeline said nothing, and I took that as my cue to continue.

"I started dating Selena. She was good company. Checked all the boxes I was looking for in someone permanent. Maybe to even marry. Except …" I paused, not wanting to discuss how sex with her hadn't been great and felt like a chore.

"She was bad at sex," Madeline supplied.

I cleared my throat, uncomfortable talking about it. "Her younger sister needed a place to stay for a few weeks, and she let her stay with her. Imagine my shock when I saw the bartender I'd had a one-night stand with coming out of an upstairs bathroom in Selena's house."

Madeline's hand flew to her mouth as her eyes went wide. "Nooo," she said, sounding surprised.

"Blaise must have left that out."

She laughed. "Yes, he did. I'll deal with him later. Continue."

"Selena said some things about Liberty, not knowing about us, and I believed her. I judged Liberty unfairly. She passed out, walking home from the bus station late one night. I thought she was drunk or on some drugs. I took her to Selena's. Then …" I paused, realizing we hadn't discussed this when she told me about her parents and Selena's lies. The Liberty I knew wouldn't have reacted the way Selena had said she did.

"She ended up leaving Selena's house. I decided to stop by her place of work and check on her. Thinking I was helping out Selena. I caught Liberty outside, throwing up in some bushes. I confronted her about it. She admitted she was pregnant. Said it was mine. I didn't know that I could trust that. Brought her here and kept her in my bedroom up here while we waited on the results of the paternity test."

Madeline held up a hand, her eyebrows raised. "You mean to tell me, you brought her to a strip club? Seriously? You have a house. No woman should have to stay at this place—unless she works here, of course."

"It's not that bad," I defended myself. "Your husband just doesn't want you here. I understand it, but that doesn't mean it's some awful place to be. Speaking of which, when he finds out you came here, he's not going to like it."

Using her thumb, she pointed over her shoulder toward the door. "He's right outside. Huck is at the back entrance. Six is at the main entrance," she told me with a roll of her eyes.

"Surprised there is no one with the vehicle," I drawled sarcastically.

"Trev," she replied.

I chuckled. "Of course."

"So, the paternity test came back, and it was yours," she said, bringing us back on topic.

"Yeah. I took her to the clubhouse and left her there for a couple of weeks."

"Please tell me you're joking." Her brows were drawn together in a frown.

"No. That way, she wasn't alone. She was safe. Nina and Goldie loved her. She was fine. Got her set up with an OB-GYN, et cetera. Then, things happened, and I thought it was for the best that she move back here and just stay at my house. She's good with landscaping and plants and flowers. She takes Ozzy out for me, so I don't have to leave work to do it or send Tex over there. I'm letting her stay there and be the dog sitter and landscaper while she's pregnant. Once the baby comes, we will figure things out." Guilt was eating at me before I even said the words.

I'd known I was going to lie or make the situation sound like something else. Telling Madeline I was fucking Liberty like a feral animal and couldn't stop would not help the way she saw me right now.

Madeline was frowning. "So, that's all you want with her?"

No. It wasn't.

I nodded. "She's thirty-one. We are at two different points in our life. We don't fit. Nothing in common."

Madeline sighed. "Oh. Well, that's not what I thought I'd hear. She's young, sure. But she's having your baby. You get to raise a child of your own. I get a sibling. It's exciting. I guess I just thought maybe you'd found someone you wanted to have a family with. Grow old with."

"You thought I would want to grow old with a woman sixteen years younger than me? I'd be old long before she got a gray hair, Madeline. You think a forty-five-year-old woman would want to be stuck with a sixty-one-year-old man? Hell, I'm a grandfather, having a baby."

Madeline shrugged. "You're a good-looking man, Dad. You don't look forty-seven, and if she loved you, she wouldn't care about age. Not now or in twenty years. But if you don't love her, then I get that."

Love her? I hadn't even considered love. That wasn't necessarily something I expected when I settled down with someone. Love was a strong emotion. I'd felt it with Etta, but I had also been young. I hadn't seen how those who claimed to love one another often destroyed each other when it ended.

"This isn't a love match. It's a one-night stand and two people trying to form some kind of friendship or relationship so that we can amicably raise a child together. Not be together."

"I guess the doctor thing is done then," she said.

I nodded. "Yeah. That wouldn't work anymore." Especially now that I knew the lies Selena had told about Liberty. I hoped I never ran into the woman again.

"That's for the best. Especially if sex wasn't good. That should be one of the top boxes. If she doesn't check it, then move on along."

I grinned. "Noted. I'll keep that in mind when I decide to try the dating thing again."

Madeline studied me for a moment. "And you're sure there is no chance you and Liberty could feel something for each other?"

I shook my head. "Not going down that road."

"Well, she's gorgeous, and you enjoy conversations with her. Was the sex any good?"

"I'm not discussing that with my daughter," I told her.

Her mouth twitched, as if she wanted to smile. "But you told me how not good the sex was with the doctor. You had no problem pointing it out. Yet you won't talk about sex with Liberty. Which means it's good and you don't want to tell me that."

She stood up. "I want to meet her. She's going to be my sibling's mom. I'll let you figure out when is best. But just because you don't want to have something more than friendship or amicable whatever with her doesn't mean I don't want to have a relationship with her. She'll be my family too."

I hadn't expected that. Picturing it made me uneasy. Seeing Liberty blending with my daughter and grandkids as seamlessly as she had with The Judgment would mess with my head. Make me forget all the reasons why a romantic relationship with Liberty would be a bad idea. Although Madeline had just taken one of those reasons and blown it to hell.

Thirty-Two

LIBERTY

Liam had taken me to my favorite nursery in town three different times now. I'd found it the first time we went looking for things for me to plant.

The yard had a long way to go, but it wasn't exactly the best time of year for planting everything I wanted to put around the house. The things that bloomed all year in Florida was where I'd started. Since this wasn't a clubhouse, but Liam's home, I wanted it to be perfect.

"Come on in, Ozzy," I called after he ran around and did his business.

Liam had texted that he'd be here in ten minutes. It had been four weeks since my last doctor's appointment, and we were headed to Miami. Liam had said we would go to the clubhouse after and visit everyone. I'd packed an overnight bag, excited about getting to catch up with my friends.

Ozzy bounded up the stairs and into the house just as the gate opened, signaling Liam was here. I bent down and kissed him, then told him Tex would be here later before locking the door and making my way down to the driveway.

Liam parked and got out of the car. "Give me the bag," he said as he walked around the front toward me.

"I can put it in the back," I told him, smiling like a schoolgirl with a crush.

He'd pulled me in the shower with him this morning and sat down on the built-in bench, then had me straddle his lap. After he released inside me, he grabbed my face and kissed me hard. That had left lingering tingles in a way an orgasm did not.

"Why are you smiling?" he asked, taking the bag.

"Because you're hot."

He chuckled and placed my bag in the back seat, then opened my door for me. "You just like me for my cock," he said, smirking.

I stopped before getting in and looked up at him. "I adore your cock," I whispered, then slid onto my seat.

His eyes went to my bare thighs, then back to my face before his nostrils flared and his eyes heated. When he closed the door to walk back around to his side, I squirmed in my seat, already feeling needy, and he'd just been inside me three hours ago.

He sat down, then reached over and ran his hand up my thigh, moving my skirt up until he could see my panties. "Keep that shit up, and you'll go to your appointment with a messy pussy, darlin'. And I'll let you explain that to the doctor."

I giggled and moved his hand off me. "You're right. Don't make my panties wet."

He groaned and backed up the car so he could turn it around to drive back down the driveway.

Once we were on the road, he reached back over and touched my stomach. "What fruit is our baby the size of this week?"

"Well, I've read three different pregnancy sites and they all say something different. A pear, an apple, and a navel orange," I replied.

"The bump is definitely bigger," he said, rubbing it.

"I know. My jean skirt wouldn't button this morning. This one has elastic, so it fits."

He moved his hand to the gear stick to shift. "Do we find out what it is yet?" he asked.

"No. A few more weeks still. So, does that mean you want to know before it's born?"

I had been debating on this already. I wanted to know, but then a surprise seemed fun too. If there was a nursery I could decorate, then finding out before would make sense. But I didn't know where we would live. Eventually, we had to address that. I needed a plan. It was just that, although things had been really good with Liam and it'd felt different with him the past couple of weeks, he hadn't brought up anything changing.

"You don't want to know?" he asked, glancing at me.

"I haven't decided. But if you want to, then that would help make up my mind." I wanted to mention the nursery and needing to know where I'd be taking our baby when I left the hospital. There were things it would need. I would have to get those and have a place to put it.

"I'd like to know, but I don't want to make you do something you don't want to do. If you want to wait, I can too."

I shook my head. This wasn't a big deal. I had much bigger things I had to worry about. "I think I want to know too."

He narrowed his eyes. "Are you sure?"

"Yep! It's settled." Unlike our future.

"Do we need to go shopping for some new clothes for you?"

I thought about that for a moment. He would be the one buying them, and I didn't like that. I already lived at his house. I needed to contribute financially. Getting a job was a topic I hadn't wanted to push since things were going so well. But I had been looking online.

"I think I've got plenty of things that stretch right now," I told him.

He glanced over at my chest. "No bra again," he said. "We need to go buy you bigger ones."

"I can handle that this week if my not wearing one is bothering you," I said.

"Your tits draw attention. I don't like men looking."

That was why I hadn't gone and bought one already. When he acted jealous, it gave me hope. I kept thinking he'd realize why he was jealous or admit he had feelings for me.

"Men have always looked at my boobs," I pointed out.

"You weren't carrying my baby then."

The fear that that could truly be what it was, just that I was pregnant with his child and not jealousy was what kept me from trying to force him to say more. It was possible I had built all this up in my head. Because he was more than a friend to me. I was falling in love with him, and I couldn't stop. The Liam he'd been the past two weeks was a much different one. That side of Liam was impossible to protect my heart from.

I wanted to ask, *And after the baby is born, will you care if men look at me then?* but I wasn't brave enough to face that answer.

Time. We needed more time. This couldn't just be one-sided, the way I was feeling. He had to feel something too.

"I'll go get a new bra," I told him.

"I'll come with you. I need to be sure it covers you appropriately," he said.

I laughed and turned to look out the window as we drove. My eyes began to get heavy, and just before I drifted off, I felt Liam's hand brush hair from my face. The back of his fingers caressed my cheek. The words *I love you* were so close to spilling from my lips, but I held tight to them. He wasn't ready to hear that, but I had to believe that he would be one day soon.

Thirty-Three

LIBERTY

My pace picked up, the closer I got to the red door, as the noise on the other side grew louder.

The doctor's appointment had gone smoothly. We listened to the baby's heartbeat with a Doppler this time, and it remained strong. I had gained one pound, and everything else had appeared to be fine.

"You trying to get away from me?" Liam asked.

I glanced back over my shoulder at him and realized how much faster I'd been walking than him. "No, but I am anxious to see Nina and Goldie," I told him as I reached the door.

His mouth twitched with amusement, and for a moment, I was distracted by him. I had been doing that more often lately. Being struck by how handsome he was.

The nurse today had once again basically drooled all over him. However, he was different. He seemed not to even notice her interest. His eyes had remained on me the entire time, making me feel important to him.

I pushed the red door once he caught up with me, and my gaze went directly to the kitchen. It was dinnertime, and I knew Nina and Goldie would be back there, cooking. I did miss that. It had been fun, working back there together to feed everyone. Although living with Liam was far superior than my time here. Because I had him with me.

Goldie noticed me first and threw the pot holder in her hand down, then raced over to hug me with a squeal. I heard several greetings called out to Liam from the men in the room, but my attention was on the woman in front of me. She let me go, standing back to place her hands on my stomach.

"Oh my God, you are the cutest damn thing I have ever seen with this tiny baby bump," she gushed.

"Move. My turn," Nina told her as she pushed Goldie over and wrapped her arms around my neck. "It's so good to see you," she said as she hugged me tightly.

"It's good to see you too. Both of you," I replied, smiling over Nina's shoulder at Goldie.

Nina grabbed my hands as she stood back and studied me. "She's right. You make pregnancy look good. Hell, maybe I'll try it after all. If I can be promised I'll look like this."

Liam's hand slid over my hip and squeezed me gently. Nina noticed the contact, and a pleased smile touched her lips as she let go of my hands and stepped back.

"I'm glad to see things are going well," she said, giving Liam a knowing look before turning her attention back to me.

Although I knew what she was referring to, I wasn't sure how Liam would react to someone pointing it out. I decided to detour the conversation.

"Baby is healthy. Heartbeat was great," I told her.

Her smile softened. "How much longer until we know what it is?" She paused, then narrowed her eyes. "We are going to find out the sex, right?"

"We'd better!" Goldie said. "How will we be able to start buying things if we don't know?"

Liam leaned down to my ear. "I'll let these two have you. I'm going to go visit with the guys," he whispered.

I nodded, feeling my cheeks warm at the way he was treating me. The last time we had been here together, he'd barely tolerated me. Him acting as if we were a couple made me feel as if we truly were.

He glanced at the women in front of me. "She's yours—for now," he told them. "And, yes, we are going to find out the sex."

Both women squealed, Goldie clapping her hands as she grinned. Nina reached for my hand and tugged it toward the kitchen while leaning close to me.

"I don't know what excites me more—learning the sex or the fact that Prez is acting like you're his most prized possession."

Hearing that sent my stomach fluttering, but I knew it wasn't wise to let them believe that was the truth. We weren't there, and we might never be. Until Liam told me his feelings had changed, our future was still unknown.

"It's just the pregnancy," I told her as she led me behind the bar and into the kitchen.

Goldie followed behind, but close enough to hear what was being said.

"I disagree," Nina said in a singsong voice. "I've known the man for seven years, and not one time have I seen him treat a woman like that."

I shrugged. "Well, none of the others were pregnant with his child," I pointed out, trying to keep my head in reality and not let it zoom to the clouds.

Nina walked over to the oven to open it. "Mmhmm," she said with a roll of her eyes. "I'm sure that's all it is."

Goldie leaned a hip against the edge of the counter and wagged her eyebrows at me. "Jars said Prez had you wrapped up in his cut last time you were here."

Nina placed a pan of cornbread on a hot plate, then gave me a pointed look. "And that sure as hell has never happened. Judgment don't put their cut on any woman unless they're staking a claim. And when I say claim, I mean ole-lady status. That, and being put on the back of his bike."

I frowned. "The back of his bike?" I asked, wondering what that meant exactly.

Sometimes, biker talk didn't mean what it sounded like. I'd learned that by living here for two weeks.

Nina placed a hand on her hip. "Exactly what I said. If Prez puts his cut on you or puts you on the back of his bike, that is a major deal. It's saying, *She's mine*. And, honey, he ain't ever done that."

I licked my bottom lip and glanced over at where he sat on a sofa. He was talking to Brick at the moment, but there were others around him. I didn't much care for the blonde woman sitting on the armrest, entirely too close to him. I'd seen her here once before. I knew she worked at one of their clubs. Nina had called her Demi.

"I rode on the back of his bike the night I met him," I said, staring at the woman who couldn't take her hungry eyes off Liam.

Nina's hand grabbed my arm. "What?" she gasped.

I tore my focus off the stripper to look at her. She looked surprised and almost giddy.

"I, uh—he gave me a ride. That's how we ended up in my motel room before, um, well, having sex," I said, then pointed at my stomach.

Goldie stepped closer so that we were in a tight circle now. "Prez gave you a ride on his bike the first night you met him?" she asked, then swung her eyes to Nina, grinning from ear to ear.

Nina chuckled. "Oh, honey. If that man put you on the back of his bike, then he'd already decided he was gonna rock your world, and whether he admits it or not, he was considering more. He doesn't do that."

It seemed silly. He'd just given me a ride. I found it hard to believe he had never given another woman a ride on his bike. I glanced over again to see Demi taking the empty beer from Liam and handing him another. She made sure to bend over far enough that her barely covered chest was on display.

Liam didn't seem to notice and took the bottle while looking at Brick, who was talking. Demi sat back down on the armrest beside Liam, but this time, she was closer. Her legs turned toward him, as well as her body.

"Oh God," Nina groaned. "Ignore her."

I tore my gaze off the woman and forced a smile. "Who?" I asked as if I didn't know what she was talking about.

Nina pursed her lips. "You know who. Demi and her pathetic attempt to get Liam's attention. He's not touched her in a year at least. Her title as Liam's favorite has been gone, and she's struggling to get it back. She's been the oldest out of the strippers that they employee for four years now. Before, when everyone knew Liam took her to his bed more than anyone else, she had that to make her feel superior."

Hearing that Liam had liked her once, enough to have sex with her a lot, sank heavy in my stomach. What if he decided he missed whatever it was she had done that made her his favorite? Would he sleep with her again? He never claimed we were exclusive, but I also knew he wanted our baby to be safe. He wouldn't go out and have sex with her or anyone else, then come back to me, right?

"You shouldn't have told her that." Goldie's tone sounded scolding.

I blinked and tried to push all those thoughts aside. I was here with my friends, and I wanted to enjoy it. Not sit around, being jealous of other women who'd been with Liam.

"I'd rather her hear the truth instead of someone like Amethyst telling her bits of it to stir things up. We all have a past. She's in Liam's. Nothing more," Nina said, then squeezed my arm. "Let's get this food set out so the lot of them can eat. I want to talk about you and Liam. His future," she said with a wink.

I so wanted to be his future.

I helped put the food out on the long countertop and tried my best not to glance over at Liam. He was leaning forward with his elbows on his knees, saying something to Jars. His brows were drawn together, as if he was angry about something. Demi reached over and placed her hand on his shoulder.

I waited. Silently begging Liam to remove it. Shrug her off. Something. He didn't do anything. He continued speaking to Jars while Demi began massaging his shoulder. She moved closer, then turned her head, and her eyes collided with mine. A slow smile slid across her face before she turned back to Liam.

I felt sick.

Nina held out a plate for me, but I shook my head.

"I'm not hungry, but I need a little air. I forgot how packed it gets in here at mealtime," I told her with a tight smile.

I didn't miss the concerned glance she gave Goldie, but I had no time to assure them I was fine. My hormones could trigger my emotions at any time, and then the floodgates would open wide. That would be humiliating. It was already embarrassing to stand in there, with everyone knowing I was pregnant with his child, while he let a stripper he used to fuck regularly massage his shoulder.

I managed to nod and say hello to the guys I passed on my way to the door. Hopefully, none of them caught on to the reason I was leaving. It'd just make me look pathetic.

Once the red door swung closed behind me, I took a deep breath and walked down a little bit before leaning against the wall.

This was fine. I would be fine.

"Liberty?" Country's voice called out, and my head snapped up from the floor I'd been staring at.

Had he followed me out?

"Hey," I said, managing a small smile. I wanted to be alone, but considering Liam had made things ugly the last time I had seen him, I felt like I needed to be nice. He was my friend here.

A scowl came over his face as he studied me. "You okay?" he asked, then nodded his head back toward the door. "That in there got you upset?"

I swallowed against the lump in my throat.

I don't want to talk about it, Country. I'll cry. Go back inside.

I nodded. "Fine. Just a lot of people. I'm taking a breather," I explained.

He shook his head and glared at the door. "That's not right. You deserve more respect than that."

Stop it!

I sucked in a breath and let it out slowly. My eyes stung, and if he didn't stop, I'd lose it.

"That is fine," I lied. "It's been a long day, and I'm tired. I'm not worried about"—I waved a hand in that direction—"whatever that is."

He wasn't convinced. Acting had never been my strong suit.

Country walked over to me, compassion on his handsome face. "I've been worried about you. I'd have called or texted, but"—he stopped as a pained look came over him—"I didn't think that would be okay."

It wouldn't have. I was glad he'd not done either.

"Things have been good. Really good," I told him, not having to lie this time. They had been good. But there was no Demi in Ocala.

Slowly, the thought came to me that, although there was no Demi, Liam went to work every day in an office above a strip club. There were many potential Demis there. Did he have a favorite at Devil's?

Fisting my hand, I placed it on my chest and sucked in a breath. I hadn't thought of that. He didn't seem to find it inappropriate for Demi to touch him here, so what happened at Devil's? I wasn't there to see it.

"Liberty, look at me." Country sounded worried.

I just shook my head. I couldn't look at him. He'd see the devastation on my face. I didn't want his pity. I was so stupid. Liam was a biker. He was around gorgeous, younger, naked women all the time, at his disposal.

"Liberty!" Liam's voice carried loudly down the hallway.

I lifted my head to see him stalking toward me. I tensed when my eyes met his. The rage glaring back at me shifted to Country.

Oh no.

"WHAT THE FUCK ARE YOU DOING?!" he roared.

Country flinched, but he didn't back away. He squared his shoulders and stood there like an idiot. He needed to run. I'd never seen Liam like this, and I wasn't sure *I* didn't need to run. He was frightening.

"She was upset," Country said defensively, but the waver in his voice told me he was scared.

The door swung open again, and I glanced back briefly, afraid to take my eyes off Liam, to see others pouring into the hallway.

Liam moved then, and I stepped back, only to realize he had grabbed the collar on Country's shirt. Opening my mouth to stop him, I watched in horror as Liam's fist connected with Country's face, causing his head to snap back.

Oh no, oh no.

"Liam, stop!" I shouted, reaching for his arm.

His eyes swung to me, and the earlier rage had morphed into something feral as his eyes gleamed in a way that caused me to freeze.

"Go to my suite, Liberty," he ground out.

I shook my head. If I ran, he'd kill Country. Whatever was going on in his head right now was dangerous.

"No. Let him go," I begged.

Liam let out a dark rumble in his chest, and his fist slammed into Country's face again.

I screamed as blood shot from his nose and Country's head drooped forward.

"GO TO MY GODDAMN ROOM!" Liam roared as his eyes bored into me, looking unhinged.

"He will kill him if you don't," Jars said.

A sob broke free as I looked back at the other man. Jars's expression was severe. The others were silent. No one moved to help Country though. I wanted to help him and stop Liam, but the more I said, the worse it seemed to get.

"LIBERTY, NOW!" Liam shouted.

Crying, I turned and ran for the stairs. How I managed to get up them without falling while my vision was so blurry from the tears I didn't know. When I hit the top step, I paused, looking back. Country was hurt because he had been worried about me.

I didn't know that man I'd just watched. Liam had been someone else. Someone violent and cruel.

"Did you touch her?!" Liam's voice carried up the stairs.

I couldn't hear Country's response. Was he even conscious?

I heard feet shuffling, then the deep rumble of another man talking, but it wasn't loud enough for me to make out.

Had one of the others finally stepped in to help Country? Why had they just let Liam do that to him?

Pressing my palms to my eyes, I let out a ragged breath, then turned and walked to Liam's suite. Numbly, I turned the knob to open the door and went inside. His scent met my nose, and more tears prickled my eyes.

I was in love with a monster.

I stared at the bed, but didn't move. The horror of what I'd witnessed replaying in my head. I tried to understand what could have triggered that in Liam. I'd never seen anything like that.

Wrapping my arms around my stomach, I began to think about what he was going to do to me. Would he let me explain? He hadn't given Country that option. We'd done nothing wrong. I hadn't even wanted company. I had been out there because he had been letting some half-naked woman touch him. How was this fair?

The door opened, and I jumped, startled, then spun around to see Liam enter. I winced as it banged closed behind him, and I took a step back away from him as the lock clicked into place. His eyes still held that wild look that I didn't trust.

"He didn't deserve that," I choked out. "He didn't do anything." I stopped talking as he began stalking toward me.

I backed up until I hit the wall. Liam narrowed his eyes as his palms slammed against the wall on each side of my head. I sucked in a breath as my heart began to race.

"Do you want him?" he demanded, his eyes boring into me.

I shook my head. "No! He didn't do anything but ask if I was okay!"

Liam's nostrils flared. "You're not his to check on. He wants what is mine. Now, I am going to ask you again. DO YOU WANT HIM?!"

I trembled, pressing myself further against the wall. "No," I cried. "I was in the hallway because of YOU. If I wanted him, then I wouldn't have cared that you were letting some woman grope you!"

He let out a hiss through his clenched teeth. "What? Demi touching my shoulder upset you?"

Was he serious? I stared up at him, trying to decide if he was sane or not.

"Yes, Liam, I was. And you just broke Country's nose for speaking to me. Do you see some hypocrisy here?"

He shook his head. "No, I don't. Demi touching me didn't register. I don't want her."

I pointed toward the door. "And I don't want Country, but that didn't stop you from hurting him for no reason."

Liam leaned down, his face moving closer to mine. "Country wants to fuck you. There was a reason. He'd been warned to stay away. You aren't his to be concerned about. He broke that order. He paid for it."

Anger was slowly starting to take over as the most dominant emotion charging through me as I looked at Liam. He still justified what he'd done.

"Demi wants to fuck you," I said, jabbing my fingernail into his hard pec. "But I didn't go grab a handful of her hair and toss her to the ground. Did I want to? Yes. I wanted to claw out her eyeballs. But like a sane human, I walked out. Got away from it. What you did has no justification, Liam."

The corner of his lips twitched. Nothing I had just said was remotely funny. If he laughed, I was sure I'd slap him. Even after I'd witnessed a temper that terrified me so bad that I no longer knew if I could stay in his house. There was something off in his head for him to be able to do that to someone.

"I didn't notice it. The girls do that. I'm immune to it. It's just normal. I wasn't aware you'd get jealous."

The way the last word rolled off his tongue annoyed me. I wanted to shout that I wasn't jealous, but that would be a pointless lie. I'd just admitted to wanting to claw her eyes out.

I crossed my arms over my chest, lifting my chin. "So, the girls all do that. When you're at Devil's and I'm tucked away at your house, strippers are massaging your shoulders? What else do they do, Liam? That you're *immune* to?"

I couldn't do this. It hurt too much. He was going to shatter me in a way I would never recover. The deeper I got into this, the worse it would be when he ended it.

His thumb brushed my cheek, and I jerked away from his touch. He didn't get to do that. Not after all this. I wasn't going to be weak.

"What if I tell you none of them will touch me again?" he said in a raspy whisper. "I'll make sure it is clear that it isn't welcome. Would that make you happy?"

I refused to meet his eyes and glared at the wall instead while the pad of his thumb moved to my bottom lip.

"Don't do it for me," I said. "If you hadn't thought to do it already, clearly, you like it. I don't want to stand in your way."

A low chuckle caused his warm breath to tickle the side of my face. "This is sexy as fuck—you know that?"

I tensed as the area between my legs decided to wake up. My damn body was a traitor.

"Don't," I warned him. "You can't act like a psycho, hurting an innocent man after a stripper you used to fuck was all over you, and talk to me like that."

Liam stilled, and I wondered if I had pushed too far. Had I not been easy this time and he was tired of it? Why deal with my anger when he could just go crook his finger at dozens of women and one would come running?

"You heard about that, huh?" he asked.

I realized I'd said something that Nina had told me and I shouldn't have. I had to fix it.

"Just a good guess," I blurted.

His fingertips trailed down my neck. "Sure it was," he replied.

When he reached my cleavage, I started to tell him to stop, but he trailed over to my shoulder. I was not going to react to this. Even if his touch aroused me, even when I wanted to hit him.

"Once, Demi was my go-to around here. She wasn't clingy, and there was no drama. We had a no-strings setup, and it worked. But then she began to act like there was more to us. Started hinting for it. I was bored, and it ended," he said.

Closing my eyes, I tried to fight the ache beginning to stir between my legs.

"Is that my future too? What happens when I want more? And you're bored and you end it." It wasn't really a question. I was saying it more for me than for him.

Gritting my teeth, I turned to finally look at him. His hooded eyes were watching me.

"I won't be her. I won't hang around, waiting for some scrap of your attention."

Liam tucked some of my loose hair behind my ear. "You could never be her," he said softly. "You're the mother of my child."

I wanted to scream, *That's not what I meant*. I needed something more than that.

"Why did you hit Country?" I asked him.

His eyes went from my ear, which he'd been momentarily fascinated with, to look into my eyes. "I thought I'd made that clear," he replied. "He wants what is mine."

I was about to push him, but it was the only way I could force something out of him that would give me hope. That would reassure me when I was no longer pregnant, I'd be more than the mother of his child.

"And when you and I end this and we go to just being our child's parents who get along, what if he wants me then?"

I held my breath as a flicker of the man I'd seen downstairs returned to his eyes. That was good. I had pointed out what could happen. Although it wouldn't. I didn't want Country.

I loved him. Even his insanity downstairs hadn't been enough to dull the way I felt.

"I'll kill him," Liam said in a cold tone that made me shiver.

I'd come this far, so backing down now wasn't an option.

"So, after you, any man I date, you'll kill? That seems unfair. You'll be bored with me, and I'll have needs—"

My feet left the ground, cutting off what I was going to say, and Liam carried me over to the bed and dropped me on it.

"Don't fucking talk about your needs, Liberty. Not in the same sentence where you mention another man."

He grabbed my blouse and ripped it open, buttons flying free. Gasping, I stared down at my exposed breasts just as his hands cupped them. That sight never got old.

"You got needs?" he growled. "I take care of those needs. You think some other man can make that pussy squirt like I do? Hmm?" He tossed my shirt down, then grabbed my skirt.

"Don't rip it! I don't have many that fit," I reminded him.

A twisted laugh fell from his lips as he snatched it down, and I heard the sound of fabric tearing.

"I'll go buy you all the fucking clothes you want."

That was not the point. I didn't want him buying me anything. The longer he saw me as a charity case who needed someone to take care of me, the less likely it was that I would ever win his love, and I wanted that. More than anything.

"Liam," I said as his fingers slid into the sides of my panties and he jerked them down, "we don't need to do this."

He discarded his shirt as I sat there, naked, staring up at him. Unable to look away.

What had I been saying? Oh, yes, the, uh …

His jeans and boxer briefs went next as he shoved them down far enough for me to see his erection. The head was already red and swollen. He kicked off his boots, then finished with his jeans. I had been about to say something.

"What don't we need to do?" he asked, taking my waist and tossing me back further on the bed. "Is it this?" His words had barely left his mouth before his tongue licked from my entrance to my clit.

My hands went to his head as I cried out.

"That sure is a creamy pussy for something we don't need to do," he said while flicking his tongue out and lapping at me like a treat he couldn't eat fast enough.

"Liam," I moaned, lifting my hips and threading my fingers in his hair.

"You definitely needed this," he said with a dark chuckle.

I was too lost in the pleasure to care that he was showing me just how little self-control I had.

"So pretty," he murmured as his finger ran through my folds, then held me open. "Tight little cunt already clenching. Wanting my big cock to stuff it full."

Another cry passed my lips. His finger slid inside me, and he began to pump it as his tongue played with my clit. I was going to come. I opened my mouth to tell him when the warm gush happened, and this time, I saw it—the actual liquid that came shooting out of me.

"See that?" Liam said, licking up everywhere it had gone. "You need to feel that, don't you?"

His hazel eyes were almost black as he looked up at me through his lashes, cleaning me.

I'd never done that before. Only with him. Did he do some trick to make me do that?

"The next time some younger fuck tries to take what's mine, just remember," he snarled as he sat up, then grabbed my hips and flipped me onto my stomach, "whose cock this cunt craves."

His hand landed on my butt, and I jerked from the sting.

"Get that ass in the air," he ordered.

I moved to my elbows and bent my knees as I raised myself off the mattress. Liam ran his hands over my bottom, and then his lips touched the spot he'd just hit.

"I love seeing my red handprint here."

Wetness trickled down my thighs, and I wiggled my bottom. "Liam, please," I begged.

"You need me, baby?" he murmured. "No young fuck can do it like I can." His words were followed by his hard length plunging into me.

"YES!" I cried out at the relief of being filled.

"Whose dick is this?" he demanded.

I turned my head to look back at him. "Yours," I panted.

"Say my name."

"Liam."

He started thrusting into me hard. "Is this Country's cock?"

I shook my head. "No."

"Do you want it to be?"

His eyes had that wild look in them again as the bed shook beneath us.

"NO! I just want yours. I always want yours," I told him, hearing the desperation in my voice. "I wake up wanting it. I think about it all the time."

He tightened his grip on my hips. "Take it then. I want you to feel this tomorrow and remember who owns this cunt."

"YES! GOD! That feels good!" I moaned, meeting each of his thrusts. "I'm gonna come!"

"That's what I want. Coat my dick with it," he encouraged, his voice sounding hoarse.

His name tore from my chest as I convulsed from a blissful surge.

"FUUUCK!" he roared at the same time his cock jerked inside me, releasing his thick ropes of cum.

When his hands released their hold on me, I fell onto the mattress. Liam moved beside me and pulled me against his chest.

The sound of our ragged breathing filled the room. We remained silent for several minutes. The heaviness of exhaustion started to pull on me.

Liam played with the hair that was draped over my shoulder. Wrapping a strand around his finger, then letting it fall before doing it again.

I wanted to say something. He'd distracted me with sex when I was trying to make a point. But the things he'd said about younger men stopped me. Was that bothering him? Did he think I'd want someone closer to my age eventually?

"I'm not sorry I hit him," Liam said. "I'm not even sorry I broke his fucking nose. But I am sorry I yelled at you. I shouldn't have done that."

I closed my eyes and wished I were a stronger person. Perhaps one with better morals. I'd like to think I was most of the time. But if we all had our kryptonite, then Liam Walsh was mine.

Thirty-Four

LIAM

A glass of whiskey slid across the table I was sitting at, going over the background checks on the new girls who had applied for a job and made it past Tex's approval. I glanced up to see Tex move into the other entrance of the circular booth to sit across from me.

"Country's coming home from the hospital today. Surgery went well, and the damage to his nose will heal for the most part. It'll never look the same," he said, taking a drink from his own glass.

I'd already gotten the text from Brick, telling me this, but I nodded.

Liberty and I had left early the next morning after I spoke to Brick and Jars. She didn't know Brick had had to take Country to the hospital because he couldn't breathe through his nose. I didn't want anyone saying anything to her about it either. She'd worry, and I didn't think I could stand her worrying about another man. But more importantly, I didn't like the idea of her stressing over anything. It wasn't good for the baby.

"Kinda wish I'd been there," he drawled. "It's been a long time since you put a brother down for disrespect. Just like the good ole days. Hotheaded, mean-as-hell Liam, bashing in skulls."

I picked up the glass and took a drink.

"He had been warned," I said. I wasn't the same reckless idiot I'd been back then.

Tex nodded. "True. Back in the day, there was no warning."

I held up one of the background checks. "This one is trouble. I don't care that you noted she can shoot ping-pong balls from her cunt across the stage. Not worth it. Read it if you need to, but she's a no," I told him, then tossed the paper down in front of him.

He let out a disappointed sigh, but didn't pick it up. Instead, he leaned back in his seat and studied me. I wasn't in the mood for whatever he wanted to talk about. I already had a feeling I knew.

"When are you gonna admit that this woman has you hooked?" he asked.

He was like a dog with a bone. I'd known this was about Liberty. He couldn't seem to keep his nose out of my business.

"Don't see how this concerns you," I said. "Focus on the new hires."

"Well, seeing as how I had to fire two of them because they couldn't seem to stop coming on to you and the rest I've had to warn not to touch you unless they want the same fate, I feel like I'm invested."

"It's my personal life. Not club business," I retorted, trying to study the next background check.

"You broke a brother's nose so bad that he needed reconstructive surgery. Your personal life is bleeding into club business."

I slammed the paper down and glared at him. "He had been warned," I repeated.

Tex nodded and leaned forward with his elbows on the table. "I'm not saying it was wrong. I'm saying a woman is what brought out the beast. So, just say it, you want to keep her? You want that sweet, little, young baby momma in your bed permanently. The sooner you admit it, the better you'll feel. I'm trying to help you here."

I threw back the rest of my whiskey. Hearing him talk about Liberty in my bed permanently caused shit inside me that I was working on controlling to flare up. It was hard to tamp down.

Hell, I liked Country. He was a good man. But in that moment, I could have killed him. Simply because he fit her better than I did. He wouldn't be an old man too soon. They were at the same stage in life. And I hated him for that. For being what I wasn't.

"Yes," I ground out. "She's different. I feel …" I paused, not sure I could say the words out loud. I felt guilty, thinking them.

For most of my adult life, I'd believed that I'd only love one girl. No one would touch my heart the way Etta had. And until now, no one had come close to even causing a ripple.

Liberty hadn't touched my heart. She'd placed a hook in it and taken it. When she was tucked in my arms, I didn't wish it were Etta. I completely forgot Etta. Liberty's smile, those honey-brown eyes, the way her stomach looked, rounded with our child—it owned me. But saying that meant facing the other side of it. I was sixteen years older than her. Sure, right now, I was fit, had my health, I could fuck her until she passed out. But how long did I have before those things started to fade? What happened when she was still youthful and full of life while I was getting back pains or struggling with an erection—or worse, I'm diagnosed with some fatal illness and she had to give up her best years so that she could nurse me until I died?

I'd thought of it all. I lay awake at night, going over every-fucking-thing that could happen.

"What do you feel?" Tex asked when I didn't finish.

"Like I need her to breathe."

Tex's eyes widened, and then a slow smile crept over his face. "Goddamn," he muttered.

My sentiments exactly.

If there was a God, he sure as fuck wasn't a fan of mine. I had believed that the love of my life was my first love, and I'd lost her, so I'd live the rest of my life, not knowing how it felt to have… this. To go to bed at night, holding someone I didn't want to live without; to feel joy from the sound of her laughter; to have a family and watch our kids grow. I had made my peace with it.

Until Liberty.

Now, that life was all I thought about. I was mourning something I knew I couldn't keep. It would be selfish to do so, and I couldn't be selfish with her.

"Then, you're gonna put a ring on it," he said.

My chest burned, and I wished he'd brought the bottle of whiskey over here if we were gonna have this conversation.

I shook my head. "No, I'm not."

Tex dropped his glass onto the table. "Why the fuck not?"

"I don't think I can have her and lose her. I wouldn't be able to survive that."

Tex sat back, staring at me like he didn't understand it. What was so hard for him to get? Did he not see it?

"You're already planning a future breakup that might not happen? I don't want you slamming your fist in my face, too, but, Prez, that's weak. There's a country song about this, probably several, but the point is, you don't want to miss the best thing that ever happened to you because you're afraid. Yeah, it might fucking end." He paused, then let out a sigh. "And she could die. You survived that before. Don't let it be what holds you back."

It took me a minute to figure out what he was saying, and then it dawned on me that he thought that I was afraid I'd lose her like I had Etta. This had nothing to do with Etta. Yes, I had loved her, but I'd been a kid. I wasn't that kid anymore. I'd lived life.

I knew that every day was a gift and we weren't promised tomorrow. But this wasn't about death taking her from me. This was about the inevitable—time. I would grow old, and she would be years behind me. Men her age would come along, and the old man she was shackled to would be a weight.

"One day, she'll turn around, and I'll be seventy years old, and she … won't be."

Thirty-Five
LIBERTY

All the things that needed to be said had been swept under the rug, and it was my fault too. I might as well have held up the damn rug while he did the sweeping. Why? Because the idea of rocking the boat and losing what we had right now had me doing whatever I had to in order to hold on. Every day that we spent together, it felt more secure. It was no longer just me, and I knew that. He didn't say it, but he felt something. It was more than a jealous, maniacal outburst.

Liam Walsh might not love me—yet—but he was falling. I could see it in the way he looked at me. Not just when our gazes connected during sex either. I would catch him watching me doing something as simple as cooking or watching television, and I'd look up, and his eyes would tell me what he couldn't say.

So, yes, I was letting go of the entire horror that had happened with Country.

Liam had moved my OB-GYN to one here in Ocala that his daughter also used. He didn't want me going back to Miami anytime soon. It was obvious, even if he didn't say it.

The group text I had with Nina, Dolly, and Goldie helped keep me connected to them. I did miss them, but right now, I was at the only place I wanted to be. With Liam.

My next appointment, the one where we'd find out the gender, was tomorrow. We were at the halfway mark, and I still had no idea what to plan for after the baby came.

I kept waiting for him to mention turning the unused room upstairs into a nursery, but nothing. Not even a peep about the things the baby would need once it arrived. Once we knew what it was, I had to start thinking about that. And if Liam wasn't going to give me any clarity, then I had to get a good job. One with normal hours, health insurance, and security.

I'd gone online and found samples of résumés, then made one of my own in Liam's home office he never used. I printed it out and sent it in to several different places, but so far, I'd not heard from any of them.

I finished putting in the burning bush around the oak tree closest to the house, then stood up to stand back and admire them. The sound of the gate opening caught my attention, and I stepped around the tree to see a silver Mercedes SUV coming down the drive. I didn't know that car, but for them to have the code to get through the gate meant they had been invited.

Liam wasn't home yet, but it was almost six, and he'd be here soon. I took off my gardening gloves, then laid them in the tote that held my supplies Liam had bought for me. The vehicle came to a stop, and I waited to see who emerged.

The door swung open, and out stepped a woman. She was young with platinum-blonde hair draped over her shoulder that held a loose curl at the ends. Calling the woman gorgeous would be an understatement. Knowing she had the code to get into Liam's gate made my stomach feel sour.

"Hello," she said as she walked toward me with a smile on her face.

"Hello," I replied, waiting for her to explain why she was here.

Her gaze dropped to my stomach briefly before looking back at me. The breeze blew her hair, and she tucked it behind her ear, then laughed as she had to hold her sundress down too. Her laugh was lovely. I needed this woman to have some faults because she wasn't lost. And the idea of her being close to Liam was getting harder to accept by the moment.

"I'm sorry for dropping in like this," she said as she stopped a few feet away from me. "I can be impatient."

When I said nothing, her smile widened, and her eyes sparkled, reminding me of clear blue water when the sun hit it just right.

She held out her hand. "I should start by introducing myself. I'm Madeline Hughes, Liam's daughter."

I blinked, completely stunned. That wasn't what I'd expected. I knew he had a grown daughter and grandkids, but he'd not made a move to introduce me to any of them.

Did she know I was pregnant? I felt so unprepared.

Fumbling, I took her hand and shook it. "It's nice to meet you. I'm, uh …" What did I say?

He must have told her about me, right? Another one of those boat-rocking things I didn't bring up with him.

Her eyes were kind as she reassured me, "I know who you are, Liberty."

I instantly relaxed. "Oh, good. I didn't know. He hasn't said and ..." I trailed off, feeling awkward.

"Liam can be hardheaded and difficult. I hope you've figured that out by now," she told me. Then, her gaze drifted back to my stomach. "I don't know what all he's told you about me, but he's the only blood relative I have." Her eyes came back to meet mine. "And seeing as you are carrying my only sibling, I wanted to get to know you. I'd like to be friends even if Liam is making that difficult."

He was? She had been asking him about me? The reasons why he wouldn't want me to meet her or get to know her were all depressing.

"I'm glad you came by," I said, although I wasn't sure if I was or not. If she hadn't, I wouldn't have known Liam didn't want his family to know me. I could have continued to live in my own little fantasy world I'd been building. The one where I thought he was falling in love with me. But could he love me if he was ashamed of me?

The sound of the gate opening again meant he was home. I would get to see how he reacted to this. Maybe since things had started to change between us, he hadn't wanted to share me yet. I liked that thought. Who was I kidding? I liked any thought that meant Liam had strong feelings for me.

"Oops," Madeline said with a grin. "I didn't expect him home so early."

This wasn't early for him. Not anymore at least. He had started leaving the club about the time it opened to come home to me. We had dinner together, sat on the front porch swing, talked about things—just not the things that we should be talking about—watched movies, and then there was the sex. Lots of sex.

I wanted to invite her to stay for dinner, but without seeing Liam's reaction to her being here, I felt like perhaps I shouldn't just yet.

Liam parked his Harley, and I watched him sling his leg over as he got off, then start this way. He smiled at Madeline.

"Didn't know you were paying me a visit," he said to her, seeming happy about her being here.

But he didn't look my way.

"Well, I wanted to meet Liberty," she said, not worrying about upsetting him at all.

He glanced at me then and gave me a nod. "How long have you been here?"

Why had he nodded at me as if I were an acquaintance? This morning, he'd pinned me against the kitchen counter and kissed me until I lost my breath. I didn't expect him to do that in front of his daughter, but this was odd.

"Not even ten minutes," she replied.

He tilted his head toward the house. "Come on inside and get a drink. Tell me how Cree's liking the preschool life. I haven't talked to him since school started."

Madeline looked over at me as if she was going to say something.

"Flowers look good, Liberty. Nice job. Has Ozzy been out for his evening run already? Or have you not gotten to that yet?" The businesslike tone he was using as he kept his distance from me was saying more than any words could.

I cleared my throat as my face flushed. "Uh, he was out here until I started the digging. But it's been an hour. I'll, uh …" I couldn't find my words.

With Madeline's presence and the fact that Liam was treating me like I worked for him in front of her, the clarity was hitting too hard.

"I can let him out. Continue with what you were doing," he said, then looked back at Madeline. "Come on."

A small frown furrowed her brow as she gave me a glance, as if she wasn't sure what to think. I managed a smile, although I didn't know how I did it.

She reached out and squeezed my hand, as if to reassure me. "I didn't mean to interrupt you. We will make plans for lunch one day. That way, we can talk."

I wasn't going to be able to get words out past the boulder lodged in my esophagus. I just nodded, then turned and went back to the tree, acting as if I had something more to do here.

When I heard the door to the house close, I picked up my tote and walked back to the storage shed. My mind was reeling. The part of me that had been wishing for a fairy tale tried so hard to hold on while the blatant truth that had just unfolded in front of me stood there, mocking its existence.

Ozzy appeared at my side, and I dropped the gardening tools and bent down to wrap my arms around him. I buried my face into his neck, and he stayed still, as if he understood this was what I needed. No whining or wiggling around, trying to play.

As demoralizing as this was, I knew that my knowing was for the best. I could stop playing house and focus on the future Liam never spoke about.

The slamming of a door caused both Ozzy and me to jump. I stood up and looked toward the front of the house. There was no talking, but the sound of a car door closing, then the engine starting up meant Madeline was already leaving. She'd barely been inside.

I didn't think I could face Liam right now. There was a lot I had to process. Decide how I would move forward and the best course. I was doing myself a disservice, pretending this was something it wasn't. I wanted it so badly that I'd made up things in my head because that was all it could have been. Whatever signs I'd thought I'd seen, I had been so very wrong. Or just desperate.

Another door slammed, and I watched as Liam walked around the side of the house. I stayed still. If he had something to say, then I'd listen, but there were no words that could take back what had just happened.

His expression appeared as if he was in pain. That wasn't going to work. Whatever it was. He didn't get to be in pain. He hadn't just been humiliated.

When he got too close, I took a step back.

"That's good," I said, holding up a hand.

His jaw clenched, and he stared at me. His hazel eyes were full of regret, and I'd give it to him—he looked like he was hurting. Too bad I didn't care. My wounds were too deep and raw.

"That was …" he started, then stopped.

I waited. I wasn't going to make this easy on him. He ran a hand over his head, as if he had something to be frustrated about.

"I'm sorry," he finally said.

I raised my eyebrows. That was it? He was sorry?

"We aren't five, Liam. *Sorry* isn't a magical word."

He let out a deep sigh and stared off into the backyard. "I can't let Madeline be affected by this, Liberty. I don't know how else to explain it. But she's my daughter, who I only got to meet six years ago. What we have is new, and I'm trying to be the father she didn't have. Make up for all the time I lost.

And dragging her into this," he said, waving his hand between the two of us, "it's not fair. She wants me to find someone to grow old with and all that shit. She worries about me being alone, and if she thinks we are … if there is …" He stopped and let out a groan, looking like what he was saying was tearing him up inside.

There was a part of me that wanted to reach out and reassure him because my stupid ass loved him that much. It was why I played his game. Lived in the now, pretending like this was all okay while we left out things. Me meeting his family, for example, talking about our pasts, planning our future. He might want me to an extent, but he didn't want me bad enough. If he was going to love me, he would've by now.

"Tell me you understand." There was pleading in his voice.

"I do," I replied.

He studied me, or perhaps he was waiting on me to elaborate. I didn't. I had nothing else to say. Yes, I understood. He had quite literally crushed my soul, but I did understand. I understood everything I hadn't before Madeline showed up. I got it loud and clear now.

"That's it. You don't have anything else to say?"

I shook my head. "No. That's all."

"You're hurt," he said gently.

I wasn't hurt. Not this time. That was a very inadequate description of what I was going through. "I promise you I'm not."

"Yes, you are!" he demanded, raising his voice. "I stood right there"—he pointed to where we had been when he arrived—"and I ignored you. I acted like you were merely … merely …"

He looked at me as if I was supposed to fill in the blanks for him. I didn't. This game was done. I'd say he won.

"FUCK!" he shouted, running his hands over his head and staring at me with a panicked gleam in his eyes.

"Just yell at me! Hit me! Do something, Liberty. You are killing me here."

Nope. He didn't get to shatter me, then have me do his bidding. That was over.

I wasn't someone he could be proud of. The mother of his child was completely dependent on him. I had nothing to give back. I couldn't share the load. I was a burden.

He might not love me, but he was damn well gonna have a reason to respect me. I would prove to him that I was worthy of being this child's mom. That I would make our baby proud even if I had failed to give him a reason to feel that way about me.

"Say something! Please," he begged.

Ozzy barked at him, as if to tell him to shut up. At least I'd won the love of one soul in this house. I wasn't completely unlovable.

"Are you ready for me to make dinner?" I asked. "I have steaks marinating."

He stood there as if he could read my mind if he looked hard enough.

"That's it? I'm trying to talk to you about something, and you want to know if I'm ready for dinner?" he asked incredulously.

"You wanted me to talk. I was done discussing the other."

"DAMMIT, LIBERTY!"

Ozzy stepped between us, and a low growl came from him as he bared his teeth.

Liam looked at his dog for a moment, then turned and stalked away. He didn't head for the house. Instead, he threw his leg over his Harley and started it up. The engine revved to life, and he spun out of the driveway while Ozzy and I stayed there in the setting sun and stared after him long after the gate closed behind him.

Thirty-Six

LIAM

Too much sunlight. I threw my arm over my eyes and groaned.

"What the fuck?" I grunted. My head felt like an entire marching band was using it as their drum.

"Wake up, sunshine." Tex's voice reminded me of nails on a chalkboard.

I winced. "Shh."

"Sorry," he replied. "I left you alone, thinking you'd wake up and pull it together, but that's not happening, and now, I've got your baby momma's sister downstairs, who wants to see you and won't leave. I don't have time for that because we have a club opening in ten minutes, so I need you to deal with your ex–doctor girlfriend or whatever she was. Then go home to Liberty. Whatever sent you over here last night, making you determined to drink every ounce of whiskey in the place, fix it."

The door closing behind him as he left was a relief. No more talking. I needed some water and a bottle of aspirin. The entire thing. Damn, how much had I drunk? I'd not had a hangover this bad in over twenty years.

What had I been thinking?

Rolling onto my side, I almost fell on the floor. Frowning, I squinted to see where the hell I was. My office. I was on the sofa. Why was I on the sofa in my office?

Pieces started to filter in, and then it all came crashing back.

Liberty.

Just like that, my chest felt like I'd ripped it open and pulled out my own heart again. The whiskey had made me forget, but that was only a temporary fix. I'd fucked up. Fisting my hands, I closed my eyes as the memory of her face yesterday taunted me. That beautiful smile and her bright, shining eyes, always there when I got home, making me feel like every bad thing that had ever happened to me was worth it because it had led me to her.

Until yesterday.

A knock on my office door started up the drumline in my head again.

Why couldn't everyone leave me alone? I had to fix what I'd done.

"GO AWAY!" I shouted, then pressed my fingers to my temples to ease the stabbing pain that came with it.

Another knock.

Who the hell was that?

Standing up, I stalked over to the door and jerked it open, ready to unleash a string of curses on whoever it was, but the sight of Selena knocked me off-balance. I'd not expected her.

Oh, wait, Tex had said something about the doctor being here.

"What do you want?" I growled.

The smile on her face brightened, as if I'd greeted her like I wanted her here. What was she up to?

"Liam, you smell like you've had better days," she said in an annoyingly cheerful tone. "Life been stressful?"

I glared at her. Talking meant more pain, and she didn't rank on the important meter for me to use my words.

She flipped her hair over her shoulder, and ... was she batting her eyelashes at me? Was this a bad drunken dream? Because I'd rather be woken up and deal with the hangover.

Stepping past me, she walked into my office. "Whew, you need lots of water. It's the best fix. Greasy food too. Although don't tell anyone I am admitting that."

Ugh, would she shut up?

"Why are you here?" I asked, my voice gravelly, matching the way my head felt.

She moved closer to me. I didn't like the look on her face. I knew that look. She was flirting.

I held up both hands. "Whoa. Personal space," I warned.

She placed her hands on her hips and pressed her lips out in a pout.

Oh God, stop. Please, someone, end this torture and get her crazy ass out of here. I have too much shit to deal with.

"I miss you. And before you tell me again, I know—*I know*—you got trapped by some bartender. I needed time to process it, but I did. And I am okay with it. I'm a pediatrician after all. I love children. It's not a turnoff for me. I think you doing the right thing and being there for the baby is truly selfless."

I held my hands up, shaking my head. She needed to go.

Where was Tex? Why hadn't he stopped her from coming up here?

"No," I said with enough force to make me wince again. "Not interested. Go away. What else do I have to say to make you leave?"

There was a flash of fury that I didn't miss in her eyes, even in my hungover state. She didn't like being told no. I'd missed that about her before, but thinking back, she had pouted about things. Oh, who cared? She was not important.

"Whatever lies she's told you about me, I should get the chance to defend myself. All she does is lie. She needed somewhere to live, and you think it's a coincidence that she was so willing to fuck a stranger? No. She wanted someone to take care of her. She's a manipulative liar. She's always been that way. She told my father things about me to make him hate me. She couldn't stand that he might love me more." She let out a fake sob and wiped at a tear that wasn't there.

When she'd started talking, I'd thought she was making assumptions about the woman I had gotten pregnant, but I realized she knew it was Liberty. She was talking about Liberty.

My blood began to heat as I stared at her.

"She's not who you think she is. Believe me. She'll probably rob you blind."

My hand was around her narrow neck before I knew what I was doing. "She doesn't have to rob me blind. I'd sign over the deed to my house if she asked. Now, you have one goddamn second to get the hell outta my club!" I said, then shook her because she was a woman and I couldn't hit her. But, God, I wanted to. I loathed the air she breathed.

"I am telling you, Liam—"

"GET OUT!" I shouted at the top of my lungs. Headache be damned. The only thing I felt was fury.

I heard footsteps, and Tex was there. He looked from her to me.

"Get her out before I throw her down the stairs," I said, not looking back at her as I walked over to my desk.

"This way, lady," Tex said.

"He won't listen to me," she cried.

"If you don't listen to me, he will do what he said. He's not in a good place right now, and you are his target at the moment. You need to run like hell."

"You'll regret it!"

"Shut the fuck up, woman!" Tex said, and I watched as Tex grabbed both her arms and shoved her through the door before he slammed it closed.

Liberty had lived with that kind of jealousy and hatred.

I pressed my fist to my chest. That wasn't easing up anytime soon. I had to fix the royal shit show I had created. If I had to get my whole family over to the house and get down on one knee, I would do it.

Screw old age. I could stay in shape. I'd do whatever was required to take care of her. There was the fear I'd lose her, but I'd be damned if I went the rest of my life without her. I'd go to my death bed, making sure she never again felt the way I'd made her feel yesterday.

Thirty-Seven

LIBERTY

I touched the ultrasound photo that I had left on the kitchen counter for Liam.

When the nurse had first shown me the little face, I had started crying. By the time she told me our baby's sex, I was in a full-blown sob. They were so worried about me that the doctor came in and someone had to bring me a glass of water. I couldn't get myself under control and explain I wasn't going crazy. My emotional wall I'd tried to hold up while I dealt with the swings fate kept aiming my way crumbled upon seeing the life inside me. The one that looked like a baby now. With little fingers and toes. It was the trigger that had cracked me.

That tiny baby's photos was the reason I'd managed to drive home. After a doctor's visit where I found out the sex of my baby, alone, without Liam, who never came home last night or called and then blew off the appointment, I'd had the good fortune to run into Selena in the parking lot at the hospital.

No, I wouldn't think about that. My new OB-GYN had told me several times that I had to calm down. Stress wasn't good for the baby. I had to be strong and survive this for him.

The letter I'd written Liam lay beside the photo, along with the keys to his car and the house. I'd made sure Ozzy had plenty time outside and filled both his food and water bowls. Thinking too hard about leaving him behind would send me into another fit of tears I might not be able to get under control.

Lifting my eyes, I looked around at the house one more time. It was never meant to be mine. This life here with Liam and our baby. But even though it was ending this way, I would hold the good memories close. I just couldn't dwell on them for now. I had to heal, and unlike with death, time could heal my soul this time. And if time didn't, I was sure my son would.

I looked down at my phone. The Uber was seven minutes away.

I bent down and kissed Ozzy on the head one more time. "Thanks for being the best friend a girl could have," I told him.

Then, I stood up, took the handle of a suitcase in each hand, and pulled them toward the front door. Ozzy whimpered when I walked out and closed the door, leaving him inside. I took one suitcase down the front doorsteps, repeated with the other one, then wheeled them down the driveway.

By the time I reached the end and the gates opened for me, my driver pulled up. Unable to help myself, I glanced back over my shoulder before handing the driver my suitcases and climbing into the back of the car.

Thirty-Eight

LIAM

It was too quiet. Ozzy walked into the foyer slowly, and he stopped when he saw me. There was no happy greeting or wagging tail. I'd spent the entire drive here going over what I would say, but in the silence, there was an alarm going off in my head.

"LIBERTY!" I called, stalking toward the back of the house to look outside. "LIBERTY!" I shouted again as my heart beat frantically inside my chest.

What had she done? It was one night. She wouldn't do this. She wouldn't leave.

"LIBERTY!"

Maybe she had gone to the store. I paused, then remembered my car was outside. She had to be here.

"LIBERTY!"

I headed for the kitchen. She normally started dinner by now. She could be in the shower after gardening.

I stormed into the kitchen, desperate to see something. A sign that she was here. I scanned the clean, tidy, unused area, until my gaze landed on keys and a note.

No!

I rushed over to it and read it to find out where she was so I could go get her. She'd tell me where she was going. She wouldn't disappear. She was hurting. She'd left because she was upset. I could fix it.

The world fell away around me the moment I saw it. That small photo. Slowly, I reached for it as my hands shook. My eyes burned, and I sucked in a ragged breath.

Written at the top of the photo were the words, *It's a boy!*

My teeth grinding together was the only sound I heard as I stared at the picture. I had missed being there when she'd found out that our baby was a … a boy. She'd been alone. I couldn't go back in time and fix that.

A hot tear rolled down my cheek, and I picked up the letter, written in her neat, feminine script.

> *Liam,*
>
> *As you can see, it's a boy. His heartbeat was once again very strong. He has all ten fingers and toes. He moves a lot, and I might be in for it when he's big enough for me to feel the kicking. But he will be worth it.*
>
> *Before I say anything else, I want to say thank you. For him. There will never be a greater gift that I receive on this earth. We might not have meant to create him, but I believe he was meant to save me.*
>
> *I was lost and lacked direction.*

He has given me a reason to find both.

You and I both know that me staying here until he was born wasn't for the best. It was kind of you to offer, and I stayed because I wanted to be with you. I wanted things you'd told me I couldn't have. That we would never have. But I stayed, believing I could make you fall in love with me. I realize that you can't make a heart love someone. It either does or doesn't.

I sent out a few résumés last week, and today, I received a call. I was offered a job. It pays well, there is a chance for promotion, I'll have normal hours, and I'll have health insurance.

It's time for me to make myself worthy to be our son's mom. I want him to be proud to call me his mother. I don't want to be an embarrassment. I've had enough of that to last a lifetime. I might not be there yet, but I will be. My new life starts now.

As for what happened with Madeline, it was something I needed. I had made up in my head all these fantasies and believed them because I wanted them. That was a wake-up call that we should both be thankful I got.

We have twenty weeks to work out the details before our son arrives. I need some time first without meeting in person or communicating at all. Until I can heal and I'm ready to face the future.

I do not intend to keep you away from our son. I will share him with you. Every kid needs their father. I know that all too well.

But for now, I'm not going to share details about my new job or where I am living. It will give me time to get my feet on the ground. Once I am ready, I'll contact you so we can discuss an arrangement that will work best for him. That's all that matters now. Giving him a happy life full of love.

I'm sure you understand and perhaps you're even relieved.

Liberty

The letter fell from my hand and fluttered slowly to the floor. I stared out the window, not moving for several minutes. When the reality of what I'd done finally sank in, I picked up the glass bowl, filled with fresh fruit, sitting beside the neatly placed keys, and smashed it against the wall while a wail that barely encompassed half of what I was feeling echoed off the walls of my house.

Thirty-Nine

LIBERTY

Buyer for a local garden center—that was the description for the job I had applied for. Out of all the jobs, this was the one I did for fun. I didn't expect to ever hear from them. Other than my love for plants and flowers, I had no experience. It had been a very emotional day for me, so when they'd called, I had taken it, no questions asked.

Now standing in the one-bedroom apartment that had come with the job, I realized I might have made a mistake.

The paperwork that had been left for me to sign and bring into the office tomorrow said the salary was seventy thousand dollars a year. I'd thought I was applying for an hourly job that was hopefully close to twenty dollars an hour. This was clearly meant for someone who had a degree or extensive experience that I did not have.

They must have gotten the applications mixed up.

It was dark outside, and I didn't want to call the contact person listed on the paper this late.

I had planned to stay in a motel until I found somewhere to live, so the email they had sent with the directions to the apartment that was ready for me to move into was shocking. Out of curiosity, I came to check it out, expecting perhaps a tiny room with a toilet and shower in the back of a storage house where the plants were kept.

Not this.

Yep, there had been a major mix-up. When I told them they'd hired Liberty, the bartender with no college degree, I'd be sent packing. I had known this was too good to be true. A job buying plants for a garden center. When had life ever started handing me favors? Never—that was when.

Not wanting to get attached to anything, I didn't walk through the rest of the apartment. I'd get a shower, sleep here, then go tell them tomorrow morning before I went on a job hunt for something I was qualified for.

Sitting down on the sofa, I laid my head back and touched my small bump. I'd been feeling weird butterfly-like flutters in my stomach this evening. It had happened yesterday, too, and I was going to ask the doctor about it, but that had all gone downhill fast. I had become an emotional wreck. It was a miracle they hadn't tried to check me into the psych ward.

I had four weeks until the next appointment, and if Liam wanted to come to that one—I couldn't be sure since he'd not cared about today's checkup—then I had to get my head ready to face him. I sure hoped four weeks would be enough time. Right now, it didn't feel as if a lifetime would be enough.

I missed him.

I laughed out loud. "How pathetic is that?" I asked aloud, then remembered I didn't have Ozzy here to hear me.

There was no one to talk to. It was just me.

I looked down at my stomach. "Not true," I said. "I have you."

The lonely feeling eased some at that thought.

"I'm going to pull it together—I promise you that. By the time you arrive, I'll have a job and an apartment." I paused and looked around. "Probably not this nice, but you can't see this place, so you won't be disappointed."

The weird butterfly feeling was back. I sat there with my hand on my stomach as it continued.

"Is that you?" I stared at my stomach.

Was that him kicking?

I grabbed my cell phone and googled it.

Quickening is when a pregnant woman starts to feel her baby's movements. It might feel like flutters, bubbles, or tiny pulses.

I dropped my phone onto the sofa and placed two hands on my stomach. "That's you!" I squealed as a sliver of joy broke through the agony.

One male had broken my heart, but it seemed another one was already working on mending it.

A knock on the door caused my head to snap up, and I stared in that direction, wide-eyed. Had they figured out their mistake already? Was that them coming to ask me to leave? Very likely.

I patted my stomach and stood up. I could take whatever happened.

When I reached the door, I unlocked it and opened it to see an older lady with short gray hair in a helmet style, wearing a blue pantsuit.

"You must be Liberty," she said as she straightened the tortoiseshell glasses perched on her long, narrow nose. "Very good. Seems you found the place and got in with no problem." She turned and picked up a massive gift basket and then held it out to me. "I am Martha Depough, HR manager for GG Center. This is for you."

I had no choice but to take it or be knocked over by it. "Oh, uh, thank you, but I—there …" I stopped and put the basket down on the table so I could see her while I explained this.

She was over by the paperwork that had been left for me. "Don't worry about this tonight. Just bring it in with you tomorrow."

"Yes, but, like I was trying to say, I believe there has been a mistake," I blurted out, hating that I had to do this. I really wanted to be able to stay here tonight.

Her brows drew together. "How so?"

I smiled. "I'm sure you saw my résumé, and I'm not qualified for a job that comes with an apartment like this, a salary that high, and"—I waved a hand at the basket, filled with food, that was almost half as tall as me—"welcome gifts such as this."

She took out her phone and tapped on the screen. "You are Liberty Virginia Dillard, birth date April 6, 1993. Your last place of work was Abernathy's. Correct?"

"Yes, that's me, but …" I held my hands out at the apartment. "I don't—I mean, I didn't think I was qualified for a job this nice. I don't have a college degree. You saw that, right?"

The woman tucked her phone back into the pocket of her blazer. "You think we made a mistake because you don't have a college degree?"

I nodded.

"Why don't you prove that we didn't make a mistake and show us that you belong here? That you are worth this apartment and the salary attached."

Was she serious? I opened my mouth and closed it. I didn't know what to say. I had been sure she would be ushering me out of here by now.

"What do you say? Do you believe you can do this job?"

I wanted to say I didn't know, but this woman seemed to have faith in me that I didn't. The small flutter in my stomach reminded me of what all I had to fight for.

"Yes. I know I can."

She smiled. "Good," she said, then headed for the door. "I will see you tomorrow morning then."

"Okay, bye. Thank you," I called out.

The door closed behind her, and I looked over at the tower of food, wrapped up in pretty packaging. It looked familiar, but I couldn't figure out where I'd seen something like it before.

Forty

LIAM

I jerked open the door before Madeline could ring the doorbell. Her vehicle pulling down my driveway had been the only moment in the past twenty-four hours that I wasn't in complete torment. The sight of her meant that Blaise had found Liberty.

"You look like you haven't slept in a week," she said, her eyes scanning me before she stepped inside.

Ozzy came walking into the foyer to see who had arrived. He wasn't in much better shape than me. He'd not eaten much since Liberty had left, and he kept pulling his dog bed to the side of my bed she'd slept on, as if he believed she would come back and he wanted to be there.

"Where is she? Did Blaise find her?" I asked, still gripping the doorknob. I wasn't going to sit and visit. I needed a goddamn address.

Madeline smiled at Ozzy. "Hello, Ozzy." Then, she lifted her eyes to me and crossed her arms over her chest.

There was disapproval in her steady gaze that I didn't have time for. She could berate me later. I just needed to get to Liberty.

"That's why I'm here. I told him not to," she informed me.

No. I shook my head. That was what had kept me sane since I'd walked in this house and found Liberty's note and the photo of our baby.

"Madeline, I have to find her," I pleaded, my hoarse voice cracking.

She raised her eyebrows. "If she wanted you to know where she was, then she would have told you. The fact that she did not means she wanted time," she replied.

Fuck. I'd have to find someone who could track her down. She didn't have a car, and her phone was going straight to voice mail. I'd driven to every motel and hotel in the city and outside the city last night. Nothing. No one had her as a guest. A few had told me that they weren't allowed to give out that information, but when I had grabbed them by the collar and pulled them over the counter, they had talked.

Blaise was the fastest way to find her.

"Madeline, please. I messed up. She needs to hear what I have to say," I begged, running my hand through my hair.

The determined gleam in my daughter's eyes wasn't softening.

I walked over and picked up the ultrasound photo that I'd been staring at when her car arrived and held it out to her. "See this? She needs me. They both do."

Madeline took the photo, and a soft smile touched her lips. "I have a brother," she said. "Congratulations, Liam."

Then, she lifted her gaze to me. "When I came here, the way she looked at you when you first walked up, that was love. Then, you treated her in a way that no woman deserves. You acted as if she were some hired hand instead of the woman carrying your child. Why, Liam? Why did you do it? My heart was breaking for her, and I was so angry with you, and you were being so stubborn, telling me that she was fine." Madeline held out the photo to me. She shook her head. "I'm sorry. I can't allow you to get her address and go to her. She was right to leave. I would have left too. Maybe now, you can acknowledge how you feel about her. Is she the live-in housekeeper, or is she the woman you want to spend forever with and raise a family with?"

Thinking about how I'd treated her was haunting me.

"You think I don't know that? I haven't slept. I can't close my eyes because when I do, I am reminded of what I've done. How I hurt her. It is ripping me to shreds inside, Madeline," I said, slamming a hand on my chest. "If I can't find her, how do I fix it?! How do I tell her that I love her? That I was scared. That I didn't think I would be enough for her. Not forever. That I thought I was saving her from a future where she was married to an old man. I couldn't see us growing old together because I was the one who was gonna be old, not her. I told myself it was selfish of me to make this more. To love her." I let out a hard laugh. "I was a fucking fool. I'll be whoever she wants me to be. I'll take her however I can have her, as long as I can have her. I'll worship her, love her, and if the day comes when she no longer wants me, I will do everything I can to change her mind. Because I can't see a future if she's not in it, here, in my bed, in my house."

Madeline lifted her chin as she stared at me, her eyes now glistening. "You should have told her all that before she left.

What was selfish was not letting her know how you feel. Making her think it was all one-sided."

"Then, Madeline, please, honey, help me. Blaise can find her faster than anyone else. If you walk out that door, still refusing to help me, I will hire someone. But every second that goes by, she's somewhere, thinking I don't love her. That I don't want us. And it is killing me."

She pressed her lips together, and a spark of hope came with the sympathetic look she gave me. She stepped forward and placed her hand on my arm. "I love you, but I won't do that. You were in control, and you screwed up. Now, Liberty has the control. Let's see what she can do with it. Give her time," she said, then scrunched her nose. "And take a shower. You stink. Try to eat something too. Sleep wouldn't hurt either."

Then, she squeezed my arm and headed for the door.

If I thought falling to my knees and begging would work, then I would do it. But I'd just been exposed to Etta's daughter. That look on her face was one I'd seen on her mother all those years ago. I wasn't going to get through to her when she had made up her mind on something.

She reached the door, then glanced over her shoulder at me. "You can try to hire someone to find her, but it'll be a waste of time. No one is going to do anything that would piss off Blaise, and every private detective in the state of Florida has received the message not to find Liberty Dillard," she said, then opened the door and walked out.

I stared at the door as she closed it.

I had to find Liberty. I'd figure out a way. No fucking Mafia boss was going to stop me. There had to be someone out there who wasn't scared of him.

Forty-One

LIBERTY

I stood at the window in my new office, looking out over the busy street below. Palm trees blew gently in the breeze as the world seemed to be in a rush to get home or go to dinner. I'd had a whirlwind of a first week here. Starting with this room. I turned around to look at the private office I'd been given the first day. I had been speechless while Martha continued to rattle on about the desk, computer, printer, my bathroom.

When we had arrived at GG Center, she had walked me past several desks with people working at them, sitting out in the open area of the main office. I was looking over them, wondering which one would be mine, when we passed them all, and she opened this door to show me my desk.

How had I managed to get this?

I smiled, shaking my head, still amazed.

This week, I had made calls to the different vendors that the company had chosen to use. Gotten to know the point of contact I'd be working with at each one. I met with the head of design, who would be making sure all the stores had the same layout, determining what the brand would look like so that I was clear on what all we were going to carry in our stores and which ones would have specialty items. There were stacks of catalogs to go through and either toss or keep, depending on what that vendor offered. I spent hours with the lady they had hired for media marketing because she'd been assigned to teach me how the software program worked for inside the office.

It had been a good week. I'd been kept so busy that it wasn't until I walked into my apartment at night that the heaviness in my chest truly affected me. I missed Liam, and although I was enjoying my job, he was never far from my mind. I wondered what he was eating at lunch when I sat down with mine. I would learn something new and think I couldn't wait to tell him, then remember we didn't have a relationship like that. I'd only lived in a fantasy in my head where I thought we did.

Heartbreak, my closest friend, was always right there by my side to nudge me when I had a moment that made me smile. It wasn't going to let me forget it was there, and I expected it never would. Learning to live each day with it clinging closely to me was the only way.

I walked over to pick up my purse, then grabbed the two files I wanted to take home and work on this weekend. I had nothing else to do. Right now, the idea of being alone for two days with no work seemed like torture. I'd have so much time to think, to feel. But I knew once the baby came, I'd love having that time with him.

The rest of the office staff had cleared out as soon as it hit five o'clock. I hadn't been ready to walk away yet. I didn't look forward to evenings the way everyone else did. But they had someone to run home to.

The elevator opened immediately, and I took it down to the first floor. The lobby, with its marble floor and walls, was almost as empty as our office had been. I waved at Zelbert, the security guard, on my way to the exit.

It might be fall, but in Florida, that just meant we weren't boiling; we were just toasting instead. I prepared myself for the uncomfortable warmth when I shoved open the door. My mind was elsewhere, and I wasn't paying attention to my surroundings, or I would have seen him. I'd not have come outside. As it was, I now stood there, frozen, unsure of what to do next.

Why was he here? Was this just incredibly bad luck?

Wallace straightened from leaning on the palm tree where he'd been standing with his focus on the building. Had he been watching it?

"Liberty." That familiar smile of his, which now made me cringe, spread across his face.

"Wallace, wasn't expecting to see you," I replied tightly, wishing I had a car in this parking lot to get in and drive away. As it was, I had to walk two blocks over to my apartment.

"I think I forgot how beautiful you are," he said, tilting his head and studying me.

"I'm tired, Wallace. I'd say it's good to see you, but I'm not a liar. If you'll excuse me, I want to go home," I told him, stepping around his tall frame.

"Wait, Liberty, please. Talk to me. How are you? How is the"—he paused, and his eyes dropped to my stomach—"baby?" He let out a small laugh. "Even pregnant, you are stunning."

My grip tightened on my purse strap hanging over my shoulder. "I'm good. Baby is great. Thanks for asking," I told him with growing annoyance.

"Let me take you to dinner. Just as friends. To catch up," he began.

I shook my head, not letting him continue. "No. You and I aren't ever going to be friends," I said.

Once again, I tried to step around him, but he continued to move when I did, keeping me there.

"You're hurt, which means you still love me. You know that. If you didn't feel something for me, then you wouldn't be trying to escape me."

The cocky gleam in his eyes had me rolling mine.

"I can promise you that my not wanting to have dinner with you isn't because I have any feelings for you. I don't. Those have been gone for a very long time. And what I did feel, it wasn't love. I just didn't realize it until I actually fell in love."

Wallace's eyes narrowed. "The father of the baby? You love him?"

I said nothing. He didn't get to know my personal life. He didn't get to know me.

"Where is he now? Hmm?" He held out his hands and looked around us. "I don't see him out here, trying to take you to dinner."

I didn't say he loved me in return, you asshole.

I stood there, waiting for him to finish whatever ridiculousness this was so I could leave.

His hardened expression softened. "I'm sorry, baby. I just miss you. I can't stop thinking about you. Worrying about you."

He reached out to touch my arm, and I moved back.

"I want to go home, Wallace. Please, leave me alone."

He sighed, then stepped to the side and waved a hand for me to go. "Another time then," he said.

God, I hoped not. I would have to start exiting the building out of the stairwell that led into the back and walk to the apartment on that street instead. It would only add a quarter of a mile. Anything was better than dealing with Wallace again.

Forty-Two

LIAM

"You not coming down to the floor tonight? Two of the new girls are onstage later. I think I did good," Tex told me as he stood in the doorway to my office.

I took another drink from the bottle of whiskey on my desk and shook my head. "I'm only here because if I had to sit in that house without her one more day, I was going to burn it to the ground."

Tex walked inside. "Let's not burn shit," he said. "It's just been a little over a week."

My bloodshot eyes lifted to meet his. "Nine days and three hours since I walked into that house to silence. No scent of whatever meal she'd made. No smile to greet me that took the darkness away. It was all gone. It is gone. Not one goddamn private detective in this motherfucking state or the surrounding ones will help me," I said as my hand tightened around the bottle I was still holding.

My chest heaved as the hole she'd left in it reminded me of how empty my life was now.

"DAMMIT!" I roared as I threw the bottle against the brick wall to my left. It shattered, and what little whiskey was left in there sprayed the area.

"Whoa!" Tex walked over to the glass. "No need to waste perfectly good Jack."

I dropped my head into my hands and closed my eyes. I couldn't keep going like this. Not knowing where she was. Not being able to hold her. Show her that I was gonna be a better man. I just needed her.

"I see you're doing better." Madeline's voice didn't give me the joy it once had.

I loved my daughter, but I felt betrayed by her. I didn't lift my head to look at her. I didn't care why she was here.

"I'd call it more of a spiral," Tex drawled.

"Yes, the glass all over the floor and the whiskey-soaked wall speak volumes." Madeline's amusement wasn't required.

"Unless you're here to tell me that Blaise is gonna help me, then please, Madeline, just go. I'm not in a good mind frame right now," I told her.

The sound of something hitting my desk caused me to finally look up. A folder was lying there, and Madeline pushed it toward me, but kept one finger on it. She tapped her long, pointy nail on it, and I lifted my eyes to look up at her questioningly.

"There. It's all there. I've held on to it as long as I can. I'm all about women sticking together, but I can't watch this anymore. Cree is asking for his Papa, and at this rate, you might drink yourself to death. So, here. Go get her, but please shower first and try not to smell like you drank the entire contents of the bar downstairs."

I grabbed the file and slung it open.
I could go get her! I could hold her!
"Liam."
I looked up at my daughter.
She placed her hands on the desk and looked at me eye level. "Make it good," she said, then straightened back up before turning and walking away.
"Thank you!" I called out to her, my focus already back on all the paperwork in this file.
"You should probably thank Blaise. He was the one who told me today that if I didn't give in and bring that to you, I was going to be bailing you out of jail or putting you in rehab soon."
"Tell him thank you for me!" Tex called out. "If he'll come in, drinks are on me. I know he's either at the bottom of the stairs or guarding the exit door."
"He is, but you know better than to invite him inside the club. If he wants a lap dance, I'll be the one giving it to him."
Tex chuckled. "I'll follow you out."
I picked up the first printout in the file. It was every detail of her childhood, starting in Charleston. How the fuck had Blaise gotten all this? I read through it, then moved on to the next page.
She had been taken to the hospital by a school nurse after arriving with a broken arm that needed a cast. The same school nurse had noted three times in one year that she had been sent to school with a high temperature, but she'd beg them not to call her stepmother. A counselor had noted six times during her three years in junior high school that Liberty was often bruised, and she was concerned about her home life; however, when asked, the child had claimed she was just clumsy.

The paper in my hand was shaking as I gripped it tightly. Every word I read, her life only seemed to get worse.

At fifteen, she'd admitted herself into the emergency room. A rape kit was required. Doctor noted that she was a minor, and they asked how to contact her parents, but she cried and begged them not to call her stepmother. The nurse left the room, and when she returned, the patient had left.

Bile burned my throat as I moved on to the next sheet. Her student loans that had gone delinquent. Grades in college courses she'd finished. They were all A's, except for a history course, where she had gotten an eighty-six percent.

The purchase of a piece-of-shit car that she'd paid one thousand dollars for in cash.

The address where she'd lived with Wallace Gabler.

I continued to scan, looking for the present. If I continued to read all the hell she'd lived through and survived, I was going to begin tearing this room apart.

My entire body tensed as I read the last page. Her job. Her apartment. A photo of a man, with the name Wallace Gabler taped over his head, was touching her arm outside of an office building. She looked angry. This was current. Her round stomach showing in the dress she was wearing meant it had been taken this week.

He had set it all up.

I was going to kill that motherfucker. Slowly.

Forty-Three

LIBERTY

My office door opened, and Martha walked inside. She glanced back out into the main area before closing it, then turned to me.

"Before the meeting, I wanted to speak with you," she said. "I wasn't sure about you. I had … a lot of feelings about the decision to hire you for this position. However, you've been, well, a pleasant surprise." She stopped, then let out a weary sigh. "What I am trying to say is, I like you. I think hiring you was a good move for the company, and I'm sorry."

I paused, staring at her, waiting for more. Why had she said she was sorry? She'd just told me I'd done a good job.

She shook her head. "I can't say any more, so don't ask me. Please understand," she said, then turned and quickly exited the room.

I sat there for a moment, trying to figure out what in the world that had been about. Glancing at the time, I realized I would have to think about that later. The staff meeting was in five minutes, and it was mandatory. We had only had one of these so far, and it had been led by a lady named Sandra. She was the operating manager. Today, however, we'd been told that the chief operating officer was meeting with us. His office was the closed door at the end of the hallway, which no one had been in since I'd started. I'd asked about it, but no one seemed to want to talk.

He had been out of town but returned and would be back in his office this morning. That had been the morning announcement. Everyone seemed nervous and began straightening things up.

Taking my company laptop with me in case I needed to make notes, I headed for the door. The conference room was down on the right, just before the large office that belonged to the COO. Others were talking quietly as they made their way to the room. The last meeting, things had been louder.

Since I worked in my office most of the day, I didn't spend much time around the others who were out in the open area. They all had a camaraderie that I didn't, but I hoped I would be accepted in time. My focus was on understanding the job and doing it well. Once that was under control, I would work on making some friendships.

Although, right now, I needed a friend. I had almost turned on my phone and texted Goldie and Nina more than once, but I was scared of the texts and voice mails I would find and the ones I wouldn't. If Liam hadn't tried to contact me, I would be shattered all over again. If he had contacted me, I was afraid I'd not have the strength to ignore it. I knew I couldn't do this forever, but I just needed a few more weeks. Then, I would turn it on and contact him. If he wanted to go to the doctor's appointment, I didn't want to keep that from him.

As much as I wanted to hate him for not loving me, I couldn't.

"You're Liberty, correct?" a guy I recognized asked, but I wasn't sure what his job was here.

"Yes," I replied.

He motioned at the seat on the side of the table where the windows were. It was the first seat, to be exact. That would put me right beside the COO.

I smiled and shook my head. "Oh, I don't think that seat is for me," I told him, preferring to take a seat at the other end. Farther away.

"No, it is," he argued. "I was told to make sure that seat is reserved for Liberty Dillard."

I frowned and looked over at it again, my gaze landing on Martha. She gave me an apologetic look again. Was this what she had said she was sorry about? Had she not wanted to sit there and had someone place me there instead?

"Okay, uh, thanks," I said to the guy and walked over to take the seat.

It felt like every eye in the room was watching me.

Behind a bar, I was in my comfort zone. The looks from others didn't bother me. I expected it. Tips were good when people were looking.

This was a different island. One I didn't know well. Among peers that were more educated. Did they know I didn't have a degree? My palms felt sweaty as I sat down and placed my laptop on the table in front of me. Crossing my legs, I attempted to dry my hands on my skirt. This wasn't a major corporation. It was a new local chain of garden centers. I had no reason to feel nervous. I was good with plants and flowers. I was going to be good at this job.

While I stared at my hands in my lap and mentally coached myself to calm down, I heard the door open again and lifted my head, ready to meet my boss.

There were moments in life when all the pieces fell into place, and you smiled, finally figuring out the puzzle. Then, there were moments when that puzzle was a nightmare you hadn't prepared for and wished it were just a dream.

I was experiencing the latter.

His eyes met mine, and it was almost as if his smile was broadcasting his win.

I had started to believe my luck was finally turning around, only to have it all come crashing down around me. I wasn't meant for luck. Fate was against me and had been since the day my Mama D had passed away. Nothing good had come after that.

My hand slid over my stomach, and I immediately regretted that thought. I was wrong. Something wonderful had come my way.

"Good morning," Wallace said to the room as he walked to stand at the head of the table.

His faded jeans—which I knew cost over three hundred dollars and were the only brand he would wear—long-sleeved white oxford, and leather loafers brought back memories I preferred to forget.

His gaze swung to mine again, and the glint of victory in his eyes was the same as when he'd won a football game when we were in high school. I wasn't a game, but right now, I couldn't be sure if he had won this or not.

He had set me up so completely and allowed me to enjoy it before taking the curtain down to see the truth behind it all.

"As most of you know, I've been to all the Gabler Groceries that are having the garden center added on to them. We have seven finished in Florida, two ready in Georgia, three in Alabama, and two in South Carolina. Those are all located in the largest areas with the highest income," he began, then walked over to pick up a remote, and the screen behind him slowly rolled down.

"We are ready to begin stocking the store in Orlando and Miami. Their additions are move-in prepped. This next week, each of your jobs will come in to full play. I need everyone here focused on our upcoming grand openings at these two stores. I know Hillary has the marketing plan already in effect, and she is going to share what she wants to accomplish this month." He paused, then turned to me. "And most importantly, Liberty Dillard, who has been working with all the vendors we are using, will be the one to choose the inventory. I have complete faith in her and look forward to seeing what she's chosen for those two stores." He flashed his grin that he'd been using to charm people since we had been in high school. "I've known Liberty for a very long time. We've had a personal relationship that has evolved over time. So, if you see me working closely with her, understand that I'm not playing favorites."

I dropped my eyes to my lap as my face heated. Great. Now, he had everyone looking at me and assuming he and I were sleeping together. Would they also think that the baby was his? I felt sick. How could I stay here? How had I not figured out in the week I had been here that GG stood for Gabler Garden, like it was so proudly displayed on the screen behind him.

The apartment, the office, the salary—all things that no one would give to a woman with no college degree or credentials. I could fix them all cocktails with my eyes closed, but that wasn't the job I'd been hired for.

I'd known this was too good to be true, and like Mama D had always told me, "If it looks like an easy pie, then it ain't gonna be worth eatin'."

Well, Mama D, I ate the damn pie.

Forty-Four
LIBERTY

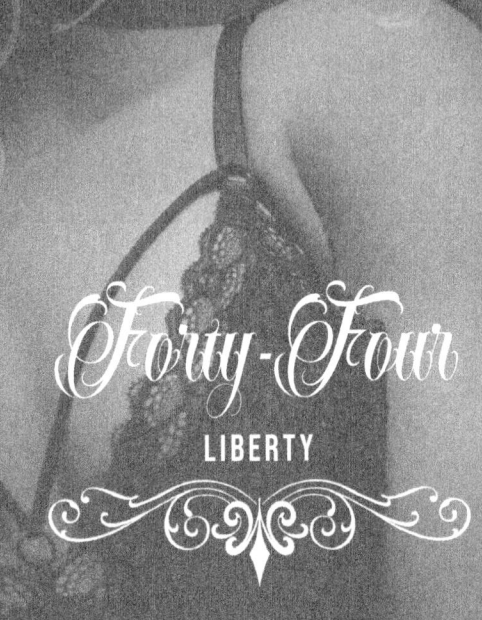

Standing outside my apartment door, I stared at it. I couldn't do this. I needed it, but I couldn't do it. As much as having a job like this along with a place to live had changed my life, it also meant I would have to allow Wallace back into my world.

I touched my stomach. I'd wanted a good job and a safe place to live before he was born, but not at this cost. Wallace was my past. He didn't get to control my life. If I stayed here, I might as well hand over my independence. This was just another man taking care of me.

Why Wallace was so determined to get me back I didn't understand. One would think being pregnant with another man's baby would be enough to send him away for good.

The only thing I could figure was that he thought of me leaving him as losing, and Wallace never liked to lose. He thought he'd won this time too. It had been all over his face today. When he stopped by my office on his way out, he told me to let him know at any time if I changed my mind about dinner. He had stood there for a moment, grinning as if he thought I was going to go with him because he'd given me all that I had wanted.

He had no idea what I wanted, and he couldn't give it to me.

Tomorrow, I'd begin looking for somewhere else to live and another job. Pressing the code outside my door, I waited for the green light and then opened the door and walked inside. Defeat weighed down my shoulders as I dropped my purse on the table by the door, then started to walk into the living area.

My heart slammed against my chest as I opened my mouth to scream when I realized who was standing in my apartment.

"Oh my God," I whispered, placing my hand over my stomach. "You." I shook my head. "How are you in my apartment?"

The shock had rattled me, but the toxic mix of anger and hurt stirred together as I straightened my shoulders and looked into Liam's eyes.

"You know what?" I said, "I don't want to know. Just leave. Today has been a bad one, and then you show up like this. I can't. I just can't."

Would it ever not hurt to look at him? Would my heart not feel as if it were breaking all over again?

"If I'd stayed outside, you'd have never let me in." His voice was hoarse, as if he were sick.

I studied him, starting to worry about his health. No. I had to stop that. He wasn't mine to be concerned about. Even if he had dark circles under bloodshot eyes. What if he was sick? He'd come to tell me. Panic caused my heart to escalate more than it already was from his appearance.

"Are you okay?" I blurted.

He shook his head. "No, I'm not. I've not been okay since I walked into our house and you were gone. I've not been okay since I picked up that photo of our son and realized I'd drunk so goddamn much, trying to numb the pain in my chest over how I'd treated you, that I slept through the ultrasound appointment. I've not been okay since I read that note and my dark, fucked-up soul was shredded."

I wrapped my arms around myself, needing some form of protection from this. His words couldn't be trusted. I had done that over and over again, only to be led to different levels of pain. Levels I hadn't known about until him.

"Don't, Liam. I can't do this. Not anymore. I'm providing for myself. Proving to you that I'm not some charity case. Earning the respect that I want from you and our child. Today hasn't been good for me. And you coming in here, saying these things, only rips off the Band-Aid I managed to put in place. So, please, leave."

I stepped back so he had a straight shot to the door. I would fall apart once he was gone. But not yet. I had to get him out of here first.

He took a step, and then the agony began again. I wanted to close my eyes so I couldn't see him go; maybe then it wouldn't hurt so much.

The second step didn't come. He stopped and was just closer to me now.

"There is a problem with that. You wanted me, but I need you." His thick, raspy voice cracked on the last word. "Liberty, you claimed my soul long before I realized your hold on it. When I did, it scared the fuck out of me. I believed things about you that were lies. And even then"—he slid a finger under my chin and tilted my head back so that I had to look at him—"I fell in love with you."

My heart could not listen to this.

Shaking my head, I took his hand from me and stepped back. "No, you don't get to come in here and say that. I know about Selena, Liam. She met me in the parking lot of the hospital after the ultrasound. She told me how you felt trapped by me. Called me names. Accused me of getting pregnant on purpose and that you resented me for it."

Tears blurred my vision, and I wished like hell I could control my crying better. I didn't want to ever cry in front of this man again.

Liam took two long strides, and before I could move again, his hands cupped my face. The fierce expression as he looked down at me kept me still instead of fighting to get free of his touch.

"She is a goddamn liar. I never once told her about you being pregnant. I never wanted her. Even when I was with her, I didn't feel anything, Liberty. I'd already been ruined by this gorgeous little bartender who had rocked my world. No woman was ever going to reach me after that. I didn't know it. Hell, I might have gone the rest of my life alone because I'd walked out of that motel room. I had no idea that a broken condom was going to be what gave me life. Gave me you."

He wiped at my tears with his thumbs as he continued to cup my face with his hands.

I would be lying if I said his words weren't threading through me, mending things I'd believed would be broken forever. I loved him. I was sure I'd love him until I took my last breath, but trusting him with my heart? I wasn't ready. There was too much wreckage on the path we'd been on. I had to make a new path. One that was safe for me and our baby.

"I need time," I finally said. Those three words had felt like I had to rip them out of my chest.

"Darlin'." The pleading way he said that one word almost undid me. "Don't do this to me. Don't let my mistakes take away the life we could have. I need you, Liberty. I'm a fucking shell without you. I can't eat. I don't sleep. Please."

The glassy sheen in his hazel eyes was going to crack me open. Hurting him, seeing him like this, was brutal. I didn't want to do it. I didn't want to be the cause of it. But loving him also meant I had to love me.

"I need time," I repeated.

I wasn't sure I trusted myself to say more. I was holding it together by a thread. The thinnest thread ever made. A heavy sigh could snap it in two.

Liam closed his eyes, and his shoulders sagged. The thread was unraveling. If he didn't walk out that door soon, I knew all my resistance would be gone.

"Okay." His husky whisper sounded so full of regret.

If I reached out and touched him, reassured him, then all of this would have been for nothing.

He lowered his head and kissed my forehead, then dropped his hands from my face. "I will do whatever you want. Not just now, but for the rest of my life. You just tell me when and where. I'll always be there."

I sucked in a breath, holding in my sob, and nodded.

His eyes drifted over me once more, pausing on my stomach. His throat flexed as he swallowed, and then he turned toward the door and walked away. When he didn't open it, I had to close my eyes so I wouldn't look at him. I wasn't sure I wouldn't run to him, begging him to stay.

Finally, it opened, and I stayed still until I heard the lock click in place. I wrapped my arms around our baby, tucked safely inside me, and sank to the floor and let the tears go freely.

"I had to do it for me," I whispered as I looked down at my stomach.

Forty-Five

LIBERTY

I made sure all my things were once again packed away in my suitcases before leaving the apartment and heading to the office. Even though Wallace had hired me to control me, I couldn't just walk away. I would turn in my resignation today, and if he made it difficult, then I would have to leave. I hoped he didn't because I could use the two weeks to find a new job and an apartment. Getting a lease would be easier if I was employed too.

Sleep hadn't come easy for me last night with all that Liam had said replaying over and over in my head.

While in the shower this morning, I had finally come up with how to handle this job and Wallace. He rarely played by anyone's rules but his, but I was going to hope for once that he did.

When I walked off the elevator, my coworkers all looked at me. Some smiled, others looked annoyed, and a few scowled.

They were young and female. I wanted to stop and tell them that Wallace Gabler wasn't someone they wanted to add to their mistakes in life, but I didn't. They could hate me if they wanted to, but I'd be gone soon, and one of them could have my office.

As soon as the door closed behind me, I sighed in relief. At least I didn't have to work out there with them all making assumptions about me. But then if I was out there and not in this fancy, private office, then they might like me more.

Rubbing my temples, I stared at the desk. I had a list of things I needed to do today for the Miami and Orlando stores, but my focus was gone.

I could think of little else but Liam. He was there, invading my head, reminding me that for once, I might get that happiness. If I wasn't terrified to trust him. Sure, he'd been convincing last night, but what happened when he got tired of me? What if he didn't love me as much as I loved him? He'd already given his heart to Etta. Was there enough left to share it with me? All these things had plagued me as I lay in bed last night.

Sitting down behind the desk, I turned on the computer and tried to decide what to do first. The door opened before I had a chance to decide. Wallace walking into the room only made things worse.

Heaving a sigh, I glared up at him.

"Good morning to you too," he said with a smile and walked over to set a cup of coffee in front of me.

I recognized it.

"Lavender mocha with a touch of honey and skim milk," he said, looking pleased with himself for remembering my order.

"I'm pregnant. I can't drink that. Too much caffeine," I told him.

He frowned. "Oh yeah. I didn't think about that." He moved the cup and sat down on the edge of my desk. "I'll get decaf tomorrow. Or we can always take a coffee break."

Not in this lifetime or in the next.

"I don't take coffee breaks. We have stores opening. No distractions, right?" I reminded him of his own words yesterday.

He smirked. "Well, that doesn't apply to you. If I'm the distraction at least."

Vomit.

I picked up the resignation letter I'd typed and printed out yesterday after the meeting. I had held on to it, wanting to be sure this was what I had to do. Seemed it was, but I'd known it would be. My things were already packed. Even if I didn't move out today, I would be ready as soon as I found somewhere to move to.

He took it from me, scowling at it. "No," he said and handed it back.

I didn't take it. "You can't control me resigning, Wallace."

"Why would you do this? You sent me a résumé. I felt like I'd won the fucking lottery when I saw your name on that paper. I handed you a job for people with four-year degrees and years of experience. You have a kick-ass apartment. But because you have to work with me, you'd give it up? Just because of me? You hate me that much?"

I opened my mouth to tell him it was more of a dislike. Hate was too strong of an emotion for how I felt about him. But the door swung open as Liam stalked inside. Tensing, I stared at him, trying to figure out why he was here, but the seething look he gave Wallace stopped me from asking.

"If you don't get off her desk and move away from her, I will burn every goddamn building your family owns to the ground," he snarled as he walked up to Wallace, towering over him.

Even when Wallace shot up off my desk, he was still a good three to four inches shorter. His shoulders weren't as wide, and his biceps were nowhere near as thick and solid as Liam's.

"SECURITY!" Wallace shouted, then sneered at Liam. "You don't get to come into my office and threaten me."

Liam's dark chuckle sent a chill down my spine. I knew I should stand up and do something, but I couldn't seem to figure out what. My eyes swung to the door. I expected security to come rushing inside, but no one appeared.

"Go ahead, little boy, why don't you call for them again? I don't think they heard you," Liam taunted him before grabbing the collar of his oxford and shoving him up against the wall. "Go on now," he urged.

"SECURITY!" Wallace yelled again. "You'll go to jail for this. I'll press charges. You shouldn't have put your hands on me."

Liam leaned closer to him. "You keep talking, little boy, and you won't live to see if I go to jail."

Finally, I shot up out of my seat. I was not letting Liam go to prison for Wallace Gabler. He wasn't worth it, and I needed him. If he was behind bars, I'd not be able to have him.

"Liam, let him go. I'll walk out with you," I told him in a calm voice.

"You wanted time," Liam said as he held Wallace up higher until his toes were struggling to stay on the ground.

"Get security, Liberty!" Wallace demanded.

Liam slammed his head back against the wall. "Be careful how you speak to her, you son of a bitch," he warned him.

"Liam"—I touched his arm—"please. Stop."

He turned to look at me, and the crazed gleam in his eyes eased some. "You wanted time. I gave you all I can manage before going insane."

"It's not even been twenty-four hours," I pointed out.

"Exactly," he replied.

"I can't breathe," Wallace gasped.

Liam turned back to the man he was strangling with his own shirt. "This is what's going to happen. Your security is currently unavailable. In fact, you'll be needing to hire new ones. The ones you had left with some of my men to have a few drinks. As for your office staff, none of them have called the police, nor will they say anything to anyone about this. If you fire one of them for it, you'll go missing."

"You can't do that," he rasped.

Liam slammed his head against the wall again. "I didn't say you could talk," he said, sounding annoyed. "I can do it, and I did. Now, I'm going to let my woman get her things, and then she's walking out the door with me. Do you understand?"

Wallace glared over at me. He felt like he was losing, and I knew he'd retaliate.

"You'll regret this," he spit.

"Dumb fucker," Liam growled, then planted his fist across his jaw.

Wallace's head slumped forward, and Liam let go of him. His body crumpled to the floor.

"Oh my God," I whispered.

"He's not dead," Liam said, moving over to me.

I looked from the heap on my floor up to Liam. He bent down and covered my mouth with his. The hard warmth of his lips and tickle of his beard was like waking up from a bad dream and realizing it wasn't real. His tongue slid over my bottom lip, and I opened for him. Grabbing his arms, I went up on my tiptoes, desperate to taste more.

In the distance, I heard someone clear their throat, but I didn't care. All I wanted was to continue savoring this.

"Could you move it outside, Liam? It'll be less of a mess to handle if we leave now," a man's voice said.

Liam groaned, pulling back from me, his eyes locked on mine. "Yeah," he replied in a gruff voice, not looking away from me.

"Come with me," he said as his hands gripped my hips.

With Wallace on the floor, unconscious, I knew I couldn't stay here.

I nodded. "My purse," I told him.

He let go of me and went to take it from my desk, then came back, sliding his arm around me. I saw the massive man standing at the door. I recognized him. He'd been in Liam's office that day at the club. When the Mafia was there.

Liam had brought the Mafia here?

I blinked up at him as he glanced over at Wallace, then back at Liam.

"Tell me you didn't kill him," the large man said.

"No, but he wouldn't shut up," Liam replied.

The man nodded, as if that made complete sense. "We will finish up here," the man told him.

Liam led me through a completely deserted office and to the elevators. I scanned the area, looking for someone, but I only saw another familiar man. This was the one who had come out of Liam's office to hurry him up after he took me out in the hallway because I'd interrupted their meeting. He didn't appear frightening. He was more of a head turner in a pretty-boy way. Not like Liam.

The man smirked at me as if he had read my thoughts. A sadistic glint in his eyes made me stiffen.

"It's fine," Liam said, pulling me closer to his side. "He's a psycho bastard, but he's with us."

I nodded and leaned against Liam until we were safely in the elevator, going down.

"He is going to press charges," I said, clinging to him. I didn't want him to go to jail.

"No, he won't," Liam replied, then kissed the top of my head. "I swear."

I shook my head. "You don't know him, Liam. He doesn't like to lose, and you just humiliated him. He will be furious."

Liam chuckled. "I doubt it, but I really hope he's stupid enough to try."

The elevator opened, and we stepped out. The lobby was like upstairs. Empty. Where was everyone?

A tattooed man with short platinum-blond hair stepped around the corner and nodded at Liam. I glanced back at him as we left, trying to figure out if he was Mafia or Judgment.

Was that how the place had been vacated? The Mafia had done all this?

"Your suitcases are already in my car," Liam said when we stepped outside.

I stopped and took a deep breath before looking at him.

"I said I needed time. And just because I left with you doesn't change that. I left because I had to choose you or Wallace, and it will always be you. That isn't even a choice. But, Liam, I want to be someone you respect. I want to do something that makes you proud. I want my son to have a mother he is proud of. I'm thirty-one, and I've not accomplished anything. I have no college degree, I can't afford a car, and now, I have no apartment."

Liam grabbed my chin, and his eyes narrowed. "For starters, that shit about your car was me being a fucking dick. Being able to afford a car doesn't give a person worth. And there are millionaires who don't have a college degree. That doesn't matter either. As for an apartment"—he shook his head—"darlin', you are my home. You will be our son's home. A structure doesn't mean shit. A house is an empty shell without the soul of the home inside of it. You're that for me. You'll be that for our son. Not every kid has that kind of mom. They aren't blessed with someone who is willing to fight for them, who will give up anything for them, who will endure pain to save them from it."

Liam brushed back some hair that had blown into my face.

"You're my hero." His words, thick with emotion, were said with pride shining in his eyes.

Forty-Six

LIAM

As I walked in the front entrance of Devil's with the mail in my hand, my thoughts were on our doctor's appointment yesterday. I'd been able to schedule some fancy-ass ultrasound that cost extra, where we could see our little guy better. He looked so much like his momma, and it made me smile.

Tex was directing a liquor delivery, and some of the new girls were working with the head of our entertainers, Divinity. Her real name was actually Melba, but if anyone called her that, she'd shove a fork in their eye.

Liberty came walking around the corner with an iPad in her hands. I stopped just to watch her. I loved having her here, and she had my files so damn organized that we'd ended up saving money on supplies for the past two months.

"Tex, what is this bill?" she asked, showing him. "It's not one I'm familiar with. It looks like paper products, but why are we buying from two distributers?"

I watched my enforcer frown. "Not sure."

"Okay, I'll call." She still hadn't spotted me when she turned to tap away on that iPad I'd gotten her so she could be mobile while doing her filing and organizing.

One of the new girls walked by and stopped when she noticed Liberty's round stomach. It was fucking adorable on her. It was difficult not touching it all the time. She was always laughing and swatting my hands away while we were working.

"Uh, so did we decide to add a kink to the show?" the girl asked with an amused smirk.

Liberty looked up from the iPad. I started in that direction, ready to fire the girl before she said another word.

"Oh, no," Liberty told her with a smile. "I only get naked for one man. Run along now and get back to work."

A grin spread across my face, and I slid one hand behind her, then covered her stomach with my other one. Liberty tilted her head back. Those honey eyes went soft as she gazed up at me lovingly. I pressed a kiss to her lips, then cut my eyes at the new dancer.

"I see you've met my queen," I drawled.

The girl's eyes widened, and she looked back at Divinity nervously before turning back to me.

"I'm so sorry. I didn't know she was …" She paused, not sure what to call her.

"Mine," I supplied.

The girl nodded, then dropped her gaze to Liberty. "I didn't mean anything by it," she said. "You're pregnant, but you look like that, so I figured you were a dancer. The whole fantasy vibe, you know. Hot, sexy pregnant woman."

Liberty laughed, and I tightened my hold on her. I loved that sound.

"Thanks, I think."

The girl nodded.

"This sexy pregnant woman is my fantasy only."

"Yes, sir," she muttered, then hurried away.

Liberty turned in my arms, and I took the iPad from her, then placed it on the bar so I could have her closer before kissing her mouth the way I wanted to. She sighed and leaned into me the best she could with our son between us. I felt the kick just as her tongue flicked against mine.

She chuckled and leaned back. "He's aggressive. Doesn't like to share."

I placed a hand over her to feel him kicking and moving around inside. "He looks just like you, so guess he's gonna act like me."

"Yeah," she agreed. "Maybe he could switch the two before he's born."

Tex placed a bottle of tequila on the bar across from us. "Nah, you're a helluva lot prettier than his ugly mug, and the world needs another Liam running around. Judgment's gotta have another Prez when this one gets old."

Liberty turned her eyes back to me.

Fate was a funny thing. Life threw you a lot of bad shit, testing you, seeing just what you could survive. Then, when you thought that was all there was on the road you were meant to walk, fate tossed you the gold medal for surviving so long. You just had to keep walking it and hope you didn't fuck it up when your prize was handed out.

Epilogue

LIBERTY

"You got this, darlin'. Just push one more time," Liam said, holding my hand beside me while my nails bit into his flesh.

"If you say that again, I'm going to hit you with the closest thing I can reach," I warned him through clenched teeth.

He grinned, then winked at me. That wasn't gonna work this time. Not when my body was being split in two.

"He's right; just one more push," the doctor encouraged.

She'd better watch it, or I was gonna hit her too. I had been pushing for an hour.

"Think about his little face," Liam whispered close to my ear.

Okay. He was right. I wanted to see that face. Hold him. I nodded closing my eyes tightly then gave it one more push, focusing on how it would feel to finally have him in my arms.

"There he is. Keep on going. You got it!" the doctor told me.

I opened my eyes and gave it everything I had left. The doctor stood up, holding a tiny red body with arms and legs stretched out as a cry filled the room.

"There he is." Liam's voice sounded thick with emotion. He kissed my head and sucked in a deep breath. "Thank you."

The nurse handed Liam the scissors for him to cut the umbilical cord, and I laughed through my tears, watching him.

Then, I held out my arms, and our son was placed in them. He stopped crying and frowned up at me.

"Hey, little guy," I said with a teary smile as I took him in. "I'm your mommy." I looked up at Liam as he watched us, one lone tear rolling down his face. "And the big, tough, emotional man beside me is your daddy."

A grin tugged at Liam's mouth, and he laughed as he wiped the tear away.

"You are so very loved," I told him as his little hand grasped my finger. "I can't wait until Ozzy sees you. You've already got a best friend waiting at home."

I glanced back up at Liam. "You want to hold him?" I asked.

He moved around to face me. "Yeah, but first …" He slid something from his pocket.

When I could see the small velvet box in his hand, my eyes flew back up to his face.

His gaze went from our son to me. "I wanted this moment to be the most special day of our lives. And I knew I had to wait until you were holding our son for the first time. There's no ring or words that could ever compete with that for first place," he said.

I let out a sob that sounded like a laugh as I stared at him, stunned. He'd not said one thing about marriage, but I had him. I didn't care what the title was. I just wanted to be with Liam. If I had his love, that was enough.

"I wasn't expecting you. But somewhere along the way, I did something that the powers that be thought I deserved an angel. I wish I knew what the fuck it was," he said, then grinned as he held up the diamond. "You own me, Liberty. I want you to have my last name. I want you by my side for the rest of my life and I'm claiming dibs on the next life too. Marry me."

In his eyes, there was more love than I ever could have hoped for in life.

I nodded. "Yes, I want that. All of it."

He took my hand and slid the ring on my finger, then leaned down to press a kiss to my lips. "I love you."

"I love you," I replied.

Straightening up, he reached out his arms. "Now, I'm ready to hold our son."

I placed him in his father's safe embrace and my heart had never felt so full.

"Hello, Hagan Arrow Walsh," he said as he stared down at the bundle in his arms with pride. "I've got a lot to thank you for."

Acknowledgments

 I struggled to get inspiration when I began Liam's story. It took me three weeks to get out only twenty-thousand words (to those who know how fast I write that is normally what I write in two days' time- at my slowest).

 I stared at those words for an entire day adding nothing to them. I was stuck and deep down I knew what I had to do. It is what I tell new authors all the time when they ask me about writer's block. "If you are stuck then you are bored. If you're bored the reader will be too. Delete until you can go in a different direction. Even if it's a lot of words."

 The next morning, I woke up, sat down in front of my computer, pulled up the manuscript, and deleted the entire thing.

 Did I mention I had only one week left to finish this story if I wanted it to release on time?

 That Sunday morning, I began writing the story that began in my dreams the night before. The words poured out of me so fast I didn't stop to eat or drink. I forgot what was going on around me. I was lost in this world, with these two broken souls.

Six days later, I wrote the end to the longest book I have written for only one couple totaling eighty-five thousand words. I loved every word I'd written. That's when I know it's a good story. When it captures me. When tears fill my eyes while I'm writing scenes, and I must stop and wipe away my tears so I can see the screen.

I hope you enjoy their story as much as I did writing it. Sure, my family missed me that week. I ignored phone calls and text (after pausing to make sure everyone was safe). When I walked out of my office after having written the end, my seven-year-old said "Thank GOD! I missed you. Now take me to Target and let me buy something to make up for it."

She's a bit of a manipulator…

To the people who suffered, stood in the gap, and worked magic to make this story happen:

Britt is always the first I mention because without him, I'd have never written that many words in only six days. He was mom and dad that week. I owe him big.

Emerson for surviving without me. I would say she didn't complain but that would be a lie. There was a lot of standing at my office door and scowling at me.

My older children, who live in other states, they called and texted and were also ignored. I felt bad but I replied "Writing, deadline, will call when finished." And they didn't mind but they also didn't stop calling and texting so… anyway.

My editor, Jovana Shirley at Unforeseen Editing, who was understanding about me missing not just the first deadline but the second one too. She worked with my tight schedule, and I would be screwed without her. She's a God send.

My formatter, Melissa Stevens at The Illustrated Author. Who has never let me down. She always does a speedy turn around for me (monthly I might add). She makes my books beautiful inside. Her work is the best formatting I've ever had in my books. I am always excited to see what she does with each one. Each book seems to be better than the last!

Autumn Sexton, at Wordsmith Publicity, for saving me from losing my mind and taking over all the things that I can't keep up with anymore. Her help allows me to write this quickly. She reminds me of the things I need to do. I don't think I would have been able to keep up with this one book a month schedule without her.

Beta readers, who come through every time: Jerilyn Martinez, and Vicci Kaighan. I love y'all!

Sarah Sentz, Enchanting Romance Designs, for my book cover. Again, she nailed it. I have no visual creativity to give her any help in the matter. But she manages to create something I adore every time.

Abbi's Army, for being my support and cheering me on. I love y'all!

My readers, for allowing me to write books. Without you, this wouldn't be possible.